Funny Money

A Novel

Thomas P. Hanna

Funny Money

Copyright © 2014 by Thomas P. Hanna

All rights reserved. No part of this book may be reproduced or transmitted in any form or by any means without written permission of the author.

ISBN-10: 150101224X

ISBN-13: 978-1501012242

Cover currency image thanks to www.Kidsmoneyfarm.com

Cover image thanks to Greater Miami Convention and Visitors Bureau

Chapter 01

A prominent sign identified the impressive block-square Art Deco building as Philadelphia's 30th Street Station, the place where several regional and long-distance train systems exchanged passengers.

Inside, Sylvester Pernell, a small, wiry man of fifty, in good but not expensive clothes with a small suitcase and a laptop computer in a shoulder carrying case at his feet stood with his buddy Jack Dimples, sixty-five and less well dressed, near the tall pedestal at one end of the cavernous concourse.

"I love this place," Pernell said looking around. "This room's 290 feet long, 135 feet wide, and the coffered ceiling soars 95 feet above the Tennessee marble floor. The structure beside us is the Pennsylvania Railroad War Memorial that honors their employees who died in World War Two. The figure on top is a larger than life bronze statue of the Archangel Michael lifting a dead soldier from the flames of war. The names of the 1307 honorees are inscribed on the pedestal, not that I've counted them myself of course."

"You sound like a walking tourist brochure, Sylvester," Dimple said with an amazed and amused shake of his head.

Over the PA system the disembodied voice of the station agent announced, "The 'Miami Streak' train is approaching the station. Those holding tickets for this train may proceed to the platform for boarding now. Staircase seven for the 'Miami Streak'. Please have your ticket out and ready for inspection."

"That's me. I want to get on before the crowd so I can find a good seat and look over my fellow travelers," Pernell said picking up his bags.

"So again this year I won't see you until spring, is that what you're telling me?" Dimples asked.

"That's it, Jack. I'm going south for the winter sort of like the birds," Pernell replied with a smile of anticipation.

"You mean you're going after the pigeons. That's why you're here to catch a seven A.M. train at the start of October."

"Can I help it if some people seem to want to give me their money? Anyway I'm betting that I can live the winter comfortably on what I'll pick up on the trip down. I have leads on two guys who made reservations for this train and I was planning to go this way anyway."

Norman Hill, thirty-six, and nicely but not expensively dressed, watched the two men from a distance at one spot. Jane Taylor, thirty-five, and nicely but not expensively dressed, watched them from another spot with no hint she was associated with Hill.

Terence Dutton, forty-two, nervous, bland, soft-looking, and dressed in casual clothes, watched someone from a third spot where he could have been looking at any of those four people or none of them.

"Ah yes, the lady with the travel agency who sells what she knows about the traveling public to those with cash in hand."

"Research is a wonderful thing, Jack. Every hour devoted to it can save a man like myself twenty times that in missed opportunities and wasted effort with penniless birds."

"So being able to pay someone else to do the research is worth the money to you."

"You'd better believe so," Pernell said with a laugh. "Plus she doesn't have to balls to pull stuff herself but she has a sense for picking likely marks. The first time I only paid her for some tips as a test to see if they were like she predicted they'd be. When I did a take off of two out of five with none obviously not in the category, I knew I should cultivate her."

"After a few drinks I'd ask for the details of cultivating her but not here."

"It's strictly a business relationship. We've never met face-to-face so neither could pick the other out in a lineup. There a middle person, a blind lady, who doesn't know or care what's in it, she's content to take the ten spot on top of the sealed envelope you give her and hand the envelope to whoever asks with the correct code word."

"I guess I'm sort of disappointed that it's not more of a storybook sweaty romance kind of thing but I recognize that it's safer this way," Dimple said with a shrug.

"Plus I don't risk focusing some cop who has questions about things I'm accused of doing onto her, which might cause her problems or simply make her research harder. I know she does some of it just by spending hours wading through the egotistic exaggerations on Facebook and Internet places like that, then doing more in-depth checks at other places using the computer on a few she considers so obviously looking to be taken. I tried that but I don't have the stomach for it. The lies and the wishful thinking are pathetic. But she slogs through it and makes neat reports giving the essential info to find them and a few names to drop to let you start a conversation. She's worth big money and if I had that I'd give her more than what she asks even if it might spoil her."

"So how does the travel agency tie into it?"

The station employee again announced over the PA, "This is a boarding call for the 'Miami Streak'. Please proceed immediately to stair seven."

Pernell glanced around to see where that staircase was. "She spots a few who fit the pattern when she has to make reservations for them. She chats them up as standard 'let me fill the time while I'm waiting for the confirmation of your trip to come up on my computer'. Plus she gets to see personal ID stuff and that kind of thing."

"She sells their credit card numbers?" Dimple asked.

"No! Nothing like that. She knows that might lead back to her and that's the bottom line – no obvious trace back to her."

"With somebody else I'd laugh at the presumption that you'll leave here with only a few bucks and your train ticket in your pocket and arrive in Miami with at least the start of your stake to take you through the winter but I've watched you work."

"I'm going prepared to play the long game this year. Should have thought of this years ago. First I bought a second pay-as-you-go phone to make calls on that I don't want traced as fast in case anyone's already tuned in to my main one." He wrote a phone number on a piece of paper from a small pad he kept in his pocket and handed that over. "This is for special calls only. Routine stuff goes to the other phone. Things I need to know and that it would be better that others don't know without making a big production out of it, use this one."

Dimple made sure he could read the number, then put that piece of paper into his wallet as he nodded that he understood the situation.

"Then I bought a phone charge card for cash at a small place. With that I can make calls on the train or in Miami without a paper trail that leads back to me. I'm not planning anything that should make that essential but it seems like a prudent precaution. Doesn't cost me any extra since I'd have to pay for those calls anyway if I make them."

"Some inkling this might be a big time winter?"

"Just a small itch in the back of my head that makes me wonder if maybe this'll be the year I make the big time in spite of myself."

"Sweet good luck to you with that then."

"There's always a certain thrill to living off the land as it were. Being my own guy. Not punching a clock or taking orders on what I have to do today or this week except what directly benefits me. I'm now willing to admit that when I was younger I was chicken to go that route. Now I'm more confident that I'll find ways to get by without setting myself up for a long vacation in the slammer if I misjudge and try to con the wrong guy."

"Thanks for joggling my memory gourd. Let me give you the name of somebody you might find an interesting challenge, Sylvester." Dimple took a folded in half index card with some information typed on it from his pocket and offered that to Pernell.

"You're trying to set me up with somebody's sister or auntie?"

"From what I've been told about this Agnes Beebop person that's not likely. She's a friend of a friend who's in a hospital down in

Miami. The name of the place is on there. The South Miami Healing Hospital. They didn't tell me a home address although I assume she has one," Dimple said as his friend read the card.

"You want me to get her flowers and deliver them in your name? What are you asking me to do, Jack?"

"If you have a few minutes, stop by and just tell her the folks at the Circle Squares group say hello."

"And they miss her."

"Don't go that far, no. Apparently she's what many of the group politely call *feisty* so she kept them aware of stuff going on that affected them for the worst but she was blunt about it and instead of pitying them she laughed at the ones who didn't have the good sense to protect themselves."

"Yet they want someone to tell her hello for them." Pernell let his doubts about that show.

"One of them does. That's the one I'd like to have a good word from for being helpful, too bad about the rest of the old biddies. I'm doing this other lady a favor by asking you to do it so you'd do me a favor by considering paying a visit if you can. Heck, as long as I asked I get my reward part even if you don't do it."

"Except as a favor to you, why would I even think about it?"

"Because you like interesting people. She sounds like she fits that job description. I don't know, maybe you can shake her up or something."

"Explain that."

"As I get it the story, she's in this hospital in a big part because she won't cooperate with the doctors or follow directives. She has some kind of stomach or digestive problems but they can't make a real diagnosis because she won't agree to most of the tests they want to do. She must have some *in* that they haven't put her out of the street to take care of herself, but I don't know any of that part of it."

"You think I can cast a spell over her and cure her stomach ache?"

"At least get her to talk about what she's afraid of that she won't take the tests or the pills they hope will fix her up. My lady friend hinted that Ms. Beebop is being contrary for the sake of being that way. Maybe con her into cooperating without realizing she's doing so. That's the way I envision you doing it. Cons are your thing," Dimple said.

Pernell put the index card in his pocket. "No promises but if I can do it without going too far out of my way I'll see what I can do."

"That's as much as I asked for but I asked so I'm rewardable. You have a good winter, Sylvester. Happy hunting. Enjoy Miami."

Pernell waved and walked to the stairs.

When Pernell went down the stairs to the platform, Hill and Taylor walked over to stand back to back pretending not to notice one another. "Do you see anybody that's probably watching his back?" Hill whispered, covering his mouth to disguise that as if coughing since there was no one close enough to hear them directly.

"Not a single person I have any suspicions about," Taylor said, straining not to move her lips while doing that.

"Then we're go."

"So go before the train leaves without us."

Hill hurried down the stairs to board; Taylor searched through her handbag for something in order to explain her hesitation.

At the bottom of the stairs Hill saw Pernell boarding the train at the rear car. Only when that man was aboard did Hill proceed out onto the platform where Pernell might see him. He made a speed dial call on his cell phone. "Get on at a front car. He got on the last one." Then he boarded the train by the same rear door Pernell had used.

Taylor hurried down the steps and boarded at the front end.

Finally Dutton came stumbling hurriedly down the stairs to board. He hesitated about where to do so and finally opted for the first car.

Once on the train, Pernell took a seat two-thirds of the way forward in the car. When Hill entered from the rear of the car he slipped quietly into a seat several behind Pernell, eager to observe and ready to eavesdrop if he could.

Taylor entered that car from the front end, passed Pernell without showing any interest in him, and sat beside Hill.

Dutton entered after Taylor and looked down the car. When he saw the positions of the others he scowled but hung his head and walked quickly past them all and sat farther back to observe them all with no hint yet of which he was interested in.

Chapter 02

An hour later while the train traveled between cities, Pernell entered the third coach car with his laptop in its carrying case. He moved slowly down the aisle letting an exaggerated concern about his stability in the slightly shaking car keep him from being obvious as he checked out those in the seats ahead.

About the middle of the car Mr. Crane, a nervous looking man in his forties with thin gray hair and wearing a cheap business suit, sat alone paging through a magazine. Pernell checked Crane's face against a small photo downloaded off the Internet that he was careful to keep inconspicuous in the palm of in his hand. Confirming the match, Pernell smiled confidently and sat down beside him before Mr. Crane realized what was happening.

"Please forgive my presumptuousness in approaching you, Mr. Crane. You don't know me but I know about your reputation. Simon Crane is highly regarded as a very smart businessman."

Crane quickly went from a frown about this intrusion into what he had claimed as his space to a flattered smile. "Yeah, I'm sure I'm known for that."

"I have contacts whose names aren't important who tell me you're a sharp investor with a good eye for unusual deals that'll pay off in short order and in big dividends. It's always an honor to be in the presence of a mind of that caliber."

Pernell glanced around as if to be sure they weren't being overheard so Crane nervously followed suit.

"My research led me to you as a potential partner in the deal of a lifetime. This is something that needs only a little capital to get it started but the business is good then for the indefinite future. Not just a one shot deal. But the timing's critical. It can all get away unless I can move on it very fast."

"That's often the case in business," Crane said with what he hoped sounded like the voice of sage experience.

"I need somebody with some cash who's stable enough to live with the likelihood of multiplying his money twenty-fold or more in the first year. A lot of people can't handle getting that rich that fast."

"I'm a pretty stable guy," Crane said. He leaned forward so as not to miss a word, trying hard to appear nonchalant but obviously interested.

* * *

Hill and Taylor entered from the rear of the car where they had watched Pernell move into position through the window in the connecting door. They slipped quietly into the seat immediately behind the other two men, eager to eavesdrop

Dutton entered after them since he had been watching them from inside the fourth car and was intent on keeping tabs on them. He started through the third car but as soon as he spotted the pair he dropped himself into the first empty seat he came to behind them.

* * *

"Of course in any business venture there's some risk, more in one with an unusually high profit potential. Maybe you're not willing to take risks. Maybe you don't even want to hear the details. I'd understand that. You're a busy man. That's fine. I won't bother you with the details unless you want to hear them. Right now it's still just general talk and I don't have to be concerned about my idea being pirated. If I do let you in on it, even if you decide not to get into the deal, I need your assurance on your honor of absolute confidentiality of this matter. I'm sure a business man of your experience understands the need for that."

Crane tried to sound nonchalant but missed it as he said, "You might as well tell me. What do I have to lose? If I'm not interested I'll have forgotten all about it before I get off this train."

"Okay, here's the deal. The president is soon going to announce a new national holiday for the last Sunday in October. It'll be a Sunday so government workers don't have to get a paid day off and it's right near Halloween to please the voter group who want to suppress that celebration of witches and black magic. This is intended to distract from and therefore diminish the scary stuff."

"I haven't heard about that."

"There's been no official word about it yet. That's why there's a chance to make a bundle on it if we're ready. The holiday's a carefully planned government way to promote cordiality among people and at the same time to save the Postal Service from financial disaster. They've very deliberately scheduled it two months before Christmas. The idea is to encourage everybody to send holiday greeting cards to all their friends and relatives twice a year instead of only once. They did focus group research and found that most people will be more likely to send these cards around the year-end holiday season when they're conditioned to send some anyway. If this works as well as they hope, they'll introduce other reasons to send cards up to six times a year which they figure should keep the post offices in business for the long haul. Government planners get paid to think about how to get us to do stuff years in the future."

"What'll this new holiday be called?" Crane asked, interested but confused.

"They gave that a lot of thought and expensive study before they decided it should be - are you ready for this? National Dog and Cat Day."

"What? For the love of... Why that?" Crane sputtered.

"They figured that dogs are man's best friends. Cats have their fans too. Come on, what do people ask about when they write to one another? Their pets. The idea is to give them a push to write to one another. So the Post Office can make money from all those stamps."

"But for crying out loud, how many people are gonna celebrate National Dog and Cat Day?" Crane asked louder than he realized.

Pernell glanced around to see if anyone else was paying them any attention and gestured for Crane to keep his volume down as he quietly asked him, "Have you any idea how many pet owners there are in this country? Each one of them with friends and relatives who know how much they care about their furry friends. Do you know how many billions of dollars Americans spend on their pets every year? Yes, billions with a B."

Crane wasn't convinced. "Okay, let's say the president does make it a holiday. So what?"

"So the thing is to corner the market on *Dog and Cat Day* greeting cards. With the president himself telling everybody to send them, there'll be a huge demand. I mean, how many people do you think will actually sit down and write a real note to one another? No way. They'll all be looking for preprinted messages with colored pictures and their names imprinted. Just like Christmas. But we'll be the only ones that'll have them ready.

"Duh, what about Hallmark and all those companies?"

"That's our big break. They haven't gotten wind of it yet. They'll be caught napping and not able to get anything out on such short notice. All their output will be focused on Christmas, Hanukkah, Kwanza, and New Year's. They won't be ready to do this new kind this year."

Since Crane's body language wasn't shouting total disbelief, Pernell opened his laptop and brought up a page showing four sample card designs with pictures of dogs and cats on them and showed those to Crane. He gave the man a minute to recognize that these were rough sketches of prospective cards using stock photo images, then he scrolled down to a second page of similar items. Each card start had some version of *Enjoy National Dog and Cat Day with me/us* in fancy font printed somewhere on it.

"But we'll be all set. I know some people, see. We've got artists busy designing the cards. These are a few rough starter ideas they're busy putting the professional look on. I have a printing factory all ready to start running them off. The presses are ready to go as soon as we get operating capital. That's where you and a few other selected individuals can come in. You can buy in on the ground floor. It's the chance of a lifetime. Once we've captured the market everybody'll look for our cards year after year. We'll have branded the company to cards for that holiday. It's the way people work."

"Of course I'll have to check this out before I lay out money."

"Of course," Pernell agreed. "I wouldn't want it any other way. But you've got to do it fast. Like by tomorrow. Those presses have got to be rolling soon or it's too late, a fortune down the tubes. I'm not playing games with you and I hope you won't play them with me. If you can't handle this opportunity just say so. I've got a few others on my short list. I've got to have an answer very soon."

"I don't know. This is all... It seems kind of..."

"I know it's rushed, but you can see that in this situation that can't be helped. It's now or never. If I had seen this thing coming six months ago it would have been different - but also the potential for a big clean up wouldn't have been there. The established card making companies would have gotten the whole thing."

Crane slumped in his seat, his brow wrinkled in concentration and worry. "I'll have to make some phone calls to see if I can arrange for somebody to meet us with the money."

Pernell took some other papers from his case. "Then I'll give you some privacy to read this proposed contract and make your calls. Let's agree to meet outside on the platform at Washington. Check with anybody you want on this, just remember that very few people will know about the new holiday which is precisely the reason it's a gold mine. Also keep in mind that everyone you mention it to, even to check it out, is one more person who could leak the news to the wrong people and destroy the opportunity."

Pernell handed over the contract and left the car, walking back the way he had entered. Crane sat wringing his hands and pulling at his hair in indecision.

Once Pernell was out of the car and had apparently not stopped in the space between cars to look back in at Crane, Hill and Taylor got up and followed. They went into that space between cars and watched Pernell through the window in the connecting door.

Pernell stopped at an empty seat toward the middle of the fourth car, checked that his bag was okay in the overhead rack, then sat. As he took a typed page and another small photo from an envelope stuffed into the carrying case with his laptop and studied those Taylor and Hill entered that car and hurried to seats three rows behind him.

"He's good," Taylor said with genuine admiration.

Hill nodded agreement. "I'd heard he could con almost anyone and know I believe it. I should give my tipster a bonus for putting us onto this guy but extras weren't part of my deal with that slime ball no matter how useful he is."

"So the first question is answered. Yes, if anyone can pull it off, this Pernell guy could do the job. Next question is, would this Pernell fellow be interested in doing it?" Taylor asked.

Dutton, who had followed that pair out of the car where Crane was making a cell phone call, entered behind them once they were seated and distracted whispering to one another. He took a seat right behind them where he slumped down to not be seen while testing whether he could eavesdrop on them.

Hill nodded. "That question slides right into the alternative one. Can we help make him receptive to the idea?"

"So we face the old carrot or the stick decision," Taylor said. "Do we entice him or do we screw up his other plans to pressure him to take what money he can still get?"

"Go ahead, call me nasty but I love the thought of outwitting an outwitter so I vote for screwing him over from the start."

"You're jealous that he's as good at creating scams as you are."

"We aren't likely to find a better candidate so we need to know what all he has going here on the train."

Taylor mimed dialing an imaginary phone, then said into that, "Hello. Calling Sylvester Pernell. Please make yourself available to do the job for us that we can't do ourselves."

Both sucked in their breath in surprise and shock when Pernell stood and looked back down the car.

They let out that air, careful not to attract attention by being noisy about it, when Pernell headed out of the car by the door ahead so he wouldn't pass them after all.

The pair allowed sixty seconds before Hill went nonchalantly to the door where they had last seen Pernell, checked through the window that that man wasn't in the between-car space, then went out there himself. That was Taylor's signal to follow, equally nonchalantly of course.

Dutton tried to force himself to count slowly to sixty before he stood and followed them but lost control of himself at thirty-three and hurried to the door without nonchalance.

* * *

U.S. Treasury Agent Warren Winkler, fifty-four, lean and business-like in a dark suit and tan trench coat, stood in the end space between the third and fourth cars making a cell phone call. He wanted this to be in secret but the noise of the wheels on the tracks required him to speak louder than he wanted to.

"This is Agent Warren Winkler reporting in. Can you hear me? Sorry about the noise but I'm on a train and there are too many people in the main parts of the cars who don't need to know there's a treasury agent with the Bunco squad on board."

He turned his back, held the phone out of sight, and strained to see their reflections in the outside window that his nose touched in front of him as Hill and Taylor passed between cars behind him. He had expected the space to be a good place for this purpose but these were the second and third persons to pass him since he stopped here.

Winkler checked that he was alone before he continued his call. "Sorry about that. I was assigned to ride this train to be familiar with it for a special job in a few days but I have a strong feeling that there's suspicious stuff we need to know about going on on this train now. I have three people that I plan to keep an eye on."

Winkler turned his back, held the phone out of sight, and strained to see the man's reflection in the outside window as Dutton moved between cars behind him.

Dutton reacted with surprise at finding someone out here but quickly tried to cover his reaction and hurried along. Winkler turned as quickly to see who had reacted so strongly to finding someone here. He stepped over to peek around the end of the car - to find Dutton peeking back through the third car door window from inside. Both jerked back nervously.

After a moment Winkler peeked again but Dutton was moving down the car. He said into the phone, "Sorry about the interruption again but I just noticed another guy who needs watching. I'll report in as I learn anything definite. You may need to have more agents ready to meet this train at Miami."

* * *

Pernell moved down the aisle of the second car with his laptop in its case. He secretly checked Mr. Santori, a jowly, heavy-set man of sixty in an unkempt but expensive suit, currently paging through a daily newspaper, against a print out of an Internet photo in his hand. With a nod to himself, Pernell slipped the photo into his pocket, then made as if to sit in one empty seat but at the last moment squeezed in beside Santori.

"Mr. Antonio Santori. Am I correct?"

"Who are you?" Santori asked suspiciously.

"My name's Terence Tony Thompson. I was referred to you by a mutual acquaintance who prefers to remain unnamed for now."

"Why? What's he afraid of?"

"He's afraid you might not recognize an opportunity when it lands in your lap and that his standing as a business intermediary might suffer. This way if you're not interested in my proposition, there's no harm done to anyone."

"A business deal. What do you have in mind?"

"It's something unusual in the entertainment area."

When the other man gestured that he was ready to hear more Pernell said, "I'm ready to cut you in as partner in an entertainment deal I'm handling. I hear you're big on investing in projects to give people something to do with their leisure time. Let me say, a very astute strategy. Well I've got a natural. It's a sure thing. I've got the Benjamin Franklin dinosaur - or so we'll bill it. A prehistoric creature dug up by a founding father of our great nation. It can't miss."

"It's crazy!" Santori snorted. Pernell took several photos of large bones, a hole with digging tools beside it, and an artist's sketch of the traveling show from his laptop case and placed them on top of it.

Hill and Taylor entered behind these two and quietly took seats where they could listen without being obvious.

"Of course. But that's the beauty of it," Pernell said pleasantly and confidently. "Let me explain. It's got everything it takes to make a big success. I have a friend who knows a guy who has the thing. He bought it from some little museum that went kaput. What we do is build it up with a lot of PR as a 'must see'. Giving it the historical twist for good measure. We might as well capitalize on the founding fathers since they're the biggest names in town for many folks."

"Come on. The Benjamin Franklin dinosaur! We'd be laughed right out of town."

"That'd never happen. It's all a matter of how you go about it. Sure, if you just kind of quietly set up shop somewhere you may get ignored or even laughed at. The name of the game though is *splash*. Do things big and flashy and everybody takes you seriously. They're fully prepared to pay you for it too. But you can't pussyfoot around."

"What's that supposed to mean?"

"You don't just rent a hall and hang out a sign. You start a few weeks in advance with an ad blitz and you keep up the pressure."

Dutton entered behind them all and took a seat behind Hill and Taylor who were too focused on Pernell to notice him.

"That's stupid," Santori said. "Then everybody knows before you open the doors that you don't have anything serious."

"With all due respect, wrong again, my friend. The pre-event ad blitz acts like an anesthetic. As a businessman you recognize that people are pretty uncritical about advertising."

"That's true."

"After the very first few times that they hear or see an ad they recognize it and then switch it to an unconscious level of alertness. So they're getting a jiggle from it but they're not really paying attention to what's being said. Give a listen to some of the stuff that comes across the airwaves and you'll definitely have to conclude that either people are extremely stupid or they just aren't listening closely."

Winkler entered at the rear of the car and walked slowly through it without stopping, but noting where Hill, Taylor, Dutton, and Pernell were seated. He stopped at the end of the car and checked a text message on his cell phone.

Santori's expression reflected his doubts. "Okay. Let's say for conversation sake that I might be interested. What exactly do you have in mind?"

"For starters we need a trailer."

"How big is this thing?"

"It's not your super-big, giant-sized dinosaur. It's a moderate-sized one. With some of the pieces missing."

"I guess that's the reason some other museum didn't pick it up," Santori suggested.

"You're probably right. I hadn't thought about that. You're very perceptive. Anyway that's to our advantage. It gives us an excuse for not making it take up more room. It travels better this way too. It can't shake apart and have to be repaired and reassembled all the time because it's not together to begin with."

"But will people be willing to pay to come and look at just a pile of old bones? Especially when they could see better ones at any regular science museum?"

"See, that's where the real psychology comes into the game. That's the historical twist. When we associate the bones with the name of someone patriotic and historical, that's what'll really pull the crowds in. We make those bones something that everybody'll want to be able to say they saw."

"Make up a story about them? Fake it and see if it floats?"

"Believe me, it'll float. With all of the other junk being floated on a historical theme, nobody of any consequence will even notice."

"But you almost have to hide your show, don't you?" Santori asked, pretty sure he knew the answer.

"Of course you don't rent Madison Square Garden. Then people will start to closely check your credentials."

"My point exactly," Santori said.

"No, the secret is to keep it small but intensive. Shopping malls, car shows, county fairs, that kind of thing."

Santori shrugged that he got that point.

"Also you keep the price down. A buck or a buck-fifty a head's good. Enough to make it worth your while but not enough to make most people hesitate about paying it. That's part of the secret. You want people to figure they really can't lose anything. I mean, what's a buck? Combine that with the lure of being able to say they saw it, whatever it is, and you've got a sure winner. Most people don't really care what it is as long as everybody else is talking about it. So we've got us a little gold mine. It's like alchemy. Turning old bones into new gold."

"I still think you're crazy."

"Yeah, but you're also getting interested. I can see the dollar signs in your eyes," Pernell said with a grin.

Winkler walked back up the aisle getting another look at them all without actually staring at any of them.

"Tell me about the historical angle. What are you going to say? That Benjamin Franklin shot the thing or something like that? I don't think even Americans are that dumb."

"I'm thinking of something more on the lines that old Ben Franklin discovered this thing and dug it up. Since he was a famous scientist among other things, and had his hand in so many places, few people really know what all he did or didn't do."

"I guess that's true," Santori conceded.

"They'll believe almost anything about him. We say that an amateur scientist found a big bone and showed it to Franklin. Then Franklin went out and dug up the other parts of it. He was gonna donate it to the museum at the University of Pennsylvania - which as a fact he founded, by the way. But he held off until he had all of the parts. But he never did find them all so the project was forgotten and the bones lay in somebody's barn or cellar for years and years, getting moved from here to there as houses changed hands and all. Spent some celebrity time in that museum but then were put back in storage. Until we found them in a warehouse and realized their significance."

"Would it really attract crowds?"

"I don't think it can miss. It has all the right things going for it. It's a natural curiosity. It's associated with a famous person. The price is reasonable. And it's right in your own backyard for a short time only. Pretty near everything else connected with the founding fathers you have to go to the big cities of the East Coast to see. This is right here, for one week only, at your local shopping center. It can't lose, I tell you. It really can't lose."

Both men looked up as Winkler passed them coming back down the aisle a third time. Winkler took the empty seat across from Hill and Taylor - who sat back so it wasn't as obvious that they were eavesdropping. But when Winkler closed his eyes as if to nap they promptly leaned forward to hear better again.

Automatically, Santori spoke in a quieter tone. "How long would it take you to get this thing together?"

"It'll take about three full days from the word go to get the ad campaign started. Bookings for the remainder of the year could be arranged as fast. You start the ad campaign two weeks before you arrive. So we can be ready to open the doors in about three weeks. Once it's rolling, an operation like this is good for five years at least."

"That long?"

"Do you know how many shopping centers and county fairs there are?"

Santori gestured that he got the point.

Pernell continued, "I can have a team ready to man the thing in three weeks too. They have to be trained. You know, background info on Ben Franklin, on the dinosaur, and all that stuff. I mentioned the project to my history expert friend a week ago as a possibility. If I know him, by now he has the whole thing all worked out and half of the documents drafted. So there's no hang up there either."

Santori let it sound like he was impressed. "About how much are we talking about?"

"From you? Fifty thousand as seed money. That gets the ad thing going, buys the trailer, and covers incidentals until the money starts rolling in. If it was gonna take longer to get operational it'd cost more for salaries and all."

Hill and Taylor leaned even closer to hear Santori's response but when Winkler opened his eyes and looked over they were torn between hearing and acting innocent. Dutton leaned forward behind them trying to hear too, a hand cupped behind his ear.

Santori gave a snorting laugh. "You really think I'm going to bite on this don't you. I should be very insulted that you take me for such a chump. The Benjamin Franklin dinosaur! Come on, mister. You sure figured that you saw me coming down the street with greenhorn written all over me."

Pernell used his insulted tone. "Mr. Santori, I brought this deal to you in good faith because you were recommended to me as having a good head for the possibilities of the more unusual line of investments. I wouldn't bother to bring this proposal to a lot of people precisely because they're too small-minded to see its potential. If you feel that I'm trying to take you in some way I'll withdraw my offer and leave quietly. I guess I was wrong about you being a man of imagination and an innovator."

Pernell gathered up his photos. "I'm sorry that I bothered you. I'll find someone else who does recognize a good thing when it comes along and who's ready to move on it. I certainly don't need you."

When Pernell started to get up, Santori pulled him back down. "Sit down. I didn't mean that I wasn't interested. I have to be careful. That was just my way of testing you since I don't know you. Now let's go over a few of the details."

While Pernell and Santori conferred in low tones, Hill and Taylor, noting that apparently Winkler had actually fallen asleep, exited back the way they had come, glancing over the seat at the photos on Pernell's case as they did so but without distracting the negotiating pair.

After those two were out of this car, Dutton stood to follow them out but dropped back down when Winkler awoke with a jerk and slowly turned to look around, reminding himself of where he was and why he was there. Dutton rummaged around in the seat, then jumped up and hurried after Hill and Taylor, now holding a partly opened newspaper to block Winkler's view of his face.

Winkler was torn between staying put in order to see what Pernell and Santori were doing and following the suspicious-acting Dutton. He mentally flipped a coin and opted to follow the others out of the car.

* * *

A while later, Taylor entered and stood holding onto the back of the seat for balance across the aisle from Antonio Santori, a cell phone to her ear. Santori glanced her way but then pretended not to notice her.

Loud enough to be sure Santori could hear her without being too obvious about it, Taylor said into the phone, "He said that the police are following the guy just waiting for the final go-ahead to arrest him. It's the kind of scam the TV magazine shows won't be able to resist. Con artists trying to rip people off with a dumb scam that involves things supposedly connected with Thomas Jefferson or somebody from his time. I don't know all the details. Somebody's in for a big surprise though and it won't be the people who plunk down their admission money."

Taylor subtly glanced down to be sure Santori was listening and his expression assured her that he was. She continued into the phone, "He said the cops don't think it can be a one-man scam, there have to be others supplying at least the start-up money. By waiting a bit they get to scoop them all up in one well-publicized raid."

Now Taylor walked back in the direction she had come from as if listening to the reply of the person she was on the phone with. When close to the back of the car she closed the phone and put it in her small handbag - which gave her the innocent excuse to turn enough to see Santori hanging halfway out of his seat to watch her go. She smiled broadly as she went on her way out of the car.

* * *

Taylor entered the next car and stopped by the seat across the aisle from Simon Crane, cell phone to her ear, to regain her footing from the rolling of the train. Crane glanced over her way but then pretended not to notice her beyond beaming a shy smile her way in case she noticed him since she seemed not to have done so yet.

Taylor said into the phone, "It was a lucky break for him. I hear the card company is giving him a big reward for letting them know about it so they wouldn't miss such an opportunity. He said they'd have the new cards in the stores by this weekend and they'll start an ad campaign about the new holiday the very day it becomes official. It's a great idea when you think about it. Everybody loves their pets." She continued on down the aisle, phone to ear. Again she used the excuse of putting the phone in her handbag to steal a glance back the way she has come – where Crane was making a frantic call on his cell phone.

Taylor broke into a big grin and continued on her way.

* * *

At Washington's Union station Pernell stepped off the train.

He stood with his bags at his feet and far enough away to not block others getting off. He would move over to the train on an adjacent track that would continue the trip south as today's "Miami Streak" run. He checked his watch and tried not to seem interested in the others getting off.

Crane and Santori came out different doors at the front end of the train and both moved quickly into the station, determined to avoid Pernell. He was distracted looking at something toward the rear of the train and didn't see them. Hill and Taylor watched Pernell from one window of the train; Dutton watched from another window; Winkler watched from a third window.

Minutes later, Pernell stood outside the train that would be continuing south so he could see the few people still on the platform as he talked on his cell phone. "I'm not sure what went wrong but it's pretty clear that my carefully selected pigeons won't get plucked after all. That'll mean a hard winter even without snow. This after I did some good work on those two."

From the phone, Dimple reassured him, "If you're only at D.C. you still have what a full day on the train to find some alternate pigeons? Come on, Sylvester, you're enough of a pro to work this out."

"I've got a bad feeling. I'm afraid I might be forced to consider doing jobs I'd prefer to pass on once I'm down south."

"See, you can already imagine where you'll get offers. That's gotta be a good sign."

A trainman waved that they are about to leave so Pernell took one last look around and boarded the train. His expression was a mix of confusion and disappointment.

"I'm not so sure. Gotta go. Talk to you later, Jack."

Chapter 03

Winkler found Dutton standing between the cars with his back to the agent and staring at the outside window as Winkler passed behind him going between cars. Winkler knew this was suspicious but knew that it wasn't improper in itself since even good guys like himself did it at times.

In that car, Hill and Taylor sat several seats from the door they had entered through. "He's as good as we can hope to find so I say let's do it. We should set him up right away," Hill insisted.

"Okay, if you say so," Taylor agreed. "But just how do we go about setting him up?"

"By explaining to him exactly what we want him to do straight out. Any theatrics would make him suspicious."

"Suppose he doesn't bite? What then?"

"Him not bite? Don't make me laugh. He'll take the line before you can blink an eye. He's the type that never lets a chance get by him. That's why he's our man."

Hill nodded to the aisle as Pernell, having found all the seats farther forward taken, walked back and took a seat.

"Here he is now, right on cue." Hill then moved over to the seat beside Pernell. Taylor exited the car by the rear door so Pernell wouldn't see her.

For a brief second Pernell looked alarmed, then when Hill didn't flash a badge he became relieved but annoyed. "That seat's taken," Pernell grumbled.

"Yeah, by me. Let me introduce myself, Mr. Pernell. My name's Alpha. I've been watching your exploits. I'm very impressed."

"If you're some kind of a cop I expect the showing of a badge to make this legal and proper."

"Cop? Perish the thought. I'm no friend of the security forces, nor they of me. They tend to get in my way and cramp my style."

"Then beat it, you bother me, Alphabet soup."

"Now, now, don't be hasty. I didn't approach you just to see the color of your eyes. I have a business proposition for you. A lucrative one - *uh*, that means worth lots of money - if you pull it off."

"I know what lucrative means. You don't have to talk down to me," Pernell said with a touch of venom in his tone.

"That's precisely the reason I was attracted to you."

"Damn! Nobody ever wants me for my body."

"You're an accomplished master of fast-talk and thinking on the spur of the moment. That's the expertise I want to hire."

"Let's save us both a lot of time. What's the bottom line? That means..."

Hill cut him off. "I can figure out what it means, thanks. The answer is ten percent of two million dollars. That would come to..."

Pernell cut him off. "Yeah. Two hundred grand. Now I know you're a practical joker. That's a lot of money."

"Certainly, but to get it you'll have to earn it - which won't be easy although it doesn't sound hard to start with."

"Just supposing I was interested, what would I have to do?"

"Be the bagman. Pick up the two million and deliver it to me. It's that simple."

"So what's the hard part?" Pernell persisted.

"Convincing the person who has it to give it to you."

"Does that mean I have to steal it?"

"Not at all. In fact you wouldn't stand a chance of doing that."

"Then you'd better explain in detail."

"My pleasure. Persons who shall remain unnamed in a public place like this owe me the two million dollars for services rendered. For reasons too complicated to go into right now, they'd just as soon eliminate me as pay me. In fact that's what I have every reason to believe would happen if I went to collect the money myself."

"So why would they give me the money if they wouldn't give it to you?"

Hill gestured, spread palms up, to emphasize how simple the answer was. "The Code of Honor among Thieves requires them to pay up whenever I make formal application for the payment. Otherwise no other professional crooks will trust them enough to deal with them, which pretty much puts them out of business."

Pernell thought about that and made an unconscious nod and facial expression that said he knew what the man was referring to and agreed with his statement. "Okay. Tell me more."

"What I need is someone smart on his mental feet who can talk his way in there and get back out alive. That means mainly someone who can convince these guys that he's only temporary help, hired for this operation only, not a regular member of my organization."

"Why?" Pernell had his suspicions about the answer but in a case like this it was important to be sure of what the others involved thought and believed.

Hills said, "A regular member of my group might be held for ransom or have his head sent to me without the rest of him attached to it as a message. My agent also has to convince them he doesn't know anything specific about their operation."

"I don't follow."

"That'd assure them he's not a cop out to gather incriminating evidence against them. They hate that. They don't treat guys they catch doing that very well."

"Even without knowing their names I'll bet on that part."

"This bag man also has to convince these guys that somebody knows where he is, although not why, so if he doesn't show up at some particular place by a particular time there'll be an investigation. You know the kind of line I mean."

"Yeah. I think I get the picture," Pernell replied.

"The really tricky part'll be getting to the big man since the guy I had the contract with doesn't answer his own phone or front door."

"Not surprising if he's a big time operator."

"But you have to formally request the money face-to-face."

"Yeah, the Code would require that," Pernell agreed.

"That being the unavoidable situation, you'll have to talk your way past several levels of underlings, each one more cautious than the others. Does that sound like a challenge?"

"A challenge? Yeah, I guess so. It also sounds pretty damned dangerous. I'd venture a guess that these guys don't like visitors."

"Yes! You are a man who sees the whole picture! Wonderful! I had the feeling you were the right man."

"If these guys are the types I suspect they are, this job is too dangerous to give serious thought to for a mere ten percent."

"Okay, you're a negotiator too. Splendid talent but not one that'll advance your standing in this case. I've made my case and my offer. They stand - for a short time only. I'm not prepared to make a better offer."

"You need brave and very talented help. That's not in abundant supply and doesn't come cheap."

"True enough but there are other avenues open to me. They're more expensive but more certain. For one thing they don't involve my having to trust a relative stranger with all of that cash. Ten percent of two million dollars is a lot of money."

"I'm calling your bluff, Mister Alpha Whatever. I'm betting that you need me more than I need you," Pernell said.

Hill immediately rose. "Wrong, Mr. Pernell or whatever your name really is. I've got time. I can look around and find somebody else or I can use one of my alternatives. You, you're out the chance to earn two hundred thousand bucks without the trouble and risk of sweet talking it out of a string of pitiful spinsters a few thousand at a time."

Hill took a seat several rows forward in the car that had just been vacated.

Pernell sat back to contemplate his position, to focus on this opportunity he had been offered and what it really entailed and offered. He was surprised when he felt his second cell phone vibrate in his pants pocket. So far only one other person knew that number and that person knew the intention to limit calls to that phone. He trusted Joe Dimple so he had to take this because it must be important. He got up to go find a more private spot to talk as he pulled out the phone and took the call.

Hill watched Pernell head out the front end of the car. As he pulled out his own cell phone and touched some buttons he thought, *That's not the cell phone we've seen him use before and that we're equipped to listen in on. What's going on?*

* * *

Pernell stood in the space between cars to take the call, facing in so he would see anyone who came close enough that they might overhear him.

"Okay, I'm where I should be able to talk without being overheard. What's up, Joe?"

"I'm being paid to make this call, Sylvester. Guy wants to talk to you on his terms. Somehow he knows that I know you so he called me and offered me a few bucks to call you and ask you to call him from a payphone so he can find out if you want to do a paid job in Miami."

"You don't know this guy?"

"I have no clue who he is and he wouldn't give me a name."

"What did he call himself?"

"Said he's acting as agent for someone else."

"Could he be the law?"

"I can't say no to that. He never hinted at it, but I'm not sure if he'd have to if he is. And before you ask, he didn't tell me anything about the job he's looking to get done except that you'd be paid for doing it but only if you decide you want to try it."

"No pressure, only an offer?"

"That's as much as I picked up on anyway. As I said, he phones out of the blue and offers me a fifty dollar gift card in the mail for calling you and passing on the message and a phone number. As far as I know, he wouldn't know if I said I'd make the call but didn't do so."

"The gift card is for saying you'd do it, not for me calling him."

"That's what I make of it," Dimple said. "He was emphatic that you can say no you don't even want to hear the offer or say no after you know the details. But that's all between you and him. Once I make this call, I'm not involved anymore and don't have any curiosity about what the offer is or whether you agree to do it."

"Why does he want to offer it to me?"

"He said he somehow picked up on your reputation for doing stuff that means you have the skills they want to hire but you stay low key and small time. That translates as you're not on big time crime investigation radars. That's close to a quote. Almost exactly the way he described it. You have what they want to hire."

"They?"

"Him and whoever he's acting as the contact guy for. He was careful not to give me any hints about who that is. Not even if it's one person or some company or group. Not a hint," Dimple said.

"Let me play it the other way then. Why you? Why pay you to make the call to me?"

"He said he knows a fair amount about your exploits. He also knows enough about me that he believes that I'll do a thing if I say I will whether there's money involved or not but I'm a guy who doesn't snoop. I'll pass along the word but then, as I said a minute ago, I won't think any more about it and won't ask you about it later."

"I'm not happy finding out that people can learn so much about me. How is that possible?" Pernell asked.

"I'm guessing, but I wonder if your various arrests records which probably include details of what you were accused of even if you've never been convicted aren't a source. Plus maybe some of those computer snoop places. What do they call them - *flogs*?"

"Blogs. I have heard that there are a few weirdoes who have so little useful stuff to do that they spend hours searching public records for tidbits about small cons like me and think of us as Robin Hood style heroes."

"The point is that with the Internet a whole lot of stuff gets sorted and saved and then handed out or sold to anyone with any interest or a credit card," Dimple said.

"Did he say anything specific about what he thinks he knows about me and what I might have done in the past?"

"That's why I agreed to take him money and make this call. They know you're on the train and when you're due into Miami. They also know that you've wintered down there for the last few years living off the scams you pulled along the way. They know or guess that you don't pull much in Florida itself in order to stay off the radar of the authorities there. That adds up to the fact that they're somehow keeping tabs on you to the minute."

"Not a real comforting thought," Pernell said.

"But maybe better to know it than that you don't if it's the way things are. At least you'll think about how much of what you do somebody's watching and reporting on."

"That's a way to think about it."

"He didn't give me details but he said I could tell you they need something done in a sneaky way but that in and of itself it's not illegal. You wouldn't be stealing anything or sabotaging anything."

"I have to think about this."

"That what he expects and wants you to do. Nothing rash."

"Did he say to call at a specific time?"

"Any time until you get to Miami. If he hasn't heard from you he'll take that to mean you have no interest and won't push this. They only want you involved if you're a willing participant is what he said. He said you should call from a payphone on the train or maybe at a station where you have a several minute layover along the way. He knows the train schedule, I don't and I wasn't tempted to look it up."

"Okay, give me the number. It's another option since I have fewer of those than I was hoping for." He memorized the number but didn't log it into his phone's *Contacts* memory. Lots to think about but it was hard to walk away without knowing the details.

Chapter 04

At 3:20 that afternoon Beth Kurian and Anne Siskel, sorority sisters for a full quarter century now, stood in the space between train cars. "I can't believe we're doing this," Kurian giggled.

"I can't believe that I've never done anything like it before," Siskel replied. "It's harmless fun but I'm getting such a kick out of it. Who knew going to an acting workshop as part of your twenty-fifth college reunion could be so... is liberating the word for it?"

"The pure chance that we would be on the train with all these wealthy men looking to be Southern gentlemen is critical though. Without them to play to it'd be too silly."

"Are we going to keep it up? Do we dare?" Siskel whispered.

"What's the worst that can happen? Some stuffy guy we think of as a throwback – and who we definitely would throw back even if he has as much money as he's trying to make it seem - says we're not truly ladies in the old style? Heck, I'm torn since I think much of what they apparently said and did was or is so dumb so I want to be told I'm too modern and sensible to convincingly put on those airs."

"I'm going for it while we have this perfect audience for our play-acting," Siskel said. Kurian nodded agreement. Each held out her left hand to show she had removed her wedding band which would hamper the illusion they aimed to create. They struggled not to giggle.

The two women entered the car ahead, already aware of a group of prosperous looking fifty-plus gentlemen traveling together and mostly sitting together. The ladies primly take the available seats with these men behind, across from, and in front of them. Most of the men were reading newspapers and business papers but looked the ladies over with at least passing interest.

Looking out the window, Siskel said, "I do declare this is lovely enough country we're passing through although not as lovely as home of course. What do you think...eh, Lucy?"

Kurian hesitated just a moment to force back the smile that had started to run across her face before she realized it. Then she said, "I'm still too annoyed at that family of yours for the trouble they put us through, Ethel."

"They're your family too. We're sisters even though it's clear to all that you're older by several years. Some of the Beauregards show the ravages of time more than others of us."

Both were fighting to play it straight now.

"That nephew deserves what he got today. Marryin' that kinda woman. She'll make his life miserable and too bad about him," Kurian stated.

"It was very inconsiderate of them to wait until the last minute to invite us to the wedding. They only did it to get some fine gifts to offset the practical stuff they were given by her family. In a proper Beauregard household you expect the servants to work for their keep, you don't give them labor-saving devices. It was all too clear that those people don't understand a lot of things."

"I've never laid eyes on the groom before and I'll be happy not to do so again. Like I'd travel any distance to attend his funeral. Until now he was simply a twig name on that part of the family tree that we can't prune off but don't have to pay attention to."

Pernell entered the car and nonchalantly took a seat where he could see and barely hear the two women who seemed to be talking louder that they realized.

He thought, *Things are more complicated here. When I spotted those two in the other car they all but screamed out 'ready to be fleeced' and I was willing to oblige. But do I dare try to scam them with so many nearby attentive witnesses? I don't know how far they're traveling and I don't want any unnecessary fuss that might spoil things for me on the rest of my trip. I'll wait and see if they move somewhere more private where I can make my approach. In the meantime I can figure out what line to throw out for them to bite on.*

Kurian said, "I've been bravely holding it in..."

Her "sister" giggled at that but covered her mouth to not laugh.

Kurian gave her a haughty look and continued, "But it must out as we learned in school that someone famous said. I am humiliated and furious to be forced to travel in these clothes. A fine lady wears formal attire to a public event like a wedding even if she doesn't care a fig for those being joined in holy matrimony."

"Now, now, Lucy, we had little choice. The bride's sisters made clear what they would do to us if we stole attention from the bride by showing up dressed as we'd have preferred."

"'They were outrageous. 'Looking like refugees from an earlier century' was how the one sister described our dresses. The other called our choice of clothing and accessories 'backwards'."

"Not a cultivated crowd to say the least but we know that all too well," Siskel said.

"We had to rush directly from the cheapskate ceremony to catch this train because I sensed when we arrived yesterday that we wouldn't be satisfied with the proceedings and changed our travel booking. At least that spared us the burden of pretending to be polite to those people who were so below us. With neither time nor place to change before the dash to the station we must travel looking common, without the dignity proper to ladies like ourselves."

"Put that all out of your mind, sister dearest. I wonder what will be on the dinner menu."

Over the PA the conductor announced, "We are arriving at the Raleigh, North Carolina station."

Almost as one, the group of businessmen rose and exited the train, many politely saluting the ladies in passing. This left Pernell and the two women the only ones in that half of this car for now. A group of elderly women sat together at the far end of the car.

The ladies sat back and relaxed. They spoke quietly. "That was fun while it lasted and no hard feelings, no harm done," Siskel said.

"Not that it makes me antsy to go on stage with the amateur theater group in my area but it was amusing since I don't expect to see any of those men again so that Southern belle persona remains a secret between the two of us. Forever a secret."

"A ton of people in two different train cars as audiences and we never broke character while we were within earshot of them. We did good. I can't promise I'll never let my Ethel pop up again but your Lucy's a sworn secret until you say otherwise."

Pernell stood, looked around with exaggerated nonchalance, then started casually down the aisle toward the ladies.

"Do I sense a third and very attentive audience?" Siskel asked in a whisper.

"I have that sense. Should we keep going with this?" Kurian whispered back.

"Let's see where it goes. We can always break down laughing and apologize for rehearsing for a play we're hoping to be in."

"We're on."

For a time they sat primly watching the passing scenery in haughty silence but with no sign they approved of any of it.

Kurian fussed, "Train travel is hardly the socially approved mode of genteel transport today. Just anybody can ride in the same car with you. Most distressing."

"But we have no choice so I suppose we'll have to make the most of it, Lucy. It's not as if we were bein' judged by the important people of the world on the basis of what kind of transportation we use to get about. I think the train can be nice," Siskel insisted.

"You would. Mother would be shocked if she saw us here with all…those people. Common working people. 'No proper dignity', she'd say. Didn't raise my daughters to rub elbows with that lot. Somebody may knock us off our seats and rob us before we reach our station."

"You worry too much. About your safety and your reputation."

Kurian huffed, "One can never worry too much about one's family name and keeping it untarnished and gleaming as a beacon."

"A beacon of what since you're eager to say it?"

"Of right living for all the world to see and follow."

"I'm sure there's not a soul on this whole big train who would want to do us any bodily harm or to slur the fine name of Beauregard. Besides, they couldn't do any more to it than grandfather Seth and uncle Harcum have already done."

Frost covered her words as Kurian said, "Ethel, I thought we had an understanding that those names were never to mentioned between us."

"Oh poo."

"Is it too much to ask a simple, civilized thing like that? I hoped that this time you would conduct yourself in a dignified manner so I wouldn't feel it necessary to take accommodations in a different coach so as not to be associated with you in the public eye. Was I mistaken?"

"You can do as you wish, Lucy. I'm not holding you in that seat. But I am finished playing by your overstuffed and outdated 'rules of conduct for proper ladies'. You draw uncomplimentary attention to yourself precisely by acting like an oddball from some other century."

"Perhaps I would indeed prefer to be living in some simpler, more civilized century."

"You might wish it but you can't achieve it so either accept that fact or accept the fact that you're an anachronism and are going to be treated as such. This is the age of those computer machines running everything, phones that take photographs, ladies going out in public not wearin' hats, and TV advertisements shaping the common culture by showing most anything and much of it a disgrace. For better or worse, that's where we are."

"I probably cannot change it but that doesn't mean I have to like it" Kurian said with a haughty lift of her chin.

The women stirred as if uncomfortable when Pernell stopped and stared at them in open-mouthed wonder as he passed them while walking nonchalantly down the aisle. "Ladies, I beg forgiveness for my forwardness but I was literally stopped in my tracks. What faces! What practical, old fashioned American visages. You two are truly wonderful! Have you any idea?"

"What silliness," Kurian huffed.

"Forgive my directness but are you represented? Television is screaming for you. The ads are so bland. They need good faces - and personalities. Oh ladies, you two are a goldmine if you could get the right kind of exposure. Please allow me to present my business card. John Hampton, Artist's Representative. I'm the middleman who scouts... Oh ladies, you are so perfect! I can hardly believe it. I'm sorry, when I get this excited I tend to forget myself. As I started to say, I am responsible for spotting talent - that means the on-screen stars - for one of the nation's largest ad firms. I'm freelance but I do my best work for them."

Kurian sniffed, "Sir, we have not been properly introduced and we do not appreciate being made a spectacle of in public."

Siskel hurried to add, "Of course when meeting on a train like this, a person can hardly expect the social niceties like proper formal introductions. Do you really select people to be on the television?"

"Yes, ma'am, I select people to be on television and to make a lot of money for being there. To say nothing of the possibility of them ending up on the silver screen too."

Siskel gushed, "The motion pictures! That'd be so wonderful."

"Don't be silly," Kurian insisted, "You have to live out there in Hollywood to be in the pictures. I'm quite sure they don't have to send persons around the country looking on public conveyances for 'good faces' to keep their business going."

Pernell gestured his apology. "I hesitate to contradict you, ma'am, but I think you're misinformed. Not that there aren't hordes of hopefuls besieging the gates of the studios in Hollywood. No, they exist, true enough. But they don't get anywhere. The name of the game is representation. The TV and film producers can't be bothered sorting through all of those hopefuls themselves. All those dashed dreams. All those anguished looks and the tears that follow. They don't want to face any of that. They expect somebody else to do that for them. And they pay us to do exactly that. In the form of a fee for every contract actually signed."

"So with you representing us we could get... what is it they say? Our foot caught in some doors?"

"You're wonderfully perceptive, Miss..."

"Ethel. Miss Ethel Beauregard. Oh, and this is my sister Lucy. Lucy Beauregard. We're both maiden ladies."

"How very wonderful. I'm pleased to meet you both." Pernell glanced around to make sure no one else seemed to be listening even though he could see there was no one else close to them. The two women played along and reassured themselves about this also.

"I know this is forward of me but could I ask you just a little thing," Pernell said. "Call it a screen test if you wish. Would you just say 'Where's the tamale sauce?'. But you know, say it with *gusto*."

In a flat tone Kurian said, "Where's the tamale sauce?"

Siskel laughed just a bit too loudly for her fake sister's faked preference then shouted out, "Where's the *tamale* sauce? Or maybe it would be better as *where* is there tamale sauce?"

Kurian looked around anxiously to see if anyone was staring.

Ether didn't care about that as she asked, "What do you think. Do I have a feel for it?"

"That was wonderful. I hope you'll take this in the right way and not think I'm being forward but you have quite a pair of pipes."

Kurian clutched at her bosom in melodramatic shock.

Siskel laughed, "He means my lungs. That I have a loud voice."

Kurian pretended to try to cover her mistake. "Oh yes, of course. I understood what was meant. I just wasn't aware that that was considered a compliment."

"In show business it certainly is," Pernell assured them. "When you're waving to the TV audience at the annual awards ceremonies all those frailer folks will be green with envy as they give credit to your capacity of vocal projection."

Now Kurian laughed. "He means you have a loud mouth."

"Shush, Lucy! I have no idea of how these things work. What do you propose to do now that you've 'discovered' us, Mr. Hampton?"

"Initially all that's necessary are some still photos and of course a video audition tape. Good professional work on both, of course, to show you off to best advantage. Of course you'll need professional hair styling and makeup work. Fortunately I know top notch people who won't charge you an arm and a leg."

"Of course," Siskel said. Was that sarcasm?

"Charge us?" This gave Kurian another obvious opportunity to act startled and shocked.

Pernell shrugged. "It's standard procedure for the talent to pick up the tab for the preliminary stuff. Of course once you're signed to a contract with an agency these incidental expenses are just subtracted from your income before you see it, but the initial costs for everybody are out-of-pocket. Is that a problem for you ladies? Are you impoverished?"

"Certainly not," Siskel rushed to assure him.

"But we're certainly not rich," Kurian said.

"Don't be silly, dear. We're reasonably well to do ladies. After all, we come from a fine old Southern family."

"Which proves only that we're potentially bigger suckers than a lot of other people because some of us have to put on airs."

Siskel laughed nervously and fanned herself with her open hand, "I do declare, sometimes I don't know what gets into my sister."

"A little common sense I'd like to believe. Not to go throwing my money around on ridiculous pipe dreamy things."

"Heavens be, woman, we haven't even discussed any sums yet and you're falling off the catbird seat. I do declare that I don't know what you must think is being discussed here."

Pernell did his full diplomat at all costs routine. He said, "If you would rather that I simply withdraw and leave you to the scenery, please just give me an indication. I'll let you pass quietly into oblivion if you wish but I must tell you that I haven't been so excited about the possibilities of a discovery for a long time. Oh, probably not since I discovered Paul Newman making the salads in a dime cafeteria."

"The mister Paul Newman?" Siskel gasped and clutched her chest to signal she had to keep her heart from breaking through in its wild pounding.

"I think you're simply making a fool of yourself, Ethel, but I know better than to think I can stop you from doing so."

"Wouldn't you like to be on the screen? Maybe just for the laugh of being able to say you did it?" Siskel asked her fake sister.

"Not really. Also I seriously doubt that with looks like mine this Mr. Hampton or anyone less that Cecil B. DeMille or the Angel Gabriel could get me a serious chance at doing so."

"You put yourself down too much, Lucy dear. You have a very... uh, interesting face. Not really a lovely face but one with character and strength of personality. Mr. Hampton said so himself. That's what attracted his experienced eye to us."

"Silliness," Kurian snorted.

Pernell said, "If you had to pick top people out of the phone book - which is impossible to do, of course - it'd cost you about six thousand dollars, including a trip to the West coast to meet with directors and casting people. With my connections I can take care of everything for about half of that amount."

"Certainly we're not leading lady types," Siskel conceded. "Those hussies have to appear half-naked on the screen and at parties, but the motion pictures always need character actresses. Those ladies only have little parts but they're usually the ones whom everyone remembers fondly and talks about afterwards."

"The prospect of being fondly remembered for being not up to the challenge of being considered attractive don't light my fire. I believe that's one of the expressions they use these days so I'm going to get myself out of the way of success right now. If you wish to discuss the matter in specifics with Mr. Hampton please be my guest.

I'm going to see what time they start seating in the dining car. Lunch was hours ago." She discreetly tapped her watch.

"As you wish. I'll hear him out but I will spare you the details later. I'll respect your right to go your way and I shall expect the same from you."

"But of course you will. Breeding always shows eventually. Good day, sir." Kurian stood to leave.

The conductor announced over the PA, "Our next station stop will be Cary, North Carolina. Cary, North Carolina will be next in just a few minutes."

Kurian nodded a stiff goodbye and went to the front of the car

"Now, where were we?" Siskel asked, indicating that Pernell should take the now empty seat beside her.

"Let me say that your sister's decision not to get involved helps your chances considerably. Parts for a single truly wonderful face are numerous. Those requiring a pair are much less common. Now, the matter of a sum to cover the initial expenses and making arrangements for you to get the professional preliminary work done."

"About how much are we talking about, Mr. Hampton? In round numbers."

"Three thousand dollars," he answered.

"Three thousand dollars?"

"In round numbers," he added.

"I see. How soon would this sum be required?"

"As soon as possible so I can make appointments for you with the photographer, cinematographer, and beauticians. When they're doing me a favor and working for below scale rates they expect cash."

"Would you accept a personal check?"

"Of course. Yes, indeed I would. No problem."

He thought for a moment, then added, "But let me suggest that we complete our discussion over a libation in the lounge car. It would be my pleasure to buy you a drink."

"Oh, I don't customarily imbibe strong liquor."

"I'm sure they have white wine or soft drinks if you prefer."

"Maybe this one special time I will have something. In order to celebrate my being *discovered,* as I think they say."

"A wonderful idea. You're at the start of an educational and eye-opening experience and a drink seems like an appropriate way to mark the occasion."

Pernell rose and stepped aside for Siskel to get out of the seat and precede him to the lounge car at the rear of this car.

She got up but then hesitated. "No, this won't do. I have to go and properly settle things with Lucy or there will be no peace on the plantation for days and days. Thank you for your very kind offer of a libation but first things first. I have a thought. If it wouldn't be too inconvenient for you, perhaps you could wait for me in the lounge car so I don't have to look for you all over the train once I have our checkbook. If you go to talk to her with me, Lucy won't stop playing mother hen and I might be a long time calming her down."

"I respect your wishes and your insight into your sister, Miss Ethel. I'll wait for your decision in the lounge car. Take your time."

Siskel smiled her brightest naïve Belle smile and headed for the car ahead. Pernell stepped out of the way to allow three other women who were already heading that way to follow Siskel out – then he followed them all, ready to adjust his position to stay out of sight behind these others now acting as his unwitting blockers.

* * *

Siskel flopped down heavily beside Kurian in the seat closest to the front door of the first car asking, "Are we ready?"

Kurian pointed to the several bags on the large rack across the aisle and close to the door. She said, "Grab our bags and go. How did it go with Mr. Charm-you-out-of-your-money-with-my-lies?"

"It was fun to watch his performance. Even more so when we were play-acting right back at him. We saw through him from the start but I'm not sure he knows yet what we were doing."

Several rows behind them Pernell slipped into an empty seat where he was unlikely to be seen by them unless they came down the aisle. He finished adjusting what looked like some kind of a personal music system but was in fact a sound amplifier widely available with the caution in the ads that it wasn't intended to be used to eavesdrop on people in case you hadn't considered that reason to buy one. It was working fine. He could hear their every word by aiming the device over the seat tops without that looking strange or inappropriate.

"Would we have spotted him right away if we weren't already tuned in to the pretense and presumptuousness of those others? I'm not sure, but I'd like to think so," Kurian said. "What excuse did you make for leaving?"

"I had to get the checkbook for our joint bank account from my sister, Miss Lucy," Siskel replied.

"I want to take a bow for recognizing where you wanted to take things when you first dropped the name Lucy so I played right along and dubbed you Ethel. If men calling themselves Desi and Fred showed up asking what Ethel and Lucy were doing here we were in trouble though. I would have lost it and had to run howling laughing from the train."

"Going to the reunion was a good idea."

"I agree a hundred percent."

"This has been a wonderful trip. It made accepting my being a middle-aged lady less a horror and more an opportunity to let my hair down and enjoy myself more." She held up her left hand to show her wedding band was back in place. That reminded Siskel to get her ring from her handbag and put it on too.

"Jack won't know what to make of me but he's adaptable."

Kurian hesitated, then continued, "Heck, he might get into the new spirit if I don't beat him over the head with it. I was wondering lately with all the talk among the ladies of a certain age like ourselves – and yes, that describes you too, sorority sister – if I should ever become sufficiently discontented and want to be freed from the chains of convention I accepted twenty years ago. Today I can say for sure that I may want to be a bit more adventurous but I don't want to change those parts of my life. I'm happily married. There, I said it for any who aren't and want everyone to be miserable with them. I made a good choice back then and I don't want to change it."

"Wow, playing the prankster really turned you on. Watch out world. Or at least watch out con men. They were all charmers though, whether men of some means going to Raleigh to learn to act like genteel Southern gentlemen or a humble enabler who can make your dreams of fame and fortune come true. Being a belle for two hours was fun too, although I wasn't very good at it. I imagine myself as more the warrior princess type."

Both laughed as the train stopped at the station. Without even a glance toward the rear of this car, they grabbed their bags from the rack and went out the door to meet their families.

Pernell sat back and pocketed the listening system saying to himself, "Okay, no real harm done. It was good practice. They didn't buy into the line but I was convincing enough to get them to play along. I have to review what I said and my body language to see if I can spot signs that might have told me to forget it and move on. At least they don't seem to have been upset in a report it to the conductor or the police way."

He watched the two greet their husbands outside. "They were better than they realize at coming across as innocents even if their accents need work. Reminder to self, always be ready to learn stuff that'd be useful from whoever does it well. It doesn't make sense to get angry about being played in return. Why waste time and energy plotting revenge when there's no reason to believe I can turn a profit from ever seeing them again? The value of this episode is in what I can learn in order to sharpen my skill at pre-screening targets on the run. It's exciting and challenging but I need it to pay off too."

Chapter 05

The angle of the sun indicated it was morning. Pernell sat at a table in the lounge car with a cup of coffee, looking tired but resigned. When Hill entered Pernell signaled him to sit by him so he did.

"Good morning and welcome to Florida," Hill said chirpily. "Wasn't that last stop Winter Haven?"

"Yeah. Still four hours to Miami. Concerning your offer, you understand that I have a lot of things in various stages going so I can't always commitment myself on the spur of the moment."

"Make me an offer."

"I can't promise you exactly what day I can try this little trip of yours beyond saying some day in the next three weeks. If you can live with the looseness of that arrangement, I'll give the deal serious thought. If you need a commitment of day and hour I can't help you now. Maybe next year. Or around December I think I'll have a few days free."

"I'll agree to those terms if you'll assure me you'll either make the pick up within the next three weeks or let me know that you can't so I can make other arrangements."

Pernell considered that for a moment before he nodded and held out his hand to shake on it. "I'll agree to give it full and serious consideration on those terms. Give me the details. I need the specifics. If I make the pickup I keep ten percent of the amount as my fee."

Hill took out an envelope and laid it on the table. "Of course. The addresses and phone numbers you'll need are in here. Memorize them and destroy the paper. You go to the front desk and ask to see the boss. His name's in there. If you pass muster they'll take you to the big man's office. You tell him that Louie Lizardo Lumbago sent you to pick up the money he's due for services rendered. A certified copy of the signed IOU is in a plastic sleeve in there so be sure to take good care of it. They'll ask you what services. You don't know, you're only the bag person for this one job."

"Okay, I'll look through it where I have more privacy and let you know if anything I'll need isn't among this stuff. And of course if I think it's doable at all. I'll give you a definite answer before we get off in Miami. In that case a nod's as good as another handshake. If I spot a problem and won't do it, I'll be sure you know that and why."

Hill nodded and walked away, happy that things were going right.

Pernell found a spot to work in private and got busy on his laptop. He gave thanks in passing to whoever invented WiFi and to whoever arranged for it to be installed on these trains.

He was as grateful as the man was probably distressed that there was as much speculation presented as information about Louie Lizardo Lumbago and his seamy history but it gave him an idea of what he was getting himself involved in.

Lumbago had an amazing memory and devised a way to use that to win at casinos without cheating. Then he expanded his take when he tested and found he could use his skill even from outside the casino by using some other guy wearing glasses with a tiny TV camera so he could see what the assistant was seeing. He took in a lot of casino money that way. But he backed off and made a point to lose enough of it back to them to skirt the casinos banning him. An occasional new guy having a hot night kept Lumbago and the new guy flush with cash but under the radar since those forays didn't happen often enough to establish a pattern.

Then Lumbago made a bad business decision. Only he knew what pressures there might have been but what became known, as such things so often do, was that he lent a mobster named Alfonso Gargoyle a large sum to get the guy out of an awkward jam.

Long sad story in short version, the mobster denied that there had been a request, a deal worked out, and money transferred to him that he therefore owed to Lumbago. Classic sort of "It's my word against yours". Except that Lumbago wasn't nearly as naive as he was happy to be thought to be. He had witnesses and even tapes of the exchanges. When Gargoyle opted to stand tough about the debt, Lumbago took the unusual step of invoking the *Code of Honor among Thieves* as his weapon to undermine the gangster's respectability among those he wanted badly to hobnob with but now couldn't.

As Pernell researched this Alfonso Gargoyle from whom he would be requesting the due payment he had serious second thoughts. But then he reminded himself that things weren't lining up as he had hoped for this winter in Florida so money would be tight unless he found new sources.

He formulated a personal theory about why the pair who had recruited him to make the pickup needed someone else to do that and why they felt his skill set would be useful for their purposes. Their names were still secrets from him but he expected to identify from online mug shot collections before long. He weighed his options, made some initial plans about how to go about this, and decided that he had little choice but to agree to do this since he had no assurance of being offered anything better once in Miami. He would prefer to have more and better choices but was enough of a realist to accept that at the end of the day he didn't have any good ones.

*   *   *

Moments later Hill entered the dining car where he sat across from Taylor. "How did it go?" she asked.

"Like a charm."

"He'll do it?"

Hill imitated Pernell voice and gestures as he said, "I won't give you any guarantee but if I get a chance to think about it I'll give it a try." In his normal voice he said, "He'll do it. Probably tomorrow."

"And get the surprise of his life."

"One way or the other."

"Okay, then are you prepared to explain to me what this is all about now?" Taylor asked.

"It's simple if diabolical. He talks his way in there through all of Gargoyle's defenses and demands the money. Gargoyle pays off, but in counterfeit bills. They're his stock in trade but I'm not supposed to know that. I tip the cops so they pick up Pernell or whatever they finally find his real name is. Our Mr. Pernell finds himself holding a pile of funny money with the cops smiling at him. He's quick in the tight spots, he'll lead them right to the only person he has any leads to - Gargoyle. Sweet revenge."

"What's to keep him from giving them the address for the money drop too? So he can lead them to you?"

"The address I gave him is an empty house. If he leads them there the cops'll think he's playing games with them."

"Just as Gargoyle won't like him asking for the money."

"Right. This isn't a nice business he's agreed to get involved with."

"But wait a minute," Taylor objected. "If the drop-off address is a fake, how are you going to get the money from him?"

"I'm not. That's been the point from the start. I know Gargoyle won't pay off in real currency. Same way that from the start Lumbago never intended to pay me if there was any possible way he could avoid that. Unfortunately I was too naive to realize that before I agreed in a way I can't back out of to try to collect the money."

"And got me involved in the mess too."

"And that. No way I can talk my way out of it, much as I'd like to since it's all embarrassing as can be. I acted like a fool and now I'm trying to act like a wise man to right what I messed up," he said.

"But I concede that finding a smooth talking con man to go in for us may be the best possible way to do this. Twenty percent if we collect the total amount but only five percent if we get even one dollar less that the total amount he lent the guy."

"But a hundred percent satisfaction if we put both Lumbago and the other guy in the Feds' cross-hairs while we stay just clear of it ourselves. That makes us in demand to other groups as thanks."

"So if somehow Pernell manages to avoid the police, he gets to keep the money?"

Hill nodded agreement. "That's what he intends from the start. What convinced him to agree to try my scheme was realizing he could get all the money by simply picking it up and then disappearing with it. I'm sure he never had any intention of being a bagman, only of picking up the money for himself. Hell, that's why I selected an unscrupulous type."

"So he gets either roughed up by Gargoyle, a run-in with the cops that he can't talk his way out of, or two million dollars' worth of phony money that the police will probably be able to trace in no time since he won't know it's counterfeit."

"Afraid so. Not much of a bargain for poor Mr. Pernell. But I get the satisfaction of annoying Gargoyle and disrupting his operation a bit. If he has to put that much of his product on the street without any control over it he'll be forced to take a lot of evasive action to make sure it can't be traced back to him. He'll be pissed. Maybe using my proxy Mr. Pernell I'll even be able to walk the cops right on into Gargoyle's living room, as it were. That'd be extra sweet."

"You're not a terribly nice person if you do things like this."

"Alas, too true. But I'm clever enough to fool the fooler. You were the one who spent half the trip from Washington to Florida interrupting his pitches and leaking warnings so he'd need my offer."

"Oh my gosh, you're right. Shame on me. I should probably punish myself by having something extra with my breakfast."

They both laughed.

* * *

From a payphone at the Lakeland, Florida station where he had a half hour layover, Pernell called the number Dimple gave him to get the initial details about the possible job in Miami.

When the call was connected, a man said, "You have reached..." and recited the number Pernell had dialed.

"Who am I talking to?" Pernell asked in response.

"My question too. To avoid an awkward mistake. You are?"

"Sylvester."

"Good enough. Mr. Pernell, I'm the one who invited you to call this number if you have an interest in a specialized paid job you should be able to complete in less than a day once you're in Miami."

"Do you have a name?"

"We can call me Harry Agent if that makes it easier for you."

"But that's not your real name."

"You've got me there. I'm imitating you in that. A different name for each tall story. Isn't that the way you do it? From what I know of your history that means you have a remarkable memory to keep all those fake personas straight although I know you only use a few at a time. Still there must be an impressive total list."

"Each tall story?" Pernell said.

"I have no reason to imply more. The facts beyond that aren't relevant to my offer and I don't want there to be any hint that I'm holding anything I know about you over your head to pressure you. Those I represent have a tricky job they hope to get done. You might have the skills required. That's what this initial contact is about. Not getting bogged down in any accusations or legal details of the past."

"Where do you find information about me that leads you to think I might be able and be interested in whatever you want done?"

"The FBI and the records of more police departments that you may realize. Someone realizes he was scammed and files a complaint with his hometown cops or the ones where the two of you met even though neither of you live there. A report gets written up but then just filed. You've been examined, rated, and put in a cubbyhole. You're judged to be unlikely to do anything violent, careful enough to be hard to positively connect to the complaint, and hard to prosecute. The latter even if the dupe is willing to stand in the public eye and admit to the far-fetched idea he fell for, which most aren't willing to."

"I'm getting an education about what somebody using my name has been up to," Pernell said.

"But his careful planning and smooth talk are why those that I represent think you might be able to pull off their little maneuver," the agent said.

"Time for some details since I have a train to get back on."

"Fine. You'd pickup an item of some size at one location and deliver it to another. The complications are that you can't be seen doing this. The goal is to have it mysteriously appear at the delivery location. As part of that you can't use any motorized transport since those would likely be detected by some security systems listening for the sounds of motors. You would be paid a cash fee to check things out and advise me about whether it even looks doable. If you think you can do it and try you would be paid an additional cash fee. If you succeed that fee would be significantly larger."

"What size fees are we talking?" Pernell asked.

"Ten thousand to check it out. Three times that for trying but failing. Ten times that for succeeding. Plus any valid expenses you incur planning or attempting it."

"So what needs to be moved has substantial value."

"To some people. Not a whole lot on the open market."

"Line in the sand. I don't have anything to do with illegal drugs, radioactive materials, or other standard contraband. That also includes live material of any sort. Viruses to humans. Also, I have to know about any explosives that are part of its protective measures but those also can't be the payload."

"Your position is noted. This doesn't involve anything that fits any of those categories. I can tell you that it's something that's been reported missing and there is FBI and Interpol interest in recovering it but neither you nor the person willing to pay for your help will have stolen it. Moved it, yes. That's the point. And why it must be done in total secrecy."

"It's important for me to know that more than the Miami cops might be on the lookout."

"We agree and wanted you aware of it from the start."

"Why?"

"If that fact scares you off it's best to know that right away. That's why the deal is to pay you to decide how to do this - if it can be done - only after you've scouted the area to your own satisfaction."

"Tell me the pickup and delivery addresses."

"After you're in Miami. First you need to carefully weigh if this is bigger than you want to get involved in even if there shouldn't be much you could be prosecuted for. You probably wouldn't even be breaking and entering. Only transporting missing goods. It's not even official that the payload is stolen."

"So we need to talk again," Pernell said.

"Inevitably. I'll give you a new number to call and the name to use and what to say when the call is picked up. At that contact you tell me if you're in for the initial fee for checking out if it can be done. If so I give you the addresses to take a look at. We also then agree on how and where the initial fee gets delivered."

"Okay, I'm in that far. You're right, this is on a different scale than I've gotten into before. I need to think about where it might take me. Give me the number and the code words. They stay only in my head so nobody can peek in my notebook or my laptop and find them."

He listened, then repeated the items before he hung up the phone and reboarded the train.

The whole time Pernell was on the phone, Hill and Taylor had been watching him out train windows and figuratively jumping through hoops trying to figure out how to learn what he was saying and to whom. They feared he was setting them up from the start since if their positions were reversed that's what they would be trying to do. What was he planning so they could counter it?

The too obvious maneuver was for Taylor to get off the train and inch as close as possible to overhear him. She had to be the one since Hill had dealt directly with Pernell and they preferred to believe he wasn't aware that Taylor was part of the operation. Too obvious because there were few people on the platform and no one else near those payphones. So she would be out in the wide open spaces with no obvious reason to be there.

    By the time they thought to have her go out and make a sham call from an adjacent payphone Pernell was hanging up. That left them not knowing what happened but knowing they didn't know that.

Chapter 06

Pernell arrived in Miami with his head chock full of ideas and questions but without further incident. He checked into the cheap hotel he had used in previous years and where he had made an open-ended reservation.

After getting dinner, he decided as his first expedition to visit Agnes Beebop. He had checked his Miami street map and noted that the South Miami Healing Hospital was near a Metrorail station and in an area he wanted to refamiliarize himself with for other reasons.

In the hospital lobby where he sat for a while to take advantage of their WiFi to do some online searching, he chanced to meet nurse's aide Thelma Roscovitz waiting for her ride to arrive to take her home.

They chatted in a friendly and general way for several minutes before he test dropped Beebop's name. Roscovitz laughed and wished him good luck having anything to do with the patient in private room 604 whom she spoke of with affection but also felt it important to warn him wasn't noted for being cooperative with anyone - mostly for the fun of it. Pernell switched in his head to label her as Roscoe in case he had to protect her if he had to explain how he found out Beebop's room number or anything about her.

Roscovitz, an ardent believer in simple solutions and healthy eating, commented that a few doses of lactobacilli would do wonders for Beebop but the doctors wouldn't "prescribe" it and to be ornery Beebop wouldn't eat it anyway. Then her ride arrived and she went her way.

It was now time that all dinners should have been delivered, eaten, and the trays cleared away so things would be settled to a less active time on most floors but still officially visiting hours.

Trying to follow the rules, Pernell asked what room Beebop was in. He was refused a visitor's pass and thus entry beyond the first floor since he couldn't produce ID as a family member. Staff nurse

Netta Nulty, who disliked the look of him from first glance, insisted that only family members were allowed to visit Ms. Beebop although when challenged she could show no official sign to support that. She was a Nurse Ratchet type – tough and no-nonsense because she found that worked more than because she was mean, but she did have a problem trusting others to do what she felt would be best so she micromanaged by telling them exactly what to do, when and how to do it.

He noted that Nulty was careful not to mention Beebop's room number so he didn't let on that he knew it as he stared at a house phone on which he could call to confirm the claim about visitors. He figured that if Beebop was as he had by now heard several people describe, she would all but fall out of bed to contradict this nurse and insist that any visitor be allowed up. He opted to resist irritating the nurse more than necessary at least for now.

Nulty, whom he had now labeled Nutty in his head, kept an eye on him to be sure he didn't try to sneak onto an elevator after she ordered him out of the building. He did annoy her by challenging her authority to order him out of the entry and lobby areas without involving the police and charges of a false arrest. She disliked him even more for standing his ground beyond a reasonable limit.

* * *

At a street payphone not far from the hospital, he called the contact number, gave the coded responses, and talked to the agent. He accepted the first stage of the deal, was told the pickup and delivery addresses, and the desired time window for the move to happen. They agreed when and how the $10,000 fee would reach him.

Now in a sense on-the-clock, he checked the Miami street map on his laptop, then set off to get an initial look at the exteriors of the pickup and delivery sites and the streets between them. He made notes in his head and on the laptop, although the recorded ones left out any details that would have given away to snoopers the exact addresses of particular interest. It felt good knowing he now had enough money available for his needs for at least several weeks even if nothing else happened and the challenge of plotting out the secret transfer route was stimulating and satisfying in its own way.

* * *

Later, but still within official visiting hours, he sneaked back into the hospital by going in a lowest floor entry close behind a funeral director there to pick up a corpse. The guard on duty was most interested in the TV in his booth and simply assumed they were together. Pernell was careful not to be too close to the undertaker except at the critical moment when the guard looked them over so that professional wouldn't note him or complain of being shadowed too closely by him.

Pernell then took the stairs to the sixth floor. It was a climb but worth it to him. The elevator might open with Nulty standing there but he could peek out from the stairs to see around before he was seen.

He decided against putting on a lab coat when he saw a stack of those in a storeroom with the door left open. That both because that would require leaving his jacket elsewhere, a problem if he had to make a fast exit, and because that wouldn't look sneaky enough. But he did borrow a too-large trench coat that let him keep his jacket on under it and a wide-brimmed hat from a pile of lost and found items in that storeroom to look clownishly sneaky.

Beebop watched him with calm amusement when he entered her room in that outfit and carrying a small brown paper bag. He partly closed the door - after making a production number out of checking to see if anyone had noticed him and was coming to check.

He stepped to the bed and took two small unmarked containers of yogurt from the bag and then two plastic spoons. He said in a clownishly accented way, "Is forbidden fruits with no pits or skins. Friends who cannot be given the names send for you to try. I get some too for being bag boy."

"You're a pretty bad bag boy," she said with a laugh as he took the lids off the fast-food store containers.

As he took the spoons out of their individual plastic sleeves he said, "Thank you for the noticing. You should not eat this since it is forbidden but okay if you want some."

"What is it?"

"Some call it yogurt. Some say is yuck. I say is yum-yum."

"Isn't yogurt full of germs? That's what I heard. That's why I won't eat any of it." She did eye the stuff with interest though. More so when he took a spoonful into his mouth and savored it.

"Nothing to hurt you in there. But has little bit tangy taste what scares off them what only eat what has little taste. Has vanilla for the more flavor. Wanilla is bland but makes forbidden food good."

"Why did you bring this here?" she asked.

"To show friends who cannot be given the names that I am clever and can get by the guards and break the rules with bringing it here where it gets all eaten up even if all by me." At that he put his partially eaten cup aside and reached for her full one.

That was the trigger. She grabbed that cup and the second spoon and put some of the yogurt in her mouth with a smirk at the satisfaction of not letting him have it all for himself.

She held it in her mouth for a moment as she considered the tang, then she swallowed it. She made a face that yes, she was okay with the tang now that she had experienced it. She proceeded to eagerly eat the rest.

He finished his and said, "I win from the others the bet about can I sneaky be but now I don't get to eat both as I 'spected."

"Too bad for you. You did offer it to me," she said with a laugh.

"Truth that is. And the time says wizitors get out now so I do like I did and was never here." He put his cup and spoon in the open bag, then held that out for her to put hers in there too.

"Good. Don't leave any evidence that'd confuse my captors," she said.

"They mean to make you be healthy even if they don't know how to get around all the blockages. If the friends want to make me a new bet I will try to sneak in some forbidden stuff again but not making the promises. The guards here are tough and scary. The one for the particular."

"Yeah, Nurse Nulty," Beebop said.

He signaled his agreement that she knew who he was referring to, then prepared to depart with a bit of melodramatic skulking and sneaking to her amusement and satisfaction.

"She could be fun if she weren't always serious about it. Too bad, but she's afraid to let her hair down once in a while and play with those who will understand," Beebop said.

He waved and was gone out the door.

Only a few minutes later, Nurse Nulty hurried into the hospital room as if expecting to catch someone doing what they weren't allowed to do. Beebop watched her with undisguised amusement as the nurse moved around without saying a word looking for anyone else present - and trying not to let her disappointment at not finding anyone show.

Finally Beebop said in a stage whisper, "Don't look under the bed. That's where I've been keeping my gentlemen callers recently and I don't want you to find out and get pissy about it."

Having completed her search, Nulty headed out the door, still without saying a word.

Beebop called, "What about the one behind the door?"

Nulty stopped, reversed, and looked behind the door that had been wide open when she entered and did have room for someone to stand and be out of sight behind it. Beebop covered her mouth with her hands to muffle her giggle. Nulty stomped back out the door.

Beebop called, "Does this mean the one in the closet has your okay to be here?" Another burst of laughter. Nulty didn't reappear.

Beebop settled in the bed saying to herself, "I haven't had this much fun in too long. I'd rather laugh with you than at you, Nulty, but I'll take what I can get." The smile

Chapter 07

At six A.M the next morning Pernell did additional quietly nonchalant reconnoitering in the area where the paid job would take him. He had seen the relevant buildings in the evening and walked the most direct several block route between them, now he was seeing how much more he could note in the brightness of the morning and getting a better idea of the alternative routes from A to B. Again he made mental notes but this time no paper or digitally recorded ones.

* * *

At 8 A.M. he nonchalantly walked through the pickup site since the building was now open although not yet officially open for business. He was just a curious tourist looking around. He took no photos and he saw no one. During his online research on the place he had seen descriptions and three somewhat confusing photos of the section of the interior of particular interest but the eye-opening in-person view gave him a lot to rethink. It wasn't that there seemed to be recent changes, it was that the space was large and somewhat complicated so it was hard to describe as one thing. The approved official online descriptions and views didn't tell him what emergency escape routes there might be either in case his plans somehow went bad before he could get out of there with the item of interest.

The location was a four-story-high storage and utility closet. At each of the upper three levels, an access door to the main public access and use parts of the building opened in to a platform that extended into about two-thirds of the area and had utility access boxes for electric and phones near the door. The remaining space of each platform was used for storage of smaller boxed materials. The open space - which was the full four stories high - was built that way to allow storage of tall materials or ones that might need to be hung or suspended rather than stood in place. The idea was also that the large space would keep the utility boxes cooler than in small enclosed ones.

For some years the space had stored large parade puppets and other display materials that couldn't be easily disassembled. Those went out of fashion but were thought to be of substantial value if those types of items were needed again in a hurry. Many of those items were loosely wrapped in paper or cheap cloth dust covers. Enough were not covered or the covers had partly or completely fallen to the ground to give the impression that it is was all junk but too precious to discard in case it might be declared of historic value or because the city might decide to use it again on short notice when other ideas for festive special events failed.

Two flights of side-by-side metal stairs with a landing switch-back per floor allowed free access from level to level. He liked that those stairs would let him reach the upper part of a tall stored item without the need for a ladder.

A casual look without touching anything let him identify the tall package he was particularly interested in. The contents were hidden in plain view by being wrapped in decorated paper strips that made them seem innocuous and irrelevant. The whole thing was loosely wrapped in heavy Kraft paper. Yes, this was a few minutes well spent. He could plan in a realistic way now.

* * *

At 8:30 A.M. four year old Robbie Roberts was left standing by a stroller that mom tied to a pole to slow up any attempt to steal it outside a gift shop with a big No Children Allowed Inside sign on the door because of the many breakable crystal items inside.

What no one could anticipate was that the boy would be caught in a drug deal gone bad - or that Pernell, who had nothing to do with that, would happen to be passing by when that happened.

One side of the fight sauntered down the street; the other side pulled up in two large cars and jumped out, shooting.

A large delivery truck was stopped in an alley, the front facing out into that street. Its motor was running and its door unlocked. The driver had gotten out to grab some fruit from an outside stand of a produce store across from the gift shop. He prudently and almost automatically ducked into the produce store and onto the floor at the first shots.

Pernell saw the boy who was at the edge of the shooting area but would likely soon be fully in it as the on-foot combatants ducked for cover among the cars parked at the curb.

Pernell climbed into the truck by way of the driver's door which was on the side away from the shooting and drove the truck forward until it totally blocked the street. He stopped it there, turned off the engine, and got out. Now there wasn't even room for the gang cars to drive onto the sidewalks to get around the truck so in order to not be trapped there with cops surely on their way, the car drivers had to maneuver to make U-turns on the narrow street while avoiding interfering with one another. That action interrupted the gun fight.

Pernell peeked around the front of the truck and waved for the scared boy to come to him - which the boy had the good sense to do. The two of them took shelter behind the truck, ducking under the rear to be out of sight and reach when the gang members who were on foot decided to run for it down the street around the truck that way.

During the shooting, the window of the gift shop and a lot of crystal items inside were shattered by bullets – with the No Children Allowed Inside sign falling off the door as the last bit of glass in the door hit the ground.

Police sirens fast approaching prompted the combatants to flee. When it was clear that the shooting was done, Pernell led the boy back around the far side of the truck and waved him back to where he had been. The boy's mother peeked out of the shattered shop, saw the boy, and started to shout about a miracle. Pernell didn't want to be identified even as a hero since that would put him on the public radar and raise questions. He always hated questions about why he was where he was or what he was doing there. He was content that the news would ask: Was there a mystery man who helped the boy? Was the boy smarter than expected? Or was he just very lucky?

Robbie wasn't good at describing strange adults so there would be a debate. Pernell was in this area checking whether he could use it as an emergency escape route if the swap and delivery somehow went bad. It was several blocks from the site where those would happen so it wasn't obviously associated with those actions. He saw what needed to be done to protect the boy and did it. End of that story.

* * *

At nine A.M. Pernell stood outside on the street and looked over Gargoyle's eight-story headquarters with interest. An older building but in good repair it loomed over a mainly industrial area of low buildings at the edge of the city. He noted that the building was south of Central Miami near the financial district, east of Brickell Avenue but not on the beach. Within easy walk of the 8th Street station of the Metromover monorail system. It seemed peaceful with little nearby foot or vehicle traffic.

The building lobby was a large almost completely open space. Harri, a large female bodybuilder sitting behind the counter that blocked access to the elevators and stairs at the back end of the room, looked Pernell over with obvious contempt as he approached. Paulie, a large but not notably hard body matched with little evidence of much of a mind to control it, sat by the elevators, grinning stupidly. Harri waited for Pernell to speak.

He looked around for a building directory but couldn't see one so he asked Harri, "Excuse me, can you tell me where I can find a Mr. Alfonso Gargoyle?"

"Who wants to know?"

"*Duh*! I do. That seems pretty obvious."

Harri jumped up, leaned over the counter, and glowered at him in a more clearly threatening way. Pernell held his ground and noted her pin-on name tag.

"You sassin' me?"

"Only if necessary," Pernell responded calmly.

"What the heck does that mean?"

Harri clicked her fingers and waved Paulie to her side.

"Congratulations. You make a charming couple," Pernell said.

Harri grabbed for Pernell but he backed up just enough to stay beyond her reach. "I can break you into pieces, runt," she said in a definitely menacing way.

"Probably. But the important question is whether that's what you're assigned to do."

"Nobody gets upstairs without I say so."

"What has that to do with anything? I only asked if I'm in the right building to transact my business."

"Just what is your business?"

"That's between Mr. Gargoyle and myself and it's none of your business."

Harri jumped right over the counter then and came toward Pernell. Paulie came around the end of the counter excited by the action. "Maybe I'm gonna' make it my business," Harri growled.

"If Mr. Gargoyle approves - which for the record I doubt he will - of course I'll be happy to tell you all about it. But I suspect he doesn't authorize you to probe all that deep or to know much at all about what he does or claims not to."

"He authorizes me to break arms, legs, backs, ribs, and assorted other body parts of those..."

"Who come to conduct business with him? I doubt that. I doubt that very much. You'd scare away the money."

"Just what do you think you're gonna do here?"

Paulie stood there all keyed up for some fun but there was only talk so he wasn't sure what to do with himself.

Pernell said, "I'm not gonna do it, you are. Please pick up the phone and inform Mr. Gargoyle that Mr. Pernell is here to see him on a matter of financial business."

"Suppose I don't do that?"

"Then I leave here and get word to Mr. Gargoyle through other channels that he's overprotecting himself right out of the action."

"Then what?" she asked.

"He can decide what to do about you from there," Pernell said.

"If your business is so important why don't you pick up the phone over there and call him yourself?"

"Because that's your job. I'm not about to give you that lame excuse for burning off some testosterone saying I tried to get by you."

"Are you chicken?"

"Where you're involved? You bet. You've got muscles where I never even suspected they existed. I respect that."

"Who sent you?"

"I'm on a freelance job for Louie Lizardo Lumbago."

"Don't know him."

"Sorry to break it to you but, hard as that is to believe, he most likely hasn't heard of you either."

"You sassin' me again?"

"Yeah, that time I definitely was. I'm also still waiting for you to do your job by calling whoever you're supposed to call if you haven't forgotten that that's your job again and announcing that there's someone here on a business matter."

"I don't care about that."

"But you're only the muscle, not the boss. He probably does."

"I'll wrestle you for it. Pin me and I do what you want. I pin you and you get taken away in a body bag."

Pernell took out his cell phone and punched in a number. "I'll pass on your challenge." Into the phone he said, "Yeah, this is in regard to the pickup for Louie Lizardo Lumbago. I'm being forcibly kept from getting inside so I'm declaring a six-twenty-nine with nineteen-o-four complications." He listened for a moment then agreed, "Yeah, that all needs to be made public." He disconnected the call and ambled back toward the door.

Harri sneered and smirked.

The phone on the counter rang. Harri stepped back and meekly picked it up. She listened in sullen silence.

Paulie picked up her mood and sulked too, kicking viciously at imaginary items on the floor.

Harri hung up the phone and called to Pernell, "Go to the third floor." Then an idea occurred to her. She grinned mischievously and nodded to Paulie, then to Pernell, then to the elevator door behind the counter.

Pernell nonchalantly walked by the counter and to an elevator and pushed the *Call* button. Briefed by Harri now, Paulie hurried over to stand behind Pernell, glancing repeatedly at Harri who encouraged him with gestures.

A *ping* announced the elevator's arrival. The doors opened. Pernell stepped forward but then quickly to the side while keeping one foot out to the side as he braced himself by grabbing the wall.

Paulie rushed forward, glancing at Harri for directives even as he moved. He intended to shove Pernell into the elevator but the man was no longer right in front of him - except for that foot that tripped Paulie. So he stumbled into the elevator, smacked hard into the back wall and slid, stunned, to the floor. The elevator door closed with Paulie inside.

Pernell stepped to the stairs door beside the elevator and called to Harri, "I'll use the stairs. The exercise'll be good for my health."

Harri threw things around in frustration as Pernell disappeared up the stairs. The elevator doors stay closed.

After a long moment there was a hesitant banging on those doors from inside.

* * *

The third floor reception area was a sterile space of bare walls and minimal furnishings with a single chair behind a reception desk that faced the elevator and stairwell doors. Three windowless closed doors opened into other parts of the floor behind the reception desk.

Professor Kerwinski was thirty-something and the epitome of the crazy scientist type look with a fright wig of frizzy hair and thick-lensed, wire-framed glasses behind which his eye balls seemed to roll around as if free in their orbits. He sat waiting at the desk with a clipboard in front of him when Pernell entered from the stairs.

"It's usual to use the elevator except during a fire," Kerwinski noted with a note of disapproval in his voice.

"I'm not here on usual business so I don't worry about the usual things," Pernell replied.

"What's your business here?"

"Are you Alfonso Gargoyle?"

"Uh, no, but I work for him."

"Then my business is none of your business since it's with him."

"Part of my job is to screen those who claim to have business with the boss so he doesn't have to be bothered with nonsense."

"So you're a direct channel to Gargoyle?"

"More or less. By circuitous routes."

"Close enough. I'm cutting through the tangles. I have business for the ears of Mr. Gargoyle alone."

"That doesn't change anything."

"So I'm invoking the Code of Honor among Thieves..."

Before the startled Kerwinski fully realized what the visitor was doing, Pernell gave him a complex secret handshake.

"...To insist on being promptly put in contact with him without disclosing the details of that secret business."

Kerwinski was too stunned to try to hide that fact. "That does change things." To buy himself time to think he muttered, "You seem to know something about the code - which I have to note is seldom invoked. The secret handshake was probably right although I've only used it once when I was taught about it. Still I'm allowed to ask some questions."

"I'm a bagman who has been hired to do this one job for Louie Lizardo Lumbago. That's all you need to know."

"Where did you have dinner last night?"

"Irrelevant. I don't need to answer."

"Where will you take anything that might be given to you by this alleged Mr. Gargoyle?"

"To the drop-point assigned by my one-time employer."

"Who are your accomplices?"

"You and those freaks in the lobby. Other than you people, I'm working this deal alone."

"Do you expect me to believe that?"

"I'll solemnly swear to it on my word of honor under the Code if you want," Pernell offered.

"Louie Lizardo Lumbago might be a fictitious mug so how can you work for him?"

"I didn't do an FBI background check on the guy who hired me, I just agreed to his instructions to use that name when questioned here about my business."

"So who are you *actually* working for?"

"As far as I know it's Louie Lizardo Lumbago. No offense but just because you say he's not a real person doesn't mean he isn't."

"Are you daring to call Mr. Gargoyle a liar?"

"I can't do that since I haven't talked to him yet. You however I won't hesitate for a moment to suggest might be one."

"What exactly is it you want to talk to Mr. Gargoyle about again?"

"Good try but I haven't forgotten that this is all about the fact that that's for his ears only."

Before he realized he was doing it openly, Kerwinski gestured annoyance that his ploy hadn't work.

An assistant wearing a frantic expression rushed in via one of the doors, leaving that door ajar. He looked around and seemed relieved when he spotted Kerwinski. He rushed to the professor and whispered excitedly in his ear. Kerwinski started to wave him off but after the assistant's next few words the professor looked concerned, then downright scared. Kerwinski jumped to his feet and hesitated.

After a moment he gestured to Pernell that he'd be right back.

Then he and the assistant rushed out of this area through that door, again leaving it ajar.

Pernell calmly stood and waited, casually looking around. He then ambled around, nonchalantly moving toward the door the others went through. When Pernell was almost to the spot where he would be able to see in through that door Kerwinski rushed back out and closed that door firmly behind him, pressing his back to it and pushing hard against it to be sure it was fully closed. Pernell continued to act nonchalant as he ambled back to the reception desk.

Kerwinski nervously checked that each of the other doors was fully closed before he went back and sat at the desk.

"Problems in your lab? Weird secret experiments gone wrong?" Pernell asked lightly.

"Who told you that? No. Nothing's wrong. *Uh,* I just needed to stretch my legs. Whose group are you part of again?"

"I admire you're sneaky persistence but I'm doing a one-time only bag job for someone that I know only as Louie Lizardo Lumbago."

"Of course we'll need to have people verify some things."

Pernell leaned close to Kerwinski and said, "You've pushed this as far as I'm going to allow. I hereby invoke Chapter Three..."

Kerwinski gasped in surprise and awe.

"Section Five..."

Kerwinski silently mouthed a stunned *No!*

"Paragraph One. Put up or shut up. Pass me along to this Mr. Gargoyle or refuse my request to see him outright - with of course the consequences under the Code for doing that when three-five-one has been invoked."

Before Kerwinski could respond, the harried-looking assistant rushed out via another of the doors, waving a handful of continuous fanfold computer paper that trailed out ten feet behind him.

Kerwinski jumped up and literally spun around in place as he tried to decide which emergency to deal with first.

The assistant waved the papers and pointed frantically to whatever was behind the door he had used.

"I'll make you a deal," Pernell said.

"A deal? What kind of a deal?" Kerwinski asked.

"We'll pretend I didn't invoke the three-five-one and I'll hold up some fingers behind my back. Guess the number and I leave, my job undone for now. Guess wrong and you pass me along for an immediate meeting with the boss. Deal?"

Kerwinski hesitated only a second before he nodded eager agreement.

Pernell put his hand behind his back where neither Kerwinski nor the assistant could see it and held up three fingers. He nodded to Kerwinski that he was ready.

"Three," Kerwinski guessed.

Pernell moved his fourth finger into place with the others as he brought his hand around for Kerwinski to see. He gestured that it was unfortunate for his side but Kerwinski was wrong.

Kerwinski gestured toward the elevator and then hurried after the assistant to deal with the other problem.

Pernell gave that fourth finger a little kiss, then invited it to have the honor of being the one that pushed the elevator *Call* button.

Chapter 08

There was no reception area of any kind where Pernell got off the elevator at the top floor. He walked down a long, bare-walled hall with unmarked, windowless doors on alternating sides every fifteen feet.

A door opened ahead of him and a man peeked out at Pernell. Then that man was pulled back inside by unseen hands and the door closed with a *bang*. Pernell acted like he didn't notice.

A door farther along the hall opened and a short, bald man peeked out at Pernell. Then a second bald head appeared above that one to peek at him. And a third bald head appeared above that one. In quick succession, top to bottom, the heads withdrew from sight and the door closed silently. Pernell acted like he didn't notice.

A door farther along opened and an avalanche of loose paper spilled out into the hall. Several people in lilac purple jumpsuits rushed out and shoved, threw, and swept all that back inside. That door was closed again when Pernell walked passed. He acted like he didn't see a thing.

A door opened farther along and suddenly there was music blaring as a conga line of women snaked out, across the hall, and disappeared through a door on the other side. The music stopped the instant the second door closed quietly behind them. Pernell acted like nothing had happened.

Pernell strode to the only ornately decorated door along the hall, and paused to brace himself for what he had to do.

Inside, in the middle of the large and fancily appointed private office, Alfonso Gargoyle, a large, well-dressed but nasty-looking man, sat behind the large highly polished exotic wood desk.

Oscar and Webber, large, tough-looking men in expensive suits who had *bruiser* and *bodyguard* written big on them in invisible ink sat in less ornate swivel chairs between the door and the desk.

Webber held up a phone to indicate where he got this message as he said, "New text. The guys are buzzin' on the insider grapevine about a new message on a site that we all visit every day for the latest scoop and dirt. That says somebody's about to shake up somebody pretty big by using the Code to back up what he knows will be some kind of an unpopular but proper request. It'll be fun to see how that works out. I'm sure we'll hear a lot of the details."

"Just some low level clown trying to get noticed. It won't be anything real," Gargoyle said. "Who'd be dumb enough to bother with the Code anyway?"

"Lots of guys take it serious," Webber said seriously.

"Goin' against it could put you on the wrong side of a lot of what we're about," Oscar said.

Gargoyle snorted his disdain. The others noted that but didn't say anything. They would remember it though. Gargoyle swiveled his chair around so he could look out the large window.

His view was out over the financial district, not the ocean view, since he said he preferred to see money people rather than Nature. A few probably believed him. His was far from the tallest building here but he pretended not to care.

Pernell opened the door and marched in without hesitation. He stopped a few feet into the large room. Oscar and Webber turned in their chairs to stare, slow to react since in their wildest dreams they never expected anyone to dare enter like that.

Once over their initial surprise, they scrambled to their feet to stand together to form a wall of well-dressed muscle blocking Pernell's way to and view of the desk at the center of the room. After being caught off guard by him the pair looked Pernell over and decided they'd enjoy working him over.

Pernell stood perfectly still for what became an uncomfortably long moment. He was calm and carefully not projecting aggression while making the pair edgy about what to do now.

Pernell finally called, "Sorry if I'm disturbing your early nap."

The big pair shifted around a bit as they confirmed for themselves that their bulk blocked Pernell's view of the desk.

From behind that wall of actin and myosin, Gargoyle growled, "It's annoying to be interrupted when I'm doing something that's important."

"But you knew, or should have, that I was on my way up so at least you haven't been uninterrupted for long. I'm here on business,' Mr. Gargoyle. Business that's important to me and involves you."

Gargoyle tapped the bodyguards and they stepped apart to let him walk between them to see Pernell. He smirked when he got his first look at his visitor. Pernell stood his ground, not cocky but also not intimidated.

"What do you want?"

"I'm here to request immediate payment of the two million dollars owed to Louie Lizardo Lumbago for services rendered..."

Gargoyle roared with laughter. "Just like that I'm supposed to give you money? Did you guys hear that?"

Pernell continued, "...As required under the Rules of Conduct of the Code of Honor among Thieves, paragraph sixteen-dash-oh-two-point-six."

Gargoyle and the bodyguards simply stared at Pernell for a long moment as this sank in. Pernell stepped over to the two guards and handed Webber a four by six inch paper in a plastic sleeve.

As the two examined that, Pernell took a quick phone selfie with them and the paper held up where it could be identified as an I.O.U. signed by Gargoyle. He did that and stepped back away from them, taking the sleeved paper with him, before they fully realized what he was doing.

Finally Gargoyle erupted in a fury. He shouted curses, beat an imaginary foe into submission with his beefy fists, and angrily stomped his feet. That recent grapevine alert meant someone knew what was about to happen so even if Gargoyle's men would stand by and let their boss ignore or abuse the Code, gangland at large would know and those here would all be punished accordingly. Therefore Gargoyle couldn't secretly silence Pernell and as a result Pernell wasn't as intimidated as Gargoyle liked those who had to deal with him to be.

During that temper fit, Gargoyle stepped over close enough to Pernell to endanger the man with his vigorous moves. Pernell didn't flinch but did look over to be sure the two bodyguards were noting this. Those two exchanged wary looks.

An additional realization for Gargoyle was that with the way the grapevine operation was run, he could never learn who originated the tip about the Code surprise which had now put the matter on the radar of everybody of significance. It could have been this Pernell guy himself creating some insurance and protection for himself. It could have been whoever sent Pernell here setting things up to get credit among the brethren for making Alfonso Gargoyle pay up knowing how that would tarnish his reputation. Or it could have been any of a long list of known rivals and enemies and an unknown but likely much longer list of unnamed enemies.

Gargoyle noted the reactions of his bodyguards. Then he glanced up at first one, then a second, TV camera on different walls that had swiveled and zoomed in on the action in the middle of the room. He stomped his foot in frustration and muttered to himself that all that had just happened had been witnessed by security people elsewhere in the building as well as being recorded so it couldn't be easily denied by beating up another imaginary foe. He was careful to avoid Pernell during this latest venting of his annoyance.

Pernell stayed calm; Oscar and Webber worried.

Finally Gargoyle regained his composure. "Okay, you slipped that in on me. I expected a lot of hot air lead-in."

"I hope to keep it all simple since the Rules exist for a purpose and I respect them."

"I'm gonna show you stuff," Gargoyle said and walked into an adjacent room. When the others didn't move Pernell followed – alone.

* * *

The adjoining room, Gargoyle's special art gallery, was smallish - wide but shallow. It had windowless walls all around filled with framed, artfully lighted oil paintings. Gargoyle stopped by a painting of a medieval torture chamber in use. "Art often gives me ideas."

"Nice frame," Pernell said. "Bet you got a good deal on that."

They stepped to another painting of torture. Gargoyle said, "It's a challenge to hurt a guy a lot without killing him too fast which ends your fun."

"Also a challenge to hurt a guy and not get your hands dirty doing it so you get the legal liability."

Gargoyle laughed. "Come on. What would be the fun without doing it yourself?"

"I meant not doing it *to* yourself. You select some poor unlucky schmuck on the street and amuse yourself killing him, that's one thing. A guy like me who came to see you knowing your reputation so he took precautions, I'm another thing."

Gargoyle stepped to the next painting, a kneeling man begging for mercy before he is slain by a grinning swordsman. "Guy begs for mercy. The satisfaction's in knowing he won't get any."

"One moment in a scenario," Pernell said. "A single snapshot. The series of canvases showing the downfall of the swordsman because of this mistake would be the interesting exhibit."

"How so?"

"Let's use me as an example. If I disappear or turn up dead, you're in danger from several sides."

Gargoyle laughed but his face showed that he was concerned.

Pernell continued calmly, "The immediate consequence would be a disruption of your operations here and everywhere that the cops know you have something going on. If I'm not seen alive or don't signal that things are okay within a certain time, the cops'll be notified that you've kidnapped or killed me. We both know they'll jump at the chance to rush in here and break up all sort of things saying, 'Oops, sorry about that, now open that next drawer so we can be sure he's not stuffed in there'."

"I have smart lawyers."

"But the cops'll have probable cause and search warrants. It'll all have to be sorted out later - *after* they've poked through every corner of your place. Including the research area on the third floor."

Gargoyle stopped smiling. "But you still might be dead."

"There's no changing that. All I could get is revenge. Word would be out that you don't honor the Code. Which top level buddies will deal with you then? You'd be an outcast. Even well-paid muscle guys don't want to be on the wrong side of the Code. Plus there's your mother to consider."

"My momma?"

"I left copies of a videotape with several people to be sure it'll get good circulation. The TV networks will love the part where I say shame on your mother for not raising an honorable son."

Gargoyle growled, "All the more reason to make you suffer a whole lot before you die."

"When I agreed to be Lumbago's bagman I accepted that you'd do your worst to me even if there weren't gonna be bad consequences for you. With my bad ticker I'll go fast and disappoint you there too."

Gargoyle forced himself to take several deep breaths to calm himself before he said, "You don't rattle easily. Maybe you could be useful to me."

"I did some homework so I know the stuff you want those with an interest in you to know at least in sanitized versions."

"What's that mean?"

"That I've looked at several Internet sites that tout the doings of a guy who could be you but of course without using your name. Those present you as a super clever manipulator, et cetera. I don't care about that part of it but I'm told that sites like those are often paid for by the ones being puffed but without wanting to seem to be behind the supportive stuff that's said about them."

"Why wouldn't a guy want everybody to know about him?" He thought, *This guy may know more about my claims about my history and accomplishments than I might prefer.*

Pernell continued, "Mainly when it would incriminate him and could be used to help convict him. Also when he thinks those looking at the stuff have no idea he's behind it so they get the idea that somebody other than the mug himself thinks he's pretty neat."

"You should be careful who you call a mug," Gargoyle growled.

"Careful. That's a giveaway."

"Tell me the names of these internet sites so that I can have my people check them out."

"I don't have the web addresses in my head or even stored on my computer. I do a search each time but I always seem to find them."

Gargoyle leaned forward, his expression telegraphing that he was about to strongly insist on the details he had asked for.

Without giving away much of what he was thinking, Pernell continued, "There's one site that shows a bunch of nice art works supposedly in the unnamed guy's personal collection. Doesn't claim to show it all but it might be a good sized group of pieces. But real art, not this torture fantasy in frames stuff. See how diplomatic I can be, I caught myself and only said *stuff,* not the cruder term I was thinking."

"You're an art connoisseur, Sylvester?"

"Mostly an art critic. I see crap, I politely call it *stuff*. What I don't do is pretend I think it's worth hanging on my wall and showing off as an example of my poor taste." Saying that was a calculated risk but at this point he had decided to test things.

Gargoyle gave an involuntary little jerk as he considered his automatic aggressive first reaction but held himself in check long enough to consider his more deliberate second reaction. He walked to a wall and stood with his back to Pernell as he did something with his hands that the other man couldn't see because the mobster was in the way. Gargoyle stepped back and pivoted out what was now obviously a hinged wall section that worked as a door into another room.

Gargoyle glanced back at Pernell for the man's reaction. He would have preferred a look of surprised amazement and maybe eager anticipation but had to content himself with enjoying Pernell's look of mild interest. This guy was a tough audience. This performer didn't like that.

Pernell made no move until Gargoyle waved for him to follow him through the door as he stepped in and turned on overhead lights. This room was three times as deep as the torture gallery and contained a variety of art objects, not just oil paintings. A few items had overhead small spotlights on them. A few were sculptures or ceramics. All looked like they might be found in a standard art museum exhibit, not in a special side room with a warning sign for the public at the door about the sick paintings being shocking or disturbing.

Pernell's impression was that these items had been arranged by someone with an artist's eye in order to be viewed in a walk-through. This wasn't a room where anyone was intended to sit and contemplate the items, it was a place to show them off for an occasional visitor. He suspected that the collection was valued by Gargoyle mainly for the sake of the importance having it gave him in certain circles, not because the man spent much time thinking about the aesthetics.

"Very nice. The web site doesn't do your collection credit," Pernell said. He thought but didn't say, *I wonder how many of these items those in the know would recognize as stolen if they saw the photos of them included on that site even if those images have been blurred and distorted to some degree on there? I give you or your adviser whoever that might be credit for holding back in the interest of security at least to that degree by the Photoshopping.*

"I don't show this stuff to many people," Gargoyle admitted as he wondered why he had chosen to show it to this guy.

"I appreciate the honor," Pernell said as he looked around to seem politely impressed without showing too much interest in details.

"It's all older stuff, I don't get turned on by the new guys smearing paint around. Classical holds its value best." Gargoyle stopped abruptly as it dawned on him that he had twice called the material *stuff* after Pernell made that a dismissive term in this context.

"Is that a Renoir painting over there? I think I saw one like it in a book once. A Rodin sculpture over there? Maybe just by someone in the same school of artists."

Gargoyle had mixed feelings. Over several minutes standing in place not moving closer to items, Pernell asked relevant questions and showed more knowledge about some of the pieces than the mobster expected or was thrilled about. He liked to show them off as artsy acquisitions but worried that someone with too much background would recognize pieces that the art world at large had lost track of.

Finally Pernell said, "Let's get back to how I might be of use to you. Make me an offer. But let's not play games, my request for the payment can't be left standing unaddressed for long. How do you propose to get around that without technically refusing to pay up?"

"You think that's what I want to do?"

"It's what your real world reputation tells me to expect."

"A reputation talked around by my enemies and those who've lost when they tried to play and lost."

"True enough, but one with enough guys agreeing with it to give it weight. Let's be blunt. If you were gonna to turn over the money you owe for the services rendered, whatever those were, you'd have already done so but you've been delaying, hoping a scheme will coagulate in your head."

"Did you consider that I might not have that much cash on hand when you made your demand?"

Pernell quickly corrected him, "I requested, I didn't demand."

Gargoyle reluctantly gestured that he conceded that point.

"I respectfully asked you to honor the agreement I was told you made, I didn't demand anything. Well, except by invoking the Code of Honor among Thieves to move things along."

Gargoyle said, "The Code still gives me leeway time-wise. Here's the deal. You fly to Savannah and pick up a suitcase full of money owed to me. You deliver that here to me and I pay you the million bucks you came to pick up for that other guy out of that."

"That's two million - plus an additional ten percent of the total amount that I pick up in Savannah since I'll be acting as your bagman in order to make my cut acting as Lumbago's bagman."

"No, that's the price you have to pay to get your money this week instead of ten weeks from now or whenever I happen to have that amount on hand."

Pernell shrugged, "No thanks. You just made it too expensive for me risk-wise to earn my money from Lumbago. Many may choose to interpret your action as a refusal to pay on your part but on my part that's not my big concern. Which of these doors will get me out of the building with the least delay?"

"A window would be the fastest way."

"It would also clearly violate the Code, Section Three. On the treatment of bagpersons."

"Nobody but me knows what happened here. It's like we met on the moon."

"Exactly. The only people who know for sure that I came here are concerned about what happened to me because they respect the Code and they take it seriously."

"You're not being helpful."

"I'm not being foolish. If there weren't some big risk in making this pickup that you're not telling me about you'd send one of your regular guys. That greater risk for me added to your reputation for scheming to use people and cheat them add up to a big fat 'Don't go there' warning sign. On top of that you want it at no cost to you. Nice if you can get it, but you won't get it from me."

"I don't like being called a liar and a cheat."

"Yes you do. You work hard to have that reputation. I assume you think that makes you a hero to certain guys. Maybe you're right."

"I could arrange an unfortunate accident for you on the street."

"But that won't make your pickup in Savannah happen."

"I'm trying hard to cut you some slack," Gargoyle said.

"You don't do freebies so why should I?"

"To get in my good graces."

"This is strictly business for me, Mr. Gargoyle. I'm not looking to be your friend and golf partner. The fact is, after I deliver Mr. Lumbago's money I hope and expect to never have anything to do with you or yours ever again. By the way, this part of our transaction is strictly between us so nobody else will ever know you changed your mind and accepted my terms. Or that those weren't your offer from the start. Unless you tell them."

"Good point. Diplomacy can be a plus in business. Maybe I do want you to make this pickup since there could be some fuss about them turning over the money. Okay, ten percent of Lumbago's money it is." Gargoyle smirked and stuck out his hand to shake on the deal.

With a disappointed sad shake of his head Pernell waited ever so patiently, checking his watch and ignoring the hand and looking around the room.

Finally Gargoyle said, "Oh yeah, and ten percent of the amount you bring me from Savannah before I give you Lumbago's payment."

Now Pernell smiled and shook Gargoyle's hand.

"Come on, we'll have tea to celebrate our deal."

Pernell's eyebrows went up a bit at the idea of having tea but he smiled and nodded agreement.

* * *

A special part of the open roof of Gargoyle's building was a professionally designed garden of potted tropical plants arranged around a gazebo containing a matching table and several chairs. The feature was a way to be noticed by those looking from taller buildings.

Gargoyle and Pernell sat across the table from one another.

Pernell stared, instantly smitten, when the lovely Shallwee Bee, well preserved at forty-plus and currently wearing a lavishly embroidered kimono and obi, her hair in geisha style up-fashion with golden kanzashi for a topping effect, brought a tray of cups and a tea pot to the table from behind a screened-off preparation area.

Gargoyle was amused by Pernell's reaction. "This is Miss Bee. Nice, huh?"

"Hello, I am Shallwee Bee. It is a pleasure to have you with us today. Mr. Pernell."

"My pleasure indeed," Pernell said in a mere whisper.

Bee laid out the things and poured the tea.

"Tell you what, Pernell. We'll let Shallwee be our go-between. She'll be the one who'll bring you word on exactly where and when you'll make the pickup in or around Savannah. She'll bring you a plane ticket to get there but you'll come back by train since it could be a problem bringing the bag back through airport security without a lot of questions."

"I'm all in favor of having this lovely lady deliver the details. Uh, so that I know I've got the right information."

"Oops, I forgot the cookies." Bee walked out of sight behind the screen, the men watching her go with appreciation.

Gargoyle said quietly, "She knows how these things go so she'll give us a minute to talk. Right now somewhere near Savannah a ship of foreign registry is being unloaded. The goods, which have an Asian connection, will be delivered to an intermediary. You'll pick them up from him so you won't need to go near the port or to talk or *capiche* anything but English."

"I assume signals or code words have been worked out so I'll know who I'm to deal with and they'll know who I'm bagging for without a lot of hassle."

"Yeah. Shallwee'll give you those before you leave."

"Do I get a number to call if there are problems?"

"No, you're on your own. We don't know you until we're sure it's not the law interfering."

Bee stepped from behind the screen with a plate of cookies.

Pernell whispered, "Is Shallwee..? Uh, how is she..?

"You wanna take her to dinner?" Gargoyle asked.

"I'd like to ask her, yeah."

"Shallwee, Sylvester's gonna take you to dinner. See that he gets to the room that'll be reserved in his name at the Dorkman Hotel afterwards so he'll get some sleep and be ready for an early morning trip to the airport and beyond. Any questions?"

"Whoa there! I said I'd like to ask Miss Bee to have dinner with me, I didn't agree to impose myself on her if she'd rather not."

"I would very much enjoy having dinner with you, Sylvester," Bee said with a warm smile. "We will go to Luigi's and put it on Mr. Gargoyle's tab."

"I can pay for it."

Bee moved a chair closer to Pernell and sat. "But it is part of his plan to know where you go and who you talk to until your job for him is done so it is only fair that it should be his business expense."

Gargoyle laughed, "Yeah, I'll write it off my taxes."

Chapter 09

Pernell moved some of his belongings to the Dorkman Hotel where they were expecting him and had a room ready for him. He discreetly put the rest of his items in a paid storage locker elsewhere to keep it out of the reach of snoops.

Before dinner he slipped out to scout the area around what would be the delivery site. He needed to work backwards from there to decide the route with the least chance of him and the item to be moved being seen by live observers or security cameras owned and operated by anyone.

For this important purpose he had printed out a blown-up view of the relevant section of the street map on which he would mark the camera locations and likely field of view of each. He had done this in several cases in previous years so he knew what to look for. There would likely to be too many cameras to trust to his memory alone. Once he had mapped out the route and knew where every lens was watching from he might still have to make last minute changes and having a paper copy of those details could be the difference between a successful seemingly unexplainable delivery and failure.

He was also testing how closely Gargoyle's hotel employees and others were watching him. As far as he could detect so far, not very closely. Still he waited for the Metromover at a station where he probably wasn't seen doing that and stayed where he couldn't be seen from the street until the monorail was in the station so it blocked the view of anyone looking for him as he boarded. Basic steps to thwart any unseen minder or a series of spies.

* * *

Having done enough field research to let him tell himself he was making progress and with time before he was to meet Shallwee Bee for dinner, Pernell also returned to the Healing Hospital where he sidestepped Nurse Nulty and delivered another cup of "forbidden" yogurt which Beebop ate eagerly. She admitted to feeling better than she had for weeks but neither of them was ready to guess about whether that was an effect of lactobacilli in her gut or the fun of sneaking around the rules and authorities.

Before he left the hospital he spent a few minutes studying a floor map of the place so he would know his way around better. He subtly tried to find someone on staff who would pay attention to the secret to getting Beebop to eat yogurt or other foods that would be good for her but no one else present at this time would listen or risk the vengeance of the formidable Nurse Nulty whom they all said wasn't a mean person, only a strict by-the-rules one.

* * *

Luigi's was a semi-fancy urban eatery. The staff knew Ms. Bee so the pair were given the booth she preferred at one side of the good-sized room. Silk plant arrangements set into the high separator backs of the booths - that opened to face the aisle along the side wall rather than the open dining area - further visually isolated them. A waiter who was attentive but not intrusive assured their good time. A full bar was to one side at the front.

"Will Gargoyle show up later to keep me edgy?" Pernell asked, only half-kidding.

"No need. He has eyes all around in here so he's likely taking care of other business tonight," Bee answered, relaxed now.

"But wishing his business was with you? Or is that part later?"

"I'm his office assistant but it's all strictly business. His wife has eyes everywhere too and she's not a lady for even him to mess with."

"That's a big statement. Are you sure?"

"Mr. Gargoyle married into power. His wife's father and two brothers are bigger mob figures than him. That's why he has good reason to fear getting her upset with him. I see that you brought your laptop with you. You could have left it in your room since you've checked in or they would hold it in their secure storage room for you. The restaurant coat check person would take care of it too."

"It's no problem to keep it with me. Quite bluntly I'm happiest having it where I know who might be tiptoeing through my files. Also I might think of something I should ask you about or should check on about Savannah and I can do it right away before I forget what it was."

"You think it's important enough to go to that trouble?"

"Yes, but more important, I'm concerned that others might think it's that important to them. These days lots of people walk around with virtually their entire lives available for inspection on their electronic devices. So much important information that can be lost, stolen, or at least revealed and used against them. Heck, even the Supreme Court recognizes that as how it is. I'm old fashioned enough to not have that much of what's important digitized and stored but there are plenty of electronic trails that I'm happier not to have easily coming back to me."

"You don't think it's safe enough to just lock it in the safe that's in the hotel room for your use?" she asked.

"The people I'd prefer not to have snoop in my files would have too easy access to that kind of safe. Starting of course with the hotel staff who are employees of the guy who might be much interested in what and how much I know. Also various law enforcement types probably have fairly easy access. I don't know who else but I'm good with taking precautions."

In fact although he would never know it, while Pernell was having dinner Norman Hill, a hotel security staff man, and an FBI agent alerted to Gargoyle's interest in Pernell would each search his comped hotel room for his laptop and come up empty-handed.

"I'll trust you with this little secret," he said. "When I don't want to carry it with me I lock my laptop in a coin locker in a place that rents such spaces by the day or week so I can get to it twenty-four seven. But, and this is the important point, where I can get in and out of there without using the standard street doors where I'd be easily seen or followed. Many times I tote along a laptop carrying shoulder bag with a thin cardboard box in it so it looks like there's a computer in there even when there's not. That's to confuse the enemy. It doesn't inconvenience me much so I do it in case it helps."

"I agree about the hotel staff. I wouldn't recommend trusting anyone who take orders from him - myself the exception of course."

He considered where that might go but opted to not find out. He said, "I see why he likes this place. You have close to a private dining room at any booth in the place."

"Plus the food's good and the staff keep an eye on everybody who walks in the door so the guests aren't likely to get unpleasant surprises. The seafood's always good. So many things look good."

As Bee focused on the menu, the Maître d' seated Jane Taylor, wearing a heavily veiled hat, in the second booth down from theirs. She strained to see what Pernell was doing before she sank from sight into her seat.

As Pernell focused on the menu, Treasury agent Winkler walked far enough down the aisle to verify that Pernell was in this booth, then walked back to stand at the bar where he could watch who might go near that booth without being too obvious himself. He passed Taylor's table without noticing her since she had her head so far down that her forehead was almost resting on the linen tablecloth.

Dutton, wearing a long wig and cheap fake beard, stood up at his small table in the open dining area and made an exaggerated stretch. That move was an excuse to strain up onto tiptoe to verify that Pernell was in the booth where he thought he was. He then sat back down fast and self-consciously. He hadn't anticipated that his stretch would cause so many people to stare at him.

"I'm usually a beef and potatoes guy but I'm willing to try new things," Pernell said as the waiter approached to take their orders.

"I'll have the seafood platter," Bee told the waiter.

"Give me the same thing but with extra shrimp," Pernell said. The waiter nodded, took the menus, and moved off.

"Do you live here in Miami?" Bee asked.

"I've wintered here in recent years.

"And the rest of the year?" she asked.

"I spend most of my time each year farther north."

"I've never been out of Florida."

"You should see more of the country - even of the world."

"There are still things I'd like to see here though."

Taylor stood and straightened her skirt under her as an excuse to spy on Pernell. She sat down fast when she saw Winkler by the bar moving for a better look at her. She wasn't sure who he was but he seemed familiar and he was definitely too interested in her to suit her.

"As long as you're happy where you are that's okay. Maybe someday you'll find a reason to want to see other things," Pernell said.

"Florida has a lot of interesting history and places to visit."

"I know that since I was developing an interest in the smaller points of Florida history until I read some of the Tim Dorsey novels featuring the rather whacko character Serge Storms. Then I decided that being able to spout the minutia didn't seem so cool."

"Why not?" she asked.

"Okay, I admit that a big part is because I'd never get much of it down so I could remember it and rattle it off with any sense of assurance. Also because I began to worry about whether focusing on the little details like that was cause, effect, or unrelated to Serge's craziness. Wow, I'm not usually this honest about stuff like this but okay, I worried if it'd seem like I was either a Serge clone or maybe a wannabe to those who've read those books."

"You can relax, Sylvester. Your secret is safe with me."

"Nothing against Tom Dorsey since I read his books but I'm worried about me. Maybe that sounds crazy. Maybe I should shut up."

"And deprive me of the fun of your company? No, I forbid it."

They both laughed and touched hands.

Having seen the fast movement of Taylor sitting down, Dutton eased to his feet to try to see who that was in that other booth. But then he flopped back down into his chair when he saw Winkler at the bar straining to get a better look at him.

"I don't rule anything out. I hear that Savannah's nice."

"I guess. I've only passed through, never spent any time there. Not that I wouldn't be glad to see the sights. I did buy a street map of the city so I can find the address I need there in the morning. I never depend on taxi drivers to know where things are," Pernell said then stood to get a folded map from his pocket, glancing around the room as he did so.

Taylor rose slowly into view to check on Pernell. Dutton did the same. At the end of the room Winkler moved to get a better view of both of those as he and Pernell stared at one another for a moment. Taylor and Dutton dropped into their seats and lowered their heads

Pernell sat down. Winkler turned on his stool to continue to watch the room as he could see it in the mirror wall behind the bar.

Taylor and Dutton both flinched, startled by the movement, when their waiters brought their first courses.

* * *

Later Pernell and Bee strolled arm-in-arm along a back street that was well lit and felt safe at this hour. She said, "I didn't mean to put a damper on our conversation in the restaurant but I realized I wanted to talk about subjects I couldn't there where I'm sure we were being recorded."

"I appreciate the caution and this is nice in itself," he said. "Are you a magician? I don't remember the last time I've so much wanted to spend time just talking to someone."

"Maybe I'm a good witch. If it helps me get what I want I'm not opposed to being called that. But you're a critical factor. I haven't felt this way about anyone else for longer than I want to admit I could claim either."

"I'm going to trust you and admit that I'm impressed by the boss man's art collection. Something I wouldn't say where he'd learn of it and maybe try to use it against me in some way. I'm sure the art's worth a lot but knowing he's the one with it I wouldn't be surprised to learn that he can't brag about it much," he said.

"I'll return the favor and tell you that officially I don't know what you're referring to. I've never been shown the big room but twice I've peeked in when I found the door sitting open and the lights on in there. I didn't risk tripping any alarms or being seen doing that on any security camera inside. I recognized a few things but there's no way I can do anything about what little I know."

"Do you think the items are fakes? That's what I wondered."

"I expect they're the originals but it's how they ended up in that room in his office suite that won't stand up to scrutiny."

"Ah, my Sherlock Holmesbody persona processes those limited inputs and concludes that you spotted one or more items from the doorway that you had seen before and know who owned them."

"Very good. I'm not playing word games simply for the sake of doing that, I don't know enough details to know what might have happened and I don't want to seem to make a case that I'm not sure can be made," she said.

"What can you tell the curious world that'd be only too happy to find out about dirt to use against Gargoyle? If that's too open and blatant a question, scratch your nose and ignore it. Oh, and I mean do that literally so I know your silence means that. Wow, that's getting awkward isn't it?"

"On several occasions I went along in the line of duty as his secretary when my employer visited Polly Nana and we saw items from her family art collection in her big house. That's Polly Nana, widow of art dealer Poppy Nana. That's as much as I feel safe saying and can say with certainty."

"Thanks for the caution signal. What else can we talk about?"

"Let's go in here. Cameras are for sure but probably no microphones," she said and guided him into a small grocery store.

"This is a place where I need to pick up some supplies anyway."

As they shopped the aisles pushing a cart, they spoke in low tones which made them seem more like love birds than conspirators so none of the several people in there paid them much attention.

"This is my guess but only that about what happened," she said. "Poppy Nana loved beautiful things and hoarded some. I suspect those were often stolen items too dangerous to sell for a time. When he died under suspicious circumstances, his widow Polly consulted with an art dealer who sold pieces and bought some for her. Mr. Gargoyle may have had Poppy killed for some reason but there was no solid police case made against him. I suspect that the art dealer routinely told Mr. Gargoyle about every purchase and every discussion with the widow."

"Padding his wallet or protecting his hide. It makes sense."

"I'm guessing that when Mr. Gargoyle felt sure the widow's collection truly was a secret, then he moved in and took it over. He could expect - as happened - that she wouldn't complain in a public forum since there'd be so many questions about how she came to have the items reported missing elsewhere. There were no investigations that Mr. Gargoyle heard about, no news media or Internet whispers."

"What about the criminal grapevine? Any rumors there?"

"I don't know anything about such a thing so I can't even guess what was or wasn't said there. Am I hopelessly naive?"

"No, that means you're innocent like ninety-eight percent of the population. Don't feel neglected or out of it, try to forget you heard about it from me. So Gargoyle's whole deal with the art works was neatly packaged in its nasty way," he said.

"The theft, since that's what it amounted to, wasn't reported to the local police or Interpol because it was a blatant strong arm job and Polly Nana had good reason to believe that she'd be killed if she complained to anyone. Her long-term revenge in a way is that she probably didn't tell Mr. Gargoyle about which items she knew were stolen - and from whom. Surely that was in large part out of fear of his anger too but as long as he didn't try to sell the items or have them appraised by anyone he didn't control and therefore who would bluntly warn him about their history, that fact should stay secret."

"A ticking incrimination bomb."

She nodded agreement.

He said, "He probably doesn't realize it has that potential or he'd keep the whole room a total secret."

"No, that would make it worthless to him," she said. "He's a man who has to show off what he has and can do, not one to sit alone and enjoy just looking at it and knowing he has sole possession of it."

"With my assessment of Gargoyle, that scenario makes sense but I see why you don't dare to go to the authorities with it. From spending several recent winters in Miami I knew of him but never had a reason or desire to meet him. He has a reputation for violence so until I got an offer that at the time I didn't feel I could refuse I was happier being well clear of him. I suspect his reputation is partly hype for intimidation effect but I don't know enough to guess how much is that. I can see that you have no proof but once you're on the record making claims you're likely in the cross-hairs of some goon taking orders from him. When he made the first not too subtle threats against me it became personal. Now I want to hurt him as well as survive."

"I never kid myself. If he suspected me of anything serious he'd hardly blink before having me killed to silence me. For now I can't even just walk away. He's paranoid enough to convince himself I was in the process of selling him out no matter who told him otherwise."

"Would his bodyguards do that if he told them to?"

"Absolutely. Those men think I'm quaint and they're amused that he keeps me around but I'm not their type so I can't distract them with feminine wiles. They want their babes brash, tanned, and with only twenty natal anniversaries on their birthday cards."

"Is Polly Nana alive?" he asked.

"Yes, alive but not very active. I'm reluctant to ascribe ideas to my employer but I suspect he's waiting impatiently for her to die so that avenue of information about the items will be closed. Polly's probably safer ever since a niece took an interest in her and has taken charge of most of her affairs. It'd be riskier for him to arrange to have her pushed over the edge now. That young woman won't let any even vaguely suspicious things happen without a full police investigation."

"I'm going to trust my instinct and trust you with something."

"I'm doing the same telling you some of what I've said."

"This is also because I should do what I can to protect you since I realize that you're always in some potential danger. There's something you should probably know for your protection even if you might have to pretend not to understand about it. You might be wondering why he treated me as he did."

"It's not part of my job description to think about such things but yes, I wondered what that's about. He seemed more cautious dealing with you than I've seen in many of his dealings - although almost always I'm seeing those from the next room without him knowing I can see or hear what's going on," she said.

"Here's the scoop, I walked in and requested payment of a debt he's been ignoring for some time. Not for me, for someone who's paying me to try to get that money. A large amount although I'm pretty sure he could come up with it. Anyway, to do that and keep him from literally shooting the messenger I invoked the Code of Honor among Thieves. That's why he's so far hands-off me but he'd like to find a way to kill me for doing that."

"I don't think I've ever heard of such a code except as a joke."

"That's the ninety-eight percent thing I mentioned. The Code is directly associated with the criminal grapevine. As intended though, it's supposed to be written off as only a dumb rumor like Nessie, or the abominable snowman, or the world at the center of the earth. It's real though and to a particular group it's important. Not sacred but deeply respected. Criminals and law enforcement people know about it. It's an open secret although there's no commercial printed version."

"I never heard of it as a real thing."

"The existence of the Code and a secret committee who deal with serious infractions were publicly revealed about two decades ago during a print journalist's interview with a midlevel mobster then regretting his decision to embrace that life and his non-Mob criminal buddy. Each was 'clearing his conscience'."

"More cases of people doing bad stuff then later in life getting religion in some sense and hoping to erase their records," she said.

"That was it. Anyway, each of them had spent time in jail and had been arrested a lot but not indicted or convicted most times."

"What happened?"

"Both claimers were found dead the next day. Both apparent suicides, although many have doubts about that. The paper printed the interview article which immediately attracted national attention. Then the reporter and all his notes and tape recordings about anything and everything disappeared no one knows where."

"See, that's what I'm afraid of if I say too much to the wrong people. It's safer to keep quiet until there's a way to testify without getting silenced forever before you can tell what you know," she said.

"Good advice. Anyway, various people, most suspected of or known to have organized crime ties, raised doubts in the media about the accuracy and even the sincerity of the article. Then a juicy sex scandal grabbed the headlines and the nation's attention. Almost overnight the Code became an afterthought and widely believed to have been a hoax or a joke."

"Some things never seem to change," she said.

"When I read the article two years after it was published I had little doubt it was real and accurate but had no idea it would ever be relevant to me. When the Internet came along I found a place to read the actual rules and tucked that info away in the back of my head. They impressed me so I remembered them even though I'm not a memory genius type. Lone operators like me don't usually formally agree to it but some organized groups of various sizes do swear to it. For some it's a formal ritual. No one can make more than wild guesses about what percentage of the crooks and their actual numbers who swear on the Code and tiptoe around its seldom invoked rules and protections. The guesses that are made publicly are all over the field, surely to confuse the matter."

"It's good sense to at least suspect such claims," she said.

"I rattled the system when I invoked it today. Not something I did casually though. But for my protection I made sure the grapevine told all those with an interest in the Code and its enforcement about what I did. That's what has your employer treating me with kid gloves while waiting to choke me while wearing those when he can find a way to keep that off the grapevine. Fact is that those who respect its rules are better than any law enforcement group at finding out what happened and who did what."

"Thank you for trusting me and telling me this, Sylvester. I'll stay alert and won't admit I know anything about it but it should help me make sense of some of what I see or hear. I have enough time and experience around his building and people to know who not to let know how much I know. Knowing what I do now, I see you were either brave or foolish to take on the task of getting him to pay what he owes but wants to forget that fact."

"I'm still wondering the same myself. Brave or foolish? I chose to take the job of trying to get the money from Gargoyle and once I started that there's no going back without seeing it through and doing what I can to keep from having to be looking over my shoulder for the rest of my days. Things have changed and I don't need the money from that job any more but I still have to follow through."

"Only time will tell, but you seem clever and for the most part cautious so I'll bet my money on you coming out on top."

"Thank you for that vote of confidence, Shallwee. Now I have more reason to be careful and crafty. I have to survive to show that you're a good judge of characters. And yeah, I consider myself to be a character when that means a stand out, pay attention and be amused or fascinated by him guy. Let me pay for these few things and we can get out of here. I have things I have to do before it gets too late."

"Do you get late night snack attacks?" she asked as she pointed to the few items in the cart.

"Once in a while something like that happens, yeah. You never know when the craving will crawl out of your gut."

She reacted with mock shock at that idea.

"No offense intended with that bluntness." She gestured that she was teasing him so he said, "But if you've stocked up properly you don't have to be concerned."

"Will you explain this to me some day?"

"I will if I can."

"But only if it's safe for you to share the details."

"Oh heck, it's not that kind of thing. These items are tools for a game I'm playing that I hope will bring someone I only met yesterday out of what I diagnose as a depression. Simple material but they have to be sneakily used and that's the point. Yes, especially if it works, I'll tell you all about it. It'll actually say a lot about me that would be hard for me to put into other words."

"That's good enough for me. I'm going to add a package of mints to the bill if that won't break your bank." She smiled coyly.

"I have enough money to cover the cost but I may want to get some reward for being so generous."

"I'm blushing like a school girl. That hasn't happened for a long time."

"But it makes you even more interesting."

"We need to pay and get out of here before I embarrass us."

"You probably can't embarrass me but you might get us both arrested so I won't challenge you to prove that. Darn it, I really do have things I need to do tonight though," he lamented.

* * *

After he saw Shallwee off home in a taxi, Pernell walked around in casual fashion to do more scouting to decide about the feasibility of the big transfer and what methods might have the best chance of success with that. He observed things in the delivery area from a distance, alert for any avoidable potential problems.

Again he also assessed whether he was being closely watched by Gargoyle's people – and decided that such monitoring still seemed minimal.

Chapter 10

From a street payphone where he wasn't easily seen he used his prepaid card to place a call. He gave a prearranged code word, and was connected to the agent for whoever was ready to pay him to make what he now thought of as the big transfer.

"Good evening. How will we proceed?" the agent asked.

"I've thought about it and done some preliminary looking around. I'm ready to be all-in but I still need assurances that I'm not getting into something seriously illegal or damaging. I can't make further plans without knowing a lot of details about the package," Pernell said.

"Understood. Are you where we can talk for several minutes?"

"Yeah, I'm good."

"The item to be transferred is an art piece unofficially but widely referred to as *Funny Money* because several parts of it are like Christmas tree balls hung on a central branched section. Those small bits are said to be roughly shaped like money symbols that are melting like Salvador Dali's watches."

"Money symbols?"

"The shapes used to indicate dollars, euros, British pounds, and the Chinese Yuan. There may be others, those I've seen listed."

"Gotcha. I can see them in my head."

"The work was created in 2000 and stolen shortly after it was first publicly displayed. There are rumors that possibly it was stolen to keep it from being closely examined. The whispers suggest that its workmanship would give critical clues about who stole various art works from the 1930s through the 1960s. That might hint where those stolen pieces went and where they are today since most of them haven't been recovered."

"So it's of value at least as much for what it might reveal about its history as for its own inherent artistic value," Pernell said.

"And the value of the precious metal since there's supposed to be a lot of gold in it, although no one seems to know just how much. Rumored values have a way of becoming inflated."

"An important consideration."

"Here's where your part in the story starts. The person for whom I am working this project knows where it is. Turns out it was hidden in place in the recent past by adding additional elements to enclose and thus hide it's better known configurations. It's quite tall but sort of open work so its total weight isn't that great."

"For an artsy thing that makes sense. Go on."

"The person interested in hiring you is pretty certain that it can be disassembled and safely reassembled because he saw the piece *in the flesh* as it were and up close before it went missing. This person also saw a set of detailed close-up photos that can no longer be found. Those were apparently the only close-up ones taken of it before it disappeared, allegedly stolen. This person is convinced that what look like ornamental dots and lines on it are *separate and snap together here* points to facilitate taking it apart to move without damaging it."

"That would make the task a whole lot easier for sure."

"I'm told that a tall A-ladder that will likely be needed to get the item back together and then upright is available at the final site but there's always the possibility that that could be moved at any time and create a problem."

"Something I can check when I make a final inspection of the site before I make any moves," Pernell said.

"That's why the principal wanted you to do this. You'd make sure what was needed was in place on the day you chose to take the final action," the agent said.

"Okay, I have a working idea of what needs to be done. Now why does it have to be done in secret and who benefits if it's done that way?"

"Does the name Armand Clanger mean anything to you?"

"Isn't he a big money guy? He's...?"

"He's not the one paying you but he will supply the money. This part isn't going to happen in secret so I can explain. Billionaire playboy Armand Clanger has bet the world at large a substantial sum of cash that no one can find *Funny Money* and return it to Interpol without being arrested by Interpol for stealing it. He did this as far as anyone can tell for the sheer fun of making a challenge of it and to annoy Interpol who have hassled him in the past. He's secure enough that he didn't make a secret of his offer, in fact rather waved it in the faces of the people who annoyed him. He's certainly good for the money and it will hardly make a dent in his wallet."

"Now I understand the secrecy element and why there might be official types with international badges snooping around and trying to catch such a move in the act. That's an important warning."

"My employer thought it essential for you to know that aspect of it. If that changes your mind, we hope you'll keep what you've been told to yourself and we will of course still pay as much as we promised for what you've done to assess if this is possible even if you decide not to proceed."

"For now I'm still go. Knowing that additional stuff I'll go back and reconsider what can be done with minimum risk of detection or interference. Has your employer told anyone that he or she intends to try to collect on the Clanger challenge?"

"I'm told no and I believe that's the case. Think about it this way, the person trying to arrange the surprise rediscovery would likely be in trouble for not immediately reporting even a hint of where the item is. We expect that Mr. Clanger won't demand answers about how this person came to suspect where the piece was located and somehow arranged to get it to where it was found - which everyone will know instantly is not where it had been any time until some time fairly recently. The authorities will want to know, but the game is to leave them all wondering but with no one who knows identified so they can be prosecuted for not telling or for what they did."

"I kind of like the whole idea of it," Pernell said.

"We hoped you would since then you'll be careful to preserve the mystery which will make it more fun for almost everyone."

"Knowing this, I recognize the satisfaction for the principal in arranging it and the big payoff even though he'll pay me a chunk of that if I succeed and a still substantial amount even if I fail but made a good try. A money risk for him but with a big payoff is I succeed. The especially interesting challenge for me is that if I'm clever enough even if I don't manage to move the item to cause the big surprise, unless I'm caught gold-handed there's little legal risk for him or for me. I can't finger him but I've already earned the first payment just for giving my estimate of whether it can be done."

"The goal is to pull it off, get secretly paid by Clanger, and take the secret to our graves. It's important to the principal that you don't get short-changed since the background checks that were paid for to identify and then learn about you and finally contact you suggested you're among the few people most likely to be able to succeed at this."

"Will I ever meet the principal?"

"There is no plan for that to happen. Do you want to?"

"No, in fact that'd be a deal breaker. It'd warn me that he has more to his agenda that what we just mentioned. That at some point he expects to go public and take credit for the mystery surprise by telling the world all the details of how he arranged it."

"I can tell you that I'm greatly relieved to hear that you feel that way. If you even insisted on knowing the person's name, whether or not you ever have direct contact we'd be worried about *your* longer term agenda."

"Like my buddy who you used to get the initial message to me, I'm good taking the reward promised me for doing a task and not thinking more about it. I do need to ask one thing since you seem to be giving me the straight dope. Is the principal a racketeer or any kind of a public enemy?"

"No. I did my due diligence when contacted about being agent in this matter. As far as I can determine using a variety of resources this person has no criminal record or connection to any organized criminal entity."

"Still a few possible sticking points. Was the principal involved in the original theft of the piece?"

"No."

"In its being hidden in recent times?"

"No.

"Could he be shown in court to have been personally involved in arranging its return to where I'm to find it and move it?"

"No. Which means that if the principal were to stiff you after you've pulled this off you can go to the FBI with what you know but they won't pay out a reward without solid proof - and you don't have any. I repeat for what it might be worth that I'm convinced there's no possibility you'll be stiffed but I realize you can never fully put that possibility out of mind until you're in a rocking chair in a retirement village years from now."

"Another point to clarify. Mr. Clanger's challenge was made publicly to the whole world, not to just the principal. Correct?"

"Correct. In fact as far as I can determine those two have never met in more than a passing way at some social event, if even then."

"If Interpol's involved should I assume the FBI and the local police are aware of chatter about the missing piece?" Pernell asked.

"I would assume so. I don't have access to their backrooms but it would seem likely to me."

"One more and it's a biggie. How did this person find out where the item is currently hidden?"

"A biggie indeed. This whole venture depends on there being only a minimal risk of it being traced back to the principal from any contacts. The simple answer is this. Based on rumors that the art piece was 'in play' either Interpol or the FBI or both have planted what I'll call *treasure hunt* hints leading to reward money on social media."

"Like the guy hiding envelopes of cash around a city and saying where to look on Twitter or some social medium?" Pernell asked.

"Same kind of thing although I don't know which social media outlets the authorities used. Anyway, it seems that to their annoyance other untraceable sources also posted hints of the same general kind online creating a momentary fad that made it a standard news story. It faded fast though when there were hints it was all a fake."

"The Internet's a fad of the day, forgotten tomorrow world."

"Based on some details about the history of the item that my employer knows but few others do, he decoded one of the online postings to mean that because it's too hot to sell or even to keep, the piece had been abandoned. Those who did so actually want it found by Interpol since that'll take the pressure off identifying and locating them. But it's important to them that it not be reported as found by anyone with a connection to them or on a definite time table that might give a clue to them. My employer interpreted the hints on where it's currently located and had someone secretly check and verify that it's there. Oh, and all the online searching was done using a computer account that doesn't lead back to my boss - or me for that matter."

"That gives me a lot to think about but my first reaction is that there's nothing that scares me off. On the contrary if I know what's what I can better protect myself which is the bottom line."

"As it should be. Is there anything else I can answer for you?"

"Not right now but let's set up another contact number. That's in case I think of something or I need something or I need to warn you about something."

"I'm happy to arrange that with you. If you find any reason that you can't proceed unless we can arrange for you to get either information or materials, be sure to let me know. We'd all like to see you pull this off. The world needs the occasional distraction of a mystery that doesn't hurt anyone."

* * *

Next, Pernell returned to the South Miami Healing Hospital where he sat in the lobby for a short while using their WiFi as he searched *Perry or Poppy Nana*. What he found seemed to fit with the scenario Bee had laid out and gave him a list of other sites to check when he had more time.

Unknown to him at his point, that search also tripped a secret monitoring signal and brought him to the attention of Interpol and the FBI who were interested in knowing who had an interest in that deceased art dealer and collector.

Then he sidestepped Nurse Nulty when he grabbed up a large flower arrangement to hide his face as she walked past him. Once she was gone, he put the flowers back where they had been. He said to someone who had watched his little performance, "Yeah, my niece should be able to carry a thing like that up to her granny's room like she wants to but her mom's worried it'll be too big and heavy for her."

He delivered the container of forbidden yogurt he had bought at the grocery earlier. Beebop wolfed that down eagerly and said she felt better than she had for some time. Then they shared a packet of what he called *power cookies* since they were labeled as high fiber. He said those were a secret special food because the company sold them on the open market but only the enlightened people for whom they were intended knew to eat them to get *cleaned out* and *powered up*.

As preparation for this visit he had phoned Jack Dimple who checked with his contacts and reported back. Two lady friends with whom Beebop regularly played harmless tricks on one another had recently died and a third became incapacitated so Beebop was having no fun and, Pernell concluded, had become badly depressed.

"What can you tell me about the Funsters?" he asked her.

"They were the fun sisters, a quartet of merry pranksters who had a good time working one another over verbally in what others sometimes thought was an outrageous fashion but that the girls all knew was always in good fun. They're dead now."

"All of them?"

"Effectively. Two might still have heartbeats but there's no fun life left in them."

"That's so sad to hear."

"Life can be nasty that way," she said and wiped away a tear.

"I ask about them because I asked the friend of the friend up in Pennsylvania who asked me to stop in and check on you about them. He got back to me with a sad story."

"Life's full of those. They can make it not seem worth going on. What's the point?"

"Are you willing to talk about this enough that I can send word back to the woman concerned about you that she's got the basic elements to the matter straight anyway?"

"I don't see why to bother but you seem to want to push it."

"Yeah, maybe I do. Maybe I'm overstepping but if you don't fend me off strongly enough I'll try to get the facts lined up in my head. Someone in the family of one of the dead women…"

"Her name was Selma."

"Thank you. I meant no disrespect, I simply wasn't told the names."

"Laura's buried too. Winona's had a stroke and she can't talk or let anyone know what she's thinking now."

"But Agnes is still stirring herself to kick against the goad but only once in a while when being like a vegetable after decades of being alive and wary and feisty is too frustrating. She's almost but not quite given up hope."

"You're probably too optimistic. She's pretty far down the tube."

"Let me get back to my sorting out the story. Someone in Selma's family reviewed her emails and decided that your barbed comments tortured Selma."

"Totally ignoring the emails in the same vein that Selma sent back since we were teasing one another. We never wanted to or tried to trick innocents, only those who understood and returned the fun in kind and that was how it went. We were funsters, the fun sisters," Beebop said.

He nodded but waited to see if she wouldn't go on now.

She did. "The relative, a great-niece named Irene, claimed publicly that she believes her relative whom she ignored for more than twenty years was driven to suicide by those emails even with no evidence of a suicide. In fact poor Selma died in a hospice after a debilitating illness. What this Irene thinks she can gain I can't guess. She said in an interview on her local TV station that she plans to sue me for killing Selma."

She gestured that she didn't understand why all this was happening but there didn't seem to be much she could do about it.

"Has she made any legal move?"

"Nothing I've been told about. In a way what she said was all it took to make it no fun being around anymore."

"If you exchanged emails with the other funsters, then you have a computer," he noted.

"Had. I gave it away when this fuss started. Seeing it kept reminding me of how Selma was being abused by her survivor who wasn't even supposed to be involved in her estate. We're old broads and knew we wouldn't last forever so we talked about stuff like that. This Irene wasn't named to have any say in Selma's affairs."

"Did you ditch the computer trying to hide your emails?"

"A double no on that. One no because I know enough about how those work to know they're also available on the computers that received them. The second no because I wasn't ashamed or afraid of them. I'm sure that anyone without an axe to grind would recognize them as the funning they were. No, the machine went because it was a daily sad reminder of how crappy some folks are for reasons of their own."

"Did the four of you use Skype or some system to let you see one another when you were visiting?"

"No. We knew there were ways to do that but Laura and Winona had old computers without cameras with them. They could have gotten them but Winona was strongly opposed to, as she put it, having to get primped up just to go on her computer. The rest of us didn't push it and didn't risk forgetting who did or who didn't want that extra capacity. Also we didn't want to chase anyone away by putting our scary mugs on their computer screens."

"What else happened? Selma's great-niece raised a fuss. From what I've heard about you then and even recently from staff here in the hospital that wasn't enough to shake you that much."

"You're good. Yeah, then my own family members who don't care two shakes about me for years at a time got worried that that woman's claims would be bad PR for them so they claimed I was losing it and needed to be *taken care of.* Dreaded three words for anyone used to fending for herself and doing what she wants. I get a visit from a doctor I don't know and from a lawyer I don't deal with. I recognize that there's stuff being done that may affect me but I'm not being consulted or even told about it. I'm okay for money so I'm not about to be a burden but they're more concerned about what strangers will say about me that might reflect on them. Oh shoot, let's not get into all that. Enough said that when you're the *elderly* one, you're automatically considered the incompetent one and... No, won't go there. Shutting up now."

"You have good paid up insurance so you let your family put you in the hospital to be cured," he said.

"Or to die where it'd look good. Like they were going out of their way to take care of me. There are those three words again."

"Do family members visit every day?"

"Haven't seen a one of them since I got here."

"Do friends know where you are to call and check on you?"

"I admit since you're determined to make me say it, that when Selma, Laura, and Winona all got sick at almost the same time and then all became unavailable I kind of crawled into my shell and lost contact with the few others I used to call or write to now and then. I had an accident one day and my personal phone book got wet and the pages stuck together so I couldn't open it. That was the only place I had a couple of the addresses and numbers. That happened some time back and then I moved to a new address and changed my phone number right after that."

"What about Della Loughlin and the Circle Square Group?"

Beebop brightened. "I've known Della since we were in high school together. For years we'd write long chatty letters two or three times a year. It's so easy to use the phone that few people still write long chatty letters."

"Do you have her address and phone number?" he asked.

"She was a soggy pages casualty. She was my main source of information about a number of people I knew in the Philadelphia area and about who was moving to Miami each year."

Pernell took a folded index card from his pocket. "Would you like to have her address and phone number?"

"Oh, after being out of contact this long she's probably not interested in having me..."

"She's the person who persuaded my friend Jack to ask me to try to check on you and report back if you need anything. I don't know how she knew you were in this hospital but she did. I guess that all means she'd really like to hear from you and do some catching up." He held out the card and she took it.

"Thank you, Della, and thank you, Sylvester. Maybe there's reason to stay in the game and fight if I can connect with some people with good sense and a good sense of humor. Oh, I see there's an email address too. Today I guess that's the item of most use."

Pernell took his laptop from his shoulder carrying case. "Why not send her an email right now? The sooner she hears something from you the happier she'll be."

"All the funsters were old fashioned and had big desktop computers. I've seen but I've never used one of these portable ones."

"I have it all set up. You type a message, click the *Send* button like on your old machine, and it's done. If you want to."

She nodded that she'd like to do that.

While he booted up the machine, she said, "Through Della I might be able to get back in contact with others in the Philadelphia area and to also learn of ladies anywhere around the country, not just in the Miami area, to establish a new circle of games friends. New funsters."

When he had things ready she wrote, *Hello from the fog of the past, Della. I promise (threaten?) to phone you tomorrow at a respectable hour when it won't seem like a bad news call.*

"I suspect you've made her very happy. Certainly you've given her fair warning," he said.

"I know she'll get that joke."

"And will interpret it as a good sign about your renewed state of mind."

"Is that a good thing?"

"One of the best and what she very much wants to hear."

At that point Nurse Nulty bustled in with a Miami cop and a hospital security guard in tow and ordered that Pernell be arrested for trespassing.

Beebop shook her head at the sadness of it and *tsk-tsked* as she picked up the bedside phone, got an outside line, and direct dialed what she said was the home number of the hospital's top administrator. The others stared at her.

She greeted the top boss by his first name, apologized that she was forced to interrupt him at home about this but with the police about to become involved it wouldn't wait. She asked when the *Relatives Only* visitor policy had been instituted.

She stared calmly at the now antsy Nulty as she said, "There is no such policy? Then there's a misunderstanding about that. That would mean someone ordered out on the claim of such hospital backing would have the basis for a lawsuit against the place. That's unfortunate for you but good to know."

She gave the others a raised eyebrows *Isn't that interesting news* look. "Thank you and have a good evening. I hope there won't have to be more talk about such a thing. Hold a minute please. You may need to repeat that to some hospital employees or a police officer who's here in my hospital room."

Nulty turned on her heels and left. The guard and the cop followed when Beebop held out the phone for them to get the word from the top man that there was no such policy. They waved off doing that and left grumbling to one another about Nulty.

Pernell stepped to the door and checked that all three had gone down the hall before he turned back and quietly applauded Beebop. "Neat performance. You get the Brass Pair of the Day award in my opinion. I don't know if any of them believed you actually know the top man's home number but none wanted to get into whether there is or isn't such a policy in front of witnesses."

She hung up the phone. "I dialed my own home phone and let the machine take it all down. After your first visit I did check and there's no such policy, only Nurse Nulty's say-so. Since I didn't intend to get her in trouble, only to back her off, I won't take it any further. How the guard and the cop write it up I can't control."

"But you faked them out. Even offering them the phone. Wow! Congrats. You've clearly been boldly tossing the BS for some time."

"Probably about as many years as you've been alive. I started at an early age and you look to be maybe ten years behind me."

"We won't get into those numbers, I'm just tipping my hat to a master of the art of the sweet con."

"You're not wearing a hat so is that a slap? A *sweet con*?"

"I'm always wearing a figurative hat so I can tip it when I'm impressed. If I didn't mean it as a real compliment I'd probably put a big enough barb in it to be obvious. As to a sweet con, that's one to get out of an awkward or sticky situation without breaking the law or anyone getting hurt."

"Yogurt, high fiber biscuits, info about old friends I had lost contact with, and a new item for my vocabulary all in one visit. You're an interesting bringer of gifts."

"Just one of my marvelous traits. But it's just about the end of visiting hours. If I overstay, then Nulty has a basis to fuss about me. I'll stop in and see you again when I can if I can."

"Not tomorrow?"

"No, I'll be out of town on business tomorrow night and I can't be sure of my schedule after that. But when I can. I have some things I might want to ask if you'd be interested in doing to have fun while putting some money in your pocket. I can't talk about it yet because it's not sure what might need to be done. I'm keeping you in mind as someone who might have the right skills for the kind of game that needs to be played though."

"I like playing games," she said.

"So I've noticed."

As a quiet taped message announced the end of visiting hours over the PA, Pernell tipped his figurative hat and left.

In the hall he passed Nulty who was watching to see if she could catch him overstaying. He smiled and tipped his figurative hat to her as he passed her. If Beebop didn't see a reason to provoke the woman then neither did he now that his right to visit was cleared up.

* * *

As Pernell approached the door to the hotel, Natalie Nigglesby, thirtyish, toned but not svelte, stepped in front of him to stop him and get his attention. They were nose-to-nose as she flashed a badge and said, "You have some explaining to do, sir."

She had taken him by surprise but he got over it fast. "Ditto."

That stumped her. What?

"We'll start with you explaining why you're accosting me on the public street with heaven knows how many people watching and trying to hear us in spite of the noise of the street repair work they're doing there with the jack hammers and all," he said.

Oh, *that* ditto. She tried for a sneer but it only half formed so it seemed like she was about to sneeze.

She gasped in shock as he raised his hand to the level of her face. What kind of an attack was this?

"If you're gonna sneeze, please turn your head. If I have to, I'll turn it for you since I don't have to submit to germ warfare."

She stepped back, which put her at a standard social distance and more beyond his reach if he moved to force her face to the side. She sputtered out, "What's your interest in Nana?"

"Which grandmother? Even I have two of them. Both of them deceased though, rest their souls. Or are you asking about the dog in Peter Pan? Isn't her name Nana?" Yes, after his initial surprise, he was back in charge! He was ready to have fun while he tried to get her to say more than she intended.

He also gestured for them to keep their voices down even with the noise around them. She wanted that too and was happy he agreed.

"You know which Nana I'm talking about," she insisted.

"Based on my question which you sidestepped maybe because you don't actually know what you're talking about, that's in dispute. Since you're being a tough guy with a badge that you waved around but didn't let me get a good look at, are you looking to be addressed as sir or ma'am? Not that I necessarily will, but it's a point of interest."

This wasn't going as she had planned it in her head but so far she couldn't expect to make a strong case that he was lying or evading, only that he was being cutesy. She hated cutesy. "Perry Nana," she reluctantly said. "What's your interest in him?"

"The Perry also known as Poppy Nana?"

She nodded yes.

"Who wants to know?" The hint of a smile signaled he was ready to play games about this.

"The proper authorities," she said. She expected a big runaround about this but couldn't see how to evade that.

"Why do you think I'm interested in him if he's even real?"

She took a moment to register that he had faked her out and she needed to change scripts. "You searched his name online earlier tonight." She would have added, *Oh crap. I shouldn't have said that* but it was too late.

"Right, I did. Okay, let's move on to why the unnamed proper authorities know or care about my interest in art."

Since she had begun this interception as official intimidation and that had lead-ballooned, she decided to stop dancing around it. "In the last few days you did online research on Alfonso Gargoyle and visited a list of sites that reference him even though those connections aren't generally known. You've been in Gargoyle's office building. You have a comped room here in a hotel he owns. You had dinner in the restaurant here but only paid a tip. Gargoyle had dealings with Nana in the past. Due to all that we in the international community have an interest in you and in your connection to Poppy Nana."

"Bingo! Interpol. The European looking clothes designs made me suspect but there I finally have enough to convince me. You won't believe me but that's to be expected. I never heard of the Nanas until recently and since I'm newly arrived in Miami which was the couple's base of operation I decided to surf some web and find out a bit about them. It's usually called idle curiosity. Of course for professional suspicious snoops there's no such thing. I had business in the building. I accepted the offer of a free room and dinner since I have to watch my money. More than that requires a court order. Now I need my sleep in that nice comped room so good night, Interpol."

Hall and Taylor had been driving around since dinner looking for Pernell and Bee but not spotting them. They now parked down the street and watched the tete-a-tete between Pernell and a stranger who had been waiting outside the hotel for him. Who was she? Why meet out here rather than in the lobby or even the room they had earlier confirmed he was registered into? Who was she? What were the two talking about? Again, who was she? Since that was still the most basic question it came around again and again. Lots of questions but no answers - which meant frustration.

Dutton stood a short distance away watching the hotel.

He also had been searching for Pernell but had picked up on him when the man was two blocks away and walking toward the hotel. He would have liked to know where Pernell had been for that time but had to try to satisfy himself with watching him right now. And only watching since he was too far away and had none of his hearing-enhancement-from-a-distance equipment with him. Who was she? Why meet out here rather than in the lobby or even Pernell's room? Had she flashed a badge? What were they talking about? Questions but no answers. Frustration.

The hotel staffer assigned to watch for and then to watch Mr. Pernell would report that he met with a woman outside the building for a short time, then she walked off and he came inside. From his spot the man could see but not hear them. He didn't see the badge flashed. He hadn't seen the woman around before and had no idea who she was. He had done his job so he wasn't frustrated; all the questions were in the minds of the people he reported to.

* * *

Pernell walked right to the front desk and insisted on being moved to another room facing out the opposite side of the building because of the noisy emergency street repairs being made outside.

When the front desk clerk insisted that no other room was available, Pernell said thanks anyway, in that case he would get his bag and find a quiet hotel elsewhere.

Suddenly another room was available after all.

When he had checked in that afternoon he had detected and noted three video cameras and two audio bugs in the room. Once in the newly assigned room he did the same search routine although he now knew he would be alone for the night so he didn't care if they taped his snores or his bare ass stroll into the bathroom. And as he suspected, the same kinds of equipment were in the same spots. Originality wasn't a factor much in demand in certain organizations. Standardized secret wiring saved time and energy.

Chapter 11

The Dorkman was a top drawer urban hotel so Pernell had had a good night of sleep - alone.

At 5 A.M. he walked out the front door to meet Bee who gave him a manila envelope saying, "Your plane ticket and the address. Also your credentials, and the passwords you might need."

"Good. I'll dispose of those carefully once I don't need them."

"You need to leave soon to be at the airport in time."

"Yeah, I can't risk attracting attention by rushing through the airport security."

"There's four hundred dollars in small bills in the envelope to cover your incidental expenses. To avoid a paper trail you'll need to buy your train ticket at the station up there."

"Right. With cash, not a credit card. I guess that's everything."

"One more thing." Bee startled but delighted him by giving him a passionate kiss.

As he recovered from his surprise and was ready to really get into that, she pulled away. "Mr. Gargoyle suggested I give you that as an extra incentive to hurry back."

"My estimate of his cleverness just went way up." Reluctantly he headed for the taxi that has just pulled up. He looked back once, hoping she would rush to him to give him another send-off but she just waved. Pernell then got into the cab he had called for the trip to the airport for a flight to Savannah.

Once on the road, he spotted Agent Winkler and Dutton, each in a separate taxi, awkwardly following him there since their drivers wanted to go faster than his was happy with.

At the airport those two watched to see where he was flying while he played with them by making two false starts to check-in areas of different airlines as if forgetting which he was flying today.

That was another pleasant surprise to make this a nice day.

But he couldn't put off checking in long enough to risk being bumped from his seat as a no-show. Since his was the only flight of that airline taking off for more than two hours, the others were then able to figure out where he had to be going.

They rushed to get on that plane too. It was an early flight and they are able to get seats. Until they were aboard - and especially after that - the two worked at hiding their faces from Pernell and from each other.

Pernell wondered if either or both of his tails realized or at least suspected he was teasing them that way. He probably would have been content that both thought he was simply an airhead and thus would be easier to monitor or to relieve of materials of interest once he had a package large enough to seem interesting.

* * *

At 11 A.M. Pernell pulled up in a taxi outside the address he had been given, which turned out to be an office tower that looked very high-powered and official. A prominent sign identified it as *Savannah Movers and Fakers, Inc.*

He got out, looked the place over, and calmly walked inside. That taxi pulled across the street and parked.

Winkler drove an unmarked government car up and parked where he had a clear view of the building's main entry. Down the block, Dutton sat behind the wheel of a rental car parked where he had a similar view.

The reception desk inside was a raised, Plexiglas-enclosed counter from which the receptionist stared down at him and everything else in this large but empty space. Two uniformed guards, one in the booth and one at his level but standing yards away, glared at him.

The receptionist asked via a microphone, "What's the nature of your business here today?"

Pernell held up a piece of paper. "I'm to pick up a package."

For a long moment the guards and the receptionist glared and stared but nothing, including Pernell, moved.

Finally a drawer slid out of the counter. Pernell put the paper in it, and it withdrew. He hummed to himself and waited patiently while the receptionist read the paper and the guard in the booth leaned closer to read it over her shoulder.

The receptionist typed something into her computer, then she nodded grimly. Via the microphone she said, "This doesn't seem to be in order."

Pernell shrugged. "Then return my form to me and I'll have to have my principals' deal with whatever's the problem."

The drawer slid out with the paper in it. Pernell didn't reach for it, simply stood calmly waiting.

The drawer quickly closed, taking the paper back inside, while the guard inside pointed to something on the computer monitor that Pernell couldn't see from outside. The guard outside tensed, ready to grab Pernell if he made an unexpected move.

The receptionist said, "I was proficient and fixed things for you. Go through door three."

Pernell looked around casually at the several unnumbered and windowless doors around the space. He waited, saying nothing.

"You'll be late for your appointment behind door three. They won't wait much longer," the receptionist warned.

Pernell said politely, "Please be so kind as to show me which of the unmarked doors you consider to be number three."

"Number three means the third door," the receptionist said.

Pernell stayed calm, even smiled. "The third from what?"

Now one door opened a bit and stayed that way.

"Thank you," Pernell said and prepared to go to that door.

"That may not be it," the receptionist cautioned him.

"But if it's not the correct one, it looks like your incompetence, not my mistake," Pernell said.

That door silently swung shut and another popped fully open. The receptionist turned away in annoyance. The guards glared at Pernell. Pernell entered by that door.

The good-sized, bare-walled room inside had twenty porthole-like windows in the walls and ceiling that could be blocked from the other side. A straight-backed office chair in dead center was the only furniture. The door through which he entered closed with a *clank*.

After a slow and appraising look around, Pernell turned the chair to face the opposite wall from its initial position and sat in it. He folded his hands in his lap and hummed quietly as he waited.

A porthole in one wall was unblocked from the other side and the huge eye of an observer - magnified by the lens that was the glass of the window - stared at Pernell. If he saw this he didn't react. That porthole was blocked again. That sequence was repeated at another of the porthole windows. Unblock, magnified eye stared, blocked again.

At a slowly accelerating pace magnified eyes briefly appeared and disappeared at other windows, including looking down from the ceiling. Then the staring eyes appeared and disappeared several at a time in a progressively more confusing pattern. Pernell seemed not to see them as he calmly examined his hands.

Finally there was a staring eye at every porthole around the room. With a loud *snap* those eyes simultaneously disappeared. Pernell lifted a hand to check a fingernail.

After a long moment, hidden double doors that until now seemed to be only part of the wall paneling design swung open into the room and a line of eight uniformed guards marched in with parade ground precision. Each carried an identical red plaid pattern softside suitcase. Pernell stayed seated, smiling pleasantly as that team went through a complicated drill maneuver around the room to end as two lines that then become a two-person-per-side square around and all facing him.

Casually Pernell stood and waited.

All eight guards held out their suitcases. Pernell didn't move. For a long moment no one moved.

Then a key on a chain slipped from one guard's grasp and swung silently beside his hand and bag. Nothing more happened.

Pernell stepped to that guard, took that bag, sat it by his feet, and held out his hand.

The guard pulled a paper and a pen from inside his uniform jacket and handed them to Pernell who signed for the bag, handed back those items, and headed for the door through which he had entered taking that bag with him.

Pernell stood looking relaxed as he faced that closed door while the guards marched back out the way they had entered and those doors closed.

Only then did the door in front of him open so he could leave.

Pernell called back, "Interesting doing business with you."

Out front, when Pernell came out the main door carrying a large item wrapped inside a large black trash bag in a way that made it hard to estimate it shape and weight by just the way he carried it, the same taxi pulled around to pick him up.

"You earned your big tip by holding my cell phone and stuff and being ready to go when I am. To the hotel, please." He thought but didn't say, *I'll keep my tails guessing until morning. I can be at the station in plenty of time to buy my ticket for the early train without giving them a heads up on how I'll be traveling.*

As Pernell pulled away in the taxi Winkler, then Dutton, pulled out to follow in their rented or borrowed cars.

Since Gargoyle was paying for the upscale hotel that Pernell was confident he could trust to do an adequate job of protecting his new suitcase in its secure storage room, he left that in there and went to lunch. He didn't realize that Dutton was where he could briefly see the bag when he took it out of the trash bag to hand it to the front desk clerk to put in the storage room.

He had no special interest in examining the contents of the bag. There was a one-time-use seal on it so if he opened it that would be obvious from then on. He was content to have that unexpected device attest that the contents when Gargoyle broke the seal were what had been handed over to Pernell at Savannah Movers and Fakers, Inc.

Funny Money

Before he made his plane reservation to get up here today he had wondered if he would have time to fly back to Miami, leaving the bag of money in safe storage here, get other things done there, then catch an evening plane back to spend the night in Savannah and be at the station for the early train in the morning. As soon as he learned the flight time between those cities was four hours minimum he gave up that idea.

That meant he had most of today to think about details of the other jobs he had to do, to travel around the city toting a large trash bag full of crumpled newspaper to confuse, mystify, and tempt those he was aware were trying to follow him everywhere, and to amuse himself by dumping that bag where it was immediately picked up by city workers and put in a trash collection truck - then making himself conspicuous carrying what looked like an identical bulging trash bag (thank you stack of freebie local weekly newspapers and the privacy of a small public restroom while he crumpled those pages) to give anyone paying attention to him plenty to wonder about.

Plus, twice he paid his way into a movie theater but went right out a far door leaving his followers who were eager to see where he went but leery of being seen by him if they followed too closely searching for him in vain in the theater showing the films he had bought the tickets for.

All in all a mildly amusing day for him with plenty of thinking cap and planning time included.

Chapter 12

Bright and early the next morning Pernell arrived by taxi at the Savannah station. He bought his ticket to Miami, checked the small bag of his few clothes and toiletries, and boarded the third car of the 6:50 A.M. train. He kept his laptop in its shoulder carrying case and the plaid suitcase of money with him. Once he found a good seat he put the plaid bag in the overhead rack and sat down with a magazine and a newspaper from the stand in the station, ready to relax and enjoy the twelve hour trip to Miami.

Dutton, now disguised with a rust-red shoulder-length wig, a glued-on Fu Manchu mustache, and fake buck teeth entered that car but as soon as he saw Pernell in there turned and went back to the second car. Dutton carried a softside suitcase the same size as Pernell's bag but of a different red plaid pattern.

When Dutton was out of sight, Winkler, with no luggage, looked into this car from the door, then followed Dutton into the second car.

* * *

Later Pernell glanced up from his magazine to find Winkler strolling by trying not to be too obvious as he looked Pernell over.

Pernell froze when he saw this man's interest, then he forced himself to look back at his magazine and stay still. A moment later he slipped a two-inch-diameter round mirror from his pocket into the palm of his aisle-side hand and used it to watch Winkler who walked on to the back end of the car and stood there.

Pernell mumbled to himself, "Why does he seem familiar? Did I see him in the restaurant last night? This could be just a coincidence but I don't believe in those. I need to keep an eye on him."

He lifted his hand to scratch his face and used the mirror to check out the people in the seats immediately behind him but didn't spot anyone he recognized or worried about.

He turned the mirror to check on Winkler's position just as that man reacted to something he saw at the end of the car closer to Pernell. Winkler stepped out into the space between the cars and peeked back in through the window in the door.

As Pernell palmed the mirror and looked at the roof as if lost in thought, Dutton came down the aisle, his plaid bag in hand, looking both comical and conspicuous in his disguise, not the effect he was aiming for.

Dutton was so intent on not being caught looking directly at Pernell that he bumped into several seat-backs thereby drawing further unwanted attention to him.

Just beyond Pernell's seat, five people traveling together now decided to switch seats. That entailed them stepping into the aisle, temporarily blocking it - which would force Dutton to stand right beside Pernell's seat for an indefinite time. With a muttered whiny complaint, Dutton turned and fled back out of the car the way he had come. Pernell watched that with interest.

* * *

Later, Pernell woke from a cat nap with a startled jerk to find a line of several people, including Dutton, moving past his seat. Dutton was conspicuous in a different way since he was now in a new pathetic disguise. This time he wore a Van Dyke beard made by adding to the Fu Manchu with fake hair of a different shade of brown, dark glasses that made it hard for him to see anything, and an African-theme knit hat pulled down tight over his own real hair which completely hid that. His plaid bag was now inside a black plastic trash bag,

There were gasps and muttered comments of surprise as the train entered a tunnel and everything went black.

There was a bit of confused movement in the aisle during the five seconds they were in the sudden darkness, then they emerged from the tunnel and there were muttered comments of relief.

As soon as the last of those people had passed him, Pernell jumped up and checked that his bag was okay in the overhead rack.

Seeing a red plaid softside in there he sank back into his seat with a relieved sigh.

* * *

Later, Pernell took the bag from the overhead rack and walked to the end of the car where he had last seen Winkler. He might have noticed that this bag wasn't the same plaid pattern as the one he started with but he was distracted by other concerns.

Along the way, he passed Winkler, now seated, who turned to face out the window to avoid Pernell while still watching him in the reflection. Pernell tried to not react with surprise. He didn't hesitate beside the man but did look the somehow familiar stranger over.

Pernell stopped in the space between the second and third cars where he had some privacy since there was no one else in that space. He asked himself, "Darn it, why does that man seem familiar? And why does he seem so interested in me?"

He rooted around in his pants pocket and got out his cell phone. "Just a quick call to Shallwee Bee to say yes, let's be together tonight but also to pass along the coded message that all's going well."

He stared down at the bag by his feet, then looked around in fear as if expecting men with guns to rush in here and surround him.

He knelt beside the bag and ran a finger over its side. "This is not the plaid I had. I surely had another plaid. The plaid I had is not this plaid. Oh crap, I took the wrong bag out of the rack - or worse. I'm so shaken up I'm talking like a Dr. Seuss character."

Pernell hurried back into the car with the bag. He slowed as he got near his seat, looking around with an apologetic grin to see who of those seated near here might belong to this bag and be about to raise a fuss. Those who glanced up promptly looked away again.

He looked into the overhead rack above his seat, hoping there was another red plaid bag in there. No, the space was empty. This was a disaster, not just a bag mix up.

He grabbed the seat-back to steady himself and then quickly slid into the seat and pulled the suitcase onto his lap. He whispered to himself, "Who'd have guessed that losing a few million bucks in cash would startle a cool old hand like me so much that I'd literally go weak in the knees?"

He stared at the bag in his lap, then pressed a hand on the side to judge how full it was. "I want to convince myself that I'm mistaken and this is the bag I brought on board but I'm not able to fool me that much. For one big thing the seal isn't on this one. I need to find out whose this is in order to get a clue to where mine is. It feels a lot like mine did. I should find out what's in it but of course I can't do that where anybody else can see what surprise is in here for me."

He carried the bag back to the restroom and although there wasn't much room inside that space he struggled the bag in there with him without attracting too much attention in the process. Those who noticed nodded in sympathy since they knew how tight that space was. He locked the door to assure his privacy and opened the bag after double-checking that there was no seal he needed to break and not be able to repair to do that.

He stared at the contents. The bag was filled with paper-banded bundles of new currency. "I still don't believe I was wrong about this being the wrong plaid." He slid a bill out of a bundle for a closer look. It was a good quality replica of a U.S. $20 bill with *Play Money* printed in hard-to-miss big letters in two different places and *Not Legal Tender* for good measure. "It's money but it's funny money and for me right now that's not laughable. How much clearer could it be? It's clearly marked in large print as play money where the serial numbers should be. Only real dummies would take this stuff for real. The question of who's playing who for a fool is open to speculation. But if I can't get back what I actually picked up I'm in deep trouble of a different sort."

Pernell stared at the restroom mirror where his imagination now produced an apparition of Winkler's face staring at him while holding a badge up to be seen. "Yeah, suddenly I suspect there's a badge plastered on that strange guy's puss. Man, if he's a cop and he finds me with this stuff I don't know how I can talk my way out of that. But he's seen me with this bag so I can't just dump it. Or can I? There's no place to hide it in here and as soon as I step out the door anyone can see me with it. Man, things got extra complicated in a hurry. My best bet's to return this to whoever owns it and get my own bag back."

He closed the bag, checked his hair, then unlocked the door. He was good at dealing with challenges but that didn't mean he liked to have to do that or that he didn't sweat it while he was going it.

* * *

Moving as quickly as he could without attracting attention but still taking a good look in all the overhead racks, Pernell walked the length of this car. He uses the roll of the train, even when there wasn't much of one, as an excuse to grab hold of the edge of the overheads and surreptitiously move coats and other items that blocked his view of all the items up there. He held the plaid bag behind him as he went, hoping that that made it less noticeable. He also uses the roll of the train as an excuse to grab seat-backs and bend closer to see the items by people's feet or under other things on the seat beside them.

At the back of the car he checked his watch. He cautioned himself, "The next stop's in less than ten minutes. Nobody can get off with my bag before then. I need to check the whole train by that time or maybe cry forever after. One car ahead, three in the back. Gotta move my butt."

* * *

At the first car Pernell repeated his walk through, checking overhead racks and by seated travelers at a Keystone Kops speeded-up rate between the following momentary pauses.

He "accidentally" knocked a newspaper open over what turned out to be the attaché case beside a napping man to the floor.

He reacted with surprise, then with caution, when he saw a red plaid bag in an overhead. He glanced at the large woman in the seat below it trying to decide what to do. He feigned a near fall as an excuse to slide a coat on top of the bag aside revealing several stickers partially hiding damage to the side. Not his bag. He stumbled on as the woman was beginning to wonder why he was beside her so long.

As he approached, another woman lifted down a red plaid bag much like his from the overhead. Pernell looked around assessing if he could grab it from her and run if it came to that. The woman opened the bag on the seat and handed its contents, a large rag doll, to her daughter sitting there. Pernell squeezed by them and continued his search.

* * *

Dutton sat at the back end of the fourth car with no one in any seat in the several rows near him. Sweating and nervous, he busily transferred bundles of currency from Pernell's plaid bag to two smaller gym bags. He looked around regularly, alert for movement in the aisle.

* * *

Pernell moved quickly through the third car since he had checked it earlier. He stopped by his seat and put the switched plaid bag back in the overhead rack. He muttered, "This is slowing me down and I'm only advertising my connection to it by carrying it with me. I'll leave it here and worry about ditching it later."

He glanced back to where Winkler was cat-napping despite his best efforts to stay awake. "On further thought, I'll ditch it somewhere else since that guy knows I was sitting right here."

Carrying the bag, Pernell tiptoed back past Winkler without waking him and put the plaid bag in the last overhead rack of this car.

* * *

In the fourth car, Dutton was closing up the gym bags when Pernell entered at the far end and walked quickly toward him. Dutton slipped the plaid bag into a large opaque tan plastic bag with a store logo on it.

Dutton seemed ready to sit there and let Pernell pass him. But no, when Pernell was halfway down the car Dutton's nerve deserted him. He jumped up and hurried back to car five with his three bags.

Pernell noticed this but didn't change his search mode.

* * *

In car five, Dutton put the store logo bag in the overhead rack then sat several rows farther back, putting the gym bags by his feet. He opened a section of newspaper that had been left in the seat and spread it over his head as he feigned being asleep.

Pernell entered moments later and did his systematic check of this car, starting at the front end. He slowed as he approached the back end of the car since this is the end of his search area and he was desperate to find what he was looking for. He stopped two steps beyond Dutton's seat and pondered what his next move must be.

Under the newspaper tent, Dutton strained to try to see where Pernell was or what he was doing. Trying to seem as if he were only making a comfort move while actually asleep, Dutton turned his head - and when that wasn't enough - his whole body, toward the aisle without lifting the newspaper.

When he still couldn't see much, he carefully pushed up the edge of the newspaper with his fingertips.

Pernell now stood nearby facing back the way he had come but still lost in thought about what to do next. He glanced at Dutton when he saw a movement but hardly focused on the man since the bizarre newspaper disguise largely hid him.

Over the PA the conductor announced, "This station is Palatka. Palatka, Florida. Not all doors will open. Those detraining must proceed to a door where they see a crew member."

The newspaper began to tremble since Dutton was shaking with fear but Pernell was moving off down the aisle and didn't notice.

Dutton pulled the newspaper off as if it were suffocating him and took a deep breath of relief - but then caught that and froze when he saw Pernell stopped only a few seats down the aisle and glancing back his way. Then the woman who was blocking the aisle as she maneuvered to leave started forward and Pernell followed her as close as he dared without prompting a protest.

* * *

When they stopped at the Palatka station, Pernell stood in the train doorway for a moment where that gave him an elevated view down the platform. He went down to stand on the platform once he felt sure no one had yet gotten off and moved down the platform without him seeing them.

He stood away from the train to see the length of the platform, straining to see the bags being pulled or carried by the several people detraining here. No one had a red plaid bag.

Winkler looked out an open side door farther forward to check on Pernell's position but didn't get off the train.

Dutton carried his three bags forward, visible for a moment through the open doors as he passed between cars.

As the train crew members signaled to one another that they were ready to depart, Pernell stepped to the train but stopped and stepped back to watch as a man hurried out of the first car carrying a red plaid softside suitcase. The trainman at this door gestured for the passenger to get on but Pernell hesitated, feigning a coughing spell to give himself a moment to assess the bag in the distance.

The other man moved through a brightly sun lit spot as he went. Pernell muttered, "Way too much green in that plaid." He promptly boarded the train followed by the trainman.

* * *

As the train slowly pulled away at Palatka, Pernell stood at an open window in the closed side door in the space between cars. He banged his forehead gently against the door asking himself, "What do I do now? Gargoyle isn't going to be happy which means he'll want company in that state of mind."

As it picked up speed, the train passed a workman standing by the tracks with his back to it tightening a bolt on another track. Pernell's red plaid suitcase was thrown from a forward car of the train and hit the workman. Pernell thrust himself halfway through the open window for a better view of that bag shouting, "That's it!"

The angry workman jumped up and down on the bag, then kicked it aside. During this assault, the bag broke open enough to show it was empty.

"That's the bag but it's empty," Pernell told himself. "Think! What does this mean? First, that I don't have to jump off the moving train to get the bag back. Second, that the money's probably still on the train but in a different bag. The bag went overboard up ahead so the person who has it or knows where the money is now is somewhere in that direction. That means four of five cars since I couldn't tell which car the bag was tossed from. It's about twenty minutes to the next stop so I need to find that money and think about how to get rid of the bag I have. You can be sure that if I throw it off the train I'll be sure it doesn't hit some guy who'll promptly kick the funny money out of it though."

* * *

In the second car, Dutton sat with his back turned toward the aisle to block the view of anyone passing as he stuffed the folded store logo bag into one of his gym bags. After a glance around to be sure no one was near, he lifted out one bundle of the currency and ran a fingertip over it, smiling with satisfaction. Then he looked closer, staring in dismay and disbelief. They were U.S. $20 bills, fairly good quality but still fairly easy to spot as counterfeit since *Federal Research Note* was printed across the top and *Twenty Dolors* across the bottom.

Dutton flipped through the bundle to confirm that they are all alike - which they were. "Do I laugh, cry, or scream and attack somebody? These are better than the play money junk I stuck him with but still worthless since they'll never pass."

After another check that no one seemed to be watching, he dug out several more bundles. They are all the same. He slumped back in frustration, the bundles in his lap. Suddenly he realized what he was going and quickly stuffed them back out of sight. "All that work and I'm left with stuff I can't even use as toilet paper 'cause it'll block the pipes. There has to be an up-side to this but what is it?"

He opened the other bag from beside his feet and checked its contents but it is all the same inadequate stuff. "At least this maneuver should inconvenience Gargoyle. That's worth something to me. I can even dream that it'll fully compromise him. I can sleep soundly on that thought. But I'm left with worthless paper and not much else."

He put both bags by his feet and sat back. Then he became alert and nervous all over again. "I'm in big danger if Gargoyle's bag man realizes I made the switch and fingers me to somebody but I'm in a different kind of danger if some lawman finds this funny money in my bags. I have to get rid of this and avoid that Pernell guy until I can slip away. If he's discovered the bag switch he'll step outside to watch who gets off at every station from now on so I can't get off right away."

* * *

Pernell sat alone. He checked his watch. Evening was creeping up on the world outside the train. "About ten minutes 'til the next stop. At this point I don't know what else to do but wait."

He was startled when Winkler walked up and sat beside him saying, "Nice day for a train ride".

Pernell turned to look out the window without responding.

"I thought I saw you on a train going south yesterday. Hard to imagine how you could be doing the same today," Winkler said.

Pernell didn't react or respond, only stared out the window.

"I notice things like that. I'm professionally curious about any unusual behavior. Humor me and tell me how and why you're on this train now," Winkler urged.

Without turning from the window, Pernell said, "It's part of my job, I'm earning my keep. Probably the same as you. If you're snooping on who rides the train each day professionally then you're probably what, a cop of some sort?"

"Did I say I was professionally curious? I meant that in the loose sense that I wonder about things. Do you have a lot of dealings with cops of various sorts?"

"You're traveling south two days in a row too," Pernell said.

"So are you. So what?"

"That means you went to some trouble to get back north overnight and that doesn't seem like something anybody does just as a hobby. What authority do you do cop stuff for?" Pernell persisted, still without looking at the other man.

"Lawmen only make the people nervous who have something to hide," Winkler said.

"Or who follow the news and know the ways some cops break the law to screw people around. It makes law-abiding citizens with common sense wonder why this is allowed to go on and on."

"Did you pick up something in Savannah to deliver in Miami?"

"Did you get on at Savannah? I hear it's a nice city. Never spent any time there myself. Who do you work for again?"

"I saw you get on there - with your bag. That's safe isn't it?"

"Do government agents get special discounts to ride the trains? Do they give you a credit card so you can buy our own tickets or do they make the arrangements and you pick them up when you arrive?"

Both glanced up as Dutton came along the aisle from behind them with his two gym bags, looking around nervously.

Dutton stared in confusion at these two sitting together long enough for them to notice and start to focus on him. He hurried down the aisle in the direction he had been going, forcing two people coming toward him to step aside since at the moment he wasn't concerned about being polite.

Winkler leaned into the aisle to watch Dutton's back while Pernell lifted himself a bit in his seat to keep Dutton in view over the seat-backs. When Dutton was out of sight both men settled back.

"Sorry, you were telling me why you're riding the train today before we were interrupted," Winkler apologized.

"No, you were telling me who you carry a badge for. Federal, State and then which one, or local?"

Winkler reflexly patted his coat to be sure his badge was in his inside pocket. Pernell smiled a small satisfied smile.

Winkler said firmly, "You first. Who are you working for?"

"I'm checking on train travel for a travel agency group. I report on how clean the cars are, how close to on-time the trains are, and how well the crews do their jobs. My reports are important to whether travel agents all across the country will recommend riding the rails. You're a federal agent of some sort aren't you?"

Winkler checked his watch. Pernell quickly started to get up, half-crawling over Winkler face-to-face before the lawman could get out of the way. Pernell said, "Gotta go. I need to get things down."

Then Pernell deliberately lost his balance and he half-fell on Winkler who tried to push him off while Pernell was pawing at him to get traction to regain control of his movement.

During this, Pernell pulled Winkler's badge far enough from the man's inside coat pocket to glance at it, then dropped it back in. Then he rolled off Winkler, stumbled into the aisle, and hurried away in the direction that Dutton had gone.

Winkler needed a moment to recover his composure after the surprise of that unexpected close encounter with Pernell. He stiffened at a thought but a pat of his coat pocket reassured him that his badge was in place. He got up and followed Pernell out of the car.

As Pernell left the car he whispered to himself, "It can't be much worse than this. He's a treasury agent who's watching me, maybe even following me. And that strange looking guy who seemed so surprised and unhappy to see me? Haven't I seen him but not always looking exactly the same since - well, since the ride down from Philly. He's the one I have to watch for at the stops from here on. If he gets off, I get off and follow him. And I do anything I can to make sure I don't have a treasury agent tailing me when I do that. The Miami station will hold my checked bag if it comes to that."

Chapter 13

Pernell watched out the open window of the space between cars as the train picked up speed leaving the Kissimmee station. "Nobody got off there so the stuff I'm supposed to deliver must still be on the train. My best lead to it's that nervous-looking dude with two gym bags."

Pernell moved nonchalantly through the first car, from the front toward the rear, looking over the people.

Dutton entered at the rear of the first car with his two gym bags but spotted Pernell and immediately reversed and went back out.

Pernell glanced up from looking at those in the seats in time to see Dutton's back as the other man stepped from this car. Pernell sped up as he moved after Dutton but still checked the people in the seats which meant his head was swinging back and forth in way likely to attract attention and pretty much guaranteed to make him dizzy if he did it for much longer.

* * *

Dutton ducked into an empty seat in the second car, stacking his two bags on the floor at his feet. When Pernell entered the car, Dutton spread a section of newspaper from one of his bags over him as if asleep under there.

Pernell stopped in the aisle beside Dutton's seat. Soon Dutton's newspaper began to quiver along with him as he became more and more nervous wondering what was about to happen.

What Dutton couldn't see was that Winkler had opened the door at the end of the car that Pernell was headed toward which brought Pernell to a sudden standstill before he did a U-turn and hurried back the way he had come to go back into the first car.

Unable to stand the suspense any longer, Dutton threw off the newspaper, gasping since he had been holding his breath. He was surprised, then confused, that Pernell wasn't in sight.

When Winkler came ambling down the aisle looking over the riders Dutton noisily put the newspaper back over his face. His hands were shaking badly so the newspaper shook noisily but he kept it in place. Winkler passed right by.

* * *

Gargoyle sat in his chair in his office and watched Oscar escort in Shallwee Bee. With a gesture he then dismissed the bodyguard who moved out of sight.

"Is there a problem, Mr. Gargoyle," she asked. He would have preferred a show of concern but she was calm and confident.

"You've been talking to Pernell."

"Of course. Those were your instructions. We had dinner on your tab. The seafood was good."

"What did you tell him about?"

"The weather. How much of Florida I've seen. Where and when I would meet him to give him the ticket and other materials for his trip to Savannah in the morning."

"How much did you tell him about the Nanas?"

"The Nanas? Polly and Poppy? Why would they come up? I know next to nothing about them."

"Did you two talk about my private art collection?" he asked.

"You scary set of torture paintings? Why would I talk about them? I've told you my opinion of them. I prefer not to think about them."

"What about the other stuff? Maybe things that reminded you of the Nanas?"

"I'm sorry, what other stuff? There's nothing I can remember from my few brief times in that torture pictures room that I expect the Nanas would have had anything to do with except perhaps Mr. Nana buying them for someone on commission."

"What about in the second room?"

"Second room? Where is that? You've never shown me any space or items except that small room as your personal art gallery."

"Oh. Yeah, I guess that's right. So you couldn't have recognized anything."

"Are you asking if I remember the art objects I saw when I went with you as your assistant to the Nana house those what, two or three times some years back? There seemed to be new things each time but I don't have an eye for that stuff so I was only concerned about doing my job."

"Yeah, right. Okay. You get back to your work and I'll do the same." He dismissed her with a gesture and watched her leave. Would she give herself away with a guilty peek back to see if she had snowed him? No, she walked out with her usual confidence, not looking back.

He had received an inside tip that Pernell had done some online research on Poppy Nana within an hour of leaving Bee after dinner. That search had caught the eye of various law enforcement groups who were now interested in what Sylvester Pernell knew and what he wanted to do with what he knew.

That was a warning that Gargoyle's connections to the Nanas could be exposed. He didn't want that to happen but for now it wasn't clear what he should do to prevent it. He didn't fully trust Bee since he didn't fully trust anyone but he did believe he was a sharp enough judge of people to know when she was being honest with him and that's how he read the situation right now.

Once in her own work area, Bee pondered the new reality. She had sparked Pernell's interest in the Nanas and somehow his effort to learn about them quickly got back to her employer. She was pretty sure that Gargoyle's operations didn't include monitoring the Internet, that was a task that various law enforcement groups did. She couldn't be certain and didn't intend to try to poke around to find out, but it was most likely that her mobster boss got tips from inside some law enforcement group. Since stolen art items might be involved in the case of the Nanas that meant that more than the local police might be compromised. Should she try to warn those groups? Not without knowing who there could be trusted when she had no solid evidence.

She had enough to worry about already but she would keep her eyes and ears open in case some evidence did present itself.

* * *

Pernell entered the first car and then the restroom near the door, keeping that door barely ajar.

Winkler entered the car and moved down the aisle trying to appear casual as he searched for Pernell. Behind him, Pernell stepped out of the restroom and out the end door of the car before that closed behind Winkler. Winkler didn't notice this.

* * *

Glancing behind him, Dutton entered the third car with his bags. He stopped long enough to see Pernell entering at the far end of the second car and heading down the car toward him.

Dutton stopped as the back of a line of three people waiting to use the two restrooms at the rear end of this car.

When he saw movement at the door that would be Pernell coming into this car, Dutton pushed roughly by the others. As a man came out of the one restroom Dutton stepped into it saying, "Sorry. Emergency. None of us wants me to try to wait another minute or I'm gonna lose control and that won't be nice for any of us."

Dutton closed the door behind him as Pernell came walking at a good but not hurried pace down the car. Not seeing Dutton, Pernell continued into the fourth car.

After only a moment, Dutton opened the restroom door and peeked out, ignoring the annoyed looks of those waiting to get in there. Once sure Pernell had passed by, Dutton came out and hurried back toward the second car muttering for the sake of the audience, "Only gas. Scared me though. Now it's somebody else's problem."

Dutton was almost to the forward end of the car before he spotted Winkler coming his way from the second car. Dutton shoved his bags into the conveniently empty overhead and dropped into an empty seat beside a woman who had an almost finished handmade scarf in her lap and a tote bag with her knitting supplies by her feet.

He was relieved that she was napping and didn't stir.

When Winkler passed him, Dutton had the scarf tied around his head as a babushka and his head down as he examined the contents of the tote bag held in his lap. Winkler moved by that seat, glanced back for another look at Dutton, but then moved on down the aisle.

As the woman stirred, Dutton pulled off the scarf and shoved it into the tote bag which he dumped by her feet while he fled toward the second car with his own bags. She was too confused to protest.

* * *

In the second car, Dutton took a well-stuffed standard store plastic bag from one gym bag, then put both gym bags in the overhead rack and sat below them. After checking for watchers he took a small bag from the store bag.

This plastic sandwich bag contained several fake mustaches. Using a small mirror from the bag to check on his progress he stripped off the Van Dyke beard and applied a handle bar with noticeable streaks of gray in it to his upper lip. He took dark-rimmed glasses with thick lenses from the store bag and donned them. It took a moment to get over the dizziness they caused. He pulled on a different cheap wig from the bag, this one short and gray. Finally he settled back with a smile, confident he was now inconspicuous and unrecognizable.

* * *

A few minutes later, Dutton was relaxed enough to have dozed off. When Pernell entered at the rear of the car he moved slowly down the aisle until he saw Dutton - and promptly took two steps backwards. He waited to see if Dutton had noticed the movement. The man of the altered look hadn't since he was half-asleep, his face turned toward the window.

Pernell looked in the overhead and spotted the gym bags. He looked around to see who else might be watching him and was happy to find that no one seemed to be paying any attention to him. He grabbed Dutton's seat-back as if worried about losing his balance as an excuse for standing here a moment longer.

Staying leaning as far back as he could to stay out of Dutton's peripheral vision while still able to reach Dutton's bags, Pernell went onto tiptoes to reach far enough into the overhead space to feel those bags. He patted them and he could feel the shapes of the bundles of currency inside.

This felt like what he hoped to find so Pernell slid one gym bag toward himself so he could grab it and lift it out of the overhead rack, watching Dutton all the time as he did this.

At that moment two ten-year-old boys wearing paper *Uncle Sam* top hats bustled into the car and ran its length of the car laughing noisily.

This noise snapped Dutton fully awake and he looked around.

Pernell took two steps backwards and slumped into an empty seat before Dutton could turn far enough to get a good look at him.

Thinking that maybe he had just seen movement he should be concerned about, Dutton leaned out to look down the aisle in Pernell's direction, then got to his feet.

Pernell leaned forward in his seat, his aisle-side hand cupped over his face to make it hard for Dutton to see him while he used his mirror, palmed in his other hand, to try to keep an eye on Dutton.

Dutton stood in the aisle nervously looking first one way, then the other. The conductor approached to pass him, paying him no special attention since he was listening on his two-way radio. "Excuse me, can I squeeze by please, sir." Into the radio he said, "No, I don't know of any treasury agent aboard. Is he going to make an arrest?"

At that Dutton turned and Pernell looked up. Both stared at the conductor in surprise, which made the conductor aware that he had spoken louder than he intended. He now spoke into the radio in a barely audible whisper as he moved off down the aisle.

This left Dutton and Pernell looking at one another. Pernell ducked his head again. Dutton hurried away down the aisle, then remembered his bags so he hurried back and grabbed them, looking to see whether he would have to fight Pernell here and now.

Pernell hid behind his hand again, then used the mirror to check on Dutton's progress down the aisle. He waited until Dutton was out the door at the end of the car before he got up to follow, but cautiously.

* * *

In the third car Dutton found the only seat available now was the window seat beside large, unfriendly-looking middle-aged Murray who said, "I keep the aisle seat so I can get up and leave whenever."

Dutton considered the space in the overhead rack and the space in front of the available seat and opted to put his bags overhead but he moved other items up there around a bit to hide his bags from easy view or reach even though this space extended back over the seats behind his.

Pernell watched this through the window of the end door of the car but stayed out of view when Dutton looked that way.

Dutton had to climb over Murray to get in. Murray promptly closed his eyes to try to nap and to avoid talking.

Dutton settled into the window seat as well as he could. He tried but found it impossible to strain up enough to see over the seat-back to watch for Pernell to enter the car from behind him since his every move elicited warning grunts of displeasure from large and grumpy-looking Murray.

Pernell entered this car wearing a paper *Uncle Sam* top hat, cheap plastic sun glasses, and with wadded facial tissues in his mouth to distort his appearance. He moved slowly down the aisle, holding onto seat-backs and giving the impression that he was unstable on his feet and worried about falling.

He stopped several rows back from Dutton and stood there holding on for a long moment. Several people glanced up but decided he would be okay even if he wasn't in good shape.

Pernell moved to the seat behind Dutton, stopped and made a show of silently gasping for breath to justify staying there holding the overhead rack to keep his balance.

In fact he slid a hand into the overhead rack and pulled one of Dutton's bags into view and reach.

Moving slowly, Pernell glanced around to see if anyone seemed to be watching him but found no one doing so conspicuously. He went up onto one foot to reach the handles of the gym bag which was wedged between other items.

He had lifted that halfway out of the overhead rack when the train lurched - which made him stagger and his uplifted knee bumped Murray who grunted loudly and stirred, trying as well as his large bulk would allow to see who was right behind his seat.

This movement alerted Dutton who turned to check on what was happening back there also, grouchy Murray be damned. Dutton's movement prompted Murray to try to turn and give him a dirty look while still trying to see who or what had bumped him - which elicited a large flip-flopping move from him.

Pernell pulled on the gym bag, ready to run with it, but found that another bag blocked its way out of the rack so he abandoned that attempt and moved back up the aisle the way he had come.

Dutton saw an unfamiliar figure moving back up the aisle and strained up in his seat enough to see that that person didn't have his bags. Murray, annoyed by the movement now, poked Dutton hard with an elbow.

Dutton practically shouted, "Let me out please."

Murray pretended not to hear that and didn't move. So Dutton climbed over Murray, who shoved at Dutton's butt when it passed in front of him. Dutton shoved his butt back and deliberately rubbed it hard across the surprised Murray's face.

Murray pinched Dutton's butt hard, his expression changing from annoyance to satisfaction as he did so. Dutton had his feet in the aisle but sat down hard on Murray, swiveled and elbowed the large man hard in the face as he got up saying. "Oh, so sorry."

As Dutton pulled his bags from the overhead, Murray struggled to get up to come after him. Dutton swung one of his bags, clobbering

Murray and knocking him back into his seat, then walked away, bags in hand. Murray struggled to get up to pursue him but then, to the relief of the others watching, shrugged and settled back. Pity the next person who wanted to sit in that window seat.

* * *

Dutton moved down the aisle of the first car to a seat near the head-end of the car, looking hard for any sign of Pernell. No-nonsense type Mrs. Figby watched him from her seat across the aisle and one row back, letting her suspicions about him and most people show.

Dutton put his bags in the overhead rack that extended from over Figby's seat, then sat in an empty seat across from the bags. He glanced back to find Figby watching his every move.

Gladys Adams, sixty-plus, garrulous and determined to be friendly, hurried up from a seat farther back and sat beside Dutton all giggly and friendly. "Hello. My name's Gladys. Are you traveling all the way to Miami? I am. My first time. I love to share the excitement with others, don't you?"

Dutton stared at her with a stricken expression for a moment.

Finally he pointed to his throat and said in a raspy whisper, "Sorry, can't talk. Throat problem." He shrugged and turned toward the window.

Adams waved that off. "That's okay, my late husband often said I talk enough for four people. When I was a girl my friend Sally was shy so I had to tell the others what I thought she wanted to say."

Dutton lightly banged his head against the window.

Pernell came down the aisle far enough to recognize Dutton's situation and to check that Dutton's bags were in the rack across from his seat. When Figby turned to see who was behind her, glaring her suspicions of everyone, Pernell dropped into the seat that Adams had recently abandoned and checked his watch.

Several minutes later, Pernell stood and checked things. Now Dutton was facing out the window with his eyes closed pretending to doze to avoid encouraging Adams' chattering.

Figby was intent on a cell phone and the written instructions for it that she was holding although she wasn't speaking on the phone.

With a whistle blast as the only warning, the train entered a short tunnel. Lights didn't come on because it was only seconds before they were back out of that.

"My goodness, that was a surprise!" Adams said. "Why don't they turn on the lights? Oh, I suppose the daylight comes back fast enough not to need that. Did you know that would happen?"

But during the momentary darkness Pernell stepped forward and grabbed Dutton's bags. One came out of the rack easily but the other caught on something and wouldn't come free.

Figby took a cell phone picture of Pernell who was standing beside her pulling on the second bag as part of her learning process to see how the new device's gizmos worked. Only when she looked at the image on the phone did she really notice what he was doing.

"What are you doing? Is that my bag? Who are you?"

Figby moved around struggling to get to her feet, which would require Pernell to step aside, which he wasn't ready to do. She said, "You didn't put any bags up there. I watched who did what the whole trip. It's what I do."

So Figby shoved him and struggled up in front of him. This forced him to release the second bag, but he swung the first one out of the rack and tensed to run up the aisle with it - only to see that the conductor was coming into the car.

Seeing the bag in his hand, Figby grabbed that and held on. "Oh no you don't. That looks like my bag so either you're making a mistake or we have a problem that needs firm action. Let me check."

At this Dutton swung around to see the activity in the aisle while Adams clasped her handbag asking, "Is something happening?"

Dutton stared at Pernell for a second, then he clambered over the startled Adams to reclaim his bag and deal with Pernell.

Figby now saw the conductor. "Conductor! I need you here. There seems to be someone stealing bags or something."

Pernell released the bag and stepped away. When he released it, Figby slumped into her seat, the bag in her arms.

Dutton shouted, "No, no. That's not yours, that's my bag."

Pernell stepped aside to let the conductor by before moving quickly up the aisle and out of the car.

The conductor held out his hand. "May I please see the bag. Is there a name tag on your bag, ma'am?"

Dutton's anxiety showed as he fidgeted in the aisle because he so wanted to grab the bag but knew he dared not do so.

"Of course I have a tag on my bag," Mrs. Figby replied.

The conductor felt the bag without opening it. "Are there clothes in your bag, ma'am?"

"Of course. That's all that's in there. I'm going to spend a few days with my sister."

The conductor looked into the overhead rack and moved the bags in there around a bit. He examined a tagged bag then asked, "Is your last name Figby?"

"Indeed it is," the lady answered.

"Then this isn't your bag. Yours is here in the rack with your tag on it." Quietly on his radio he said, "Request that the federal agent on board join me in the first car. I may have something for him."

Dutton pulled the second bag from the rack and pointed to it. "That one and this are mine. See, they match."

Figby stuck out the cell phone and clicked a picture of Dutton but he was too distracted to notice. The conductor handed Dutton the bag and stepped aside so the man could hurry from the car with the two bags. The conductor waited while Figby confirmed that her bag was in the rack.

Dutton got to the end of this car where he spotted Winkler hurrying this way through the second car. Dutton ducked into the empty last seat in this car and bent down as if looking at his shoes until Winkler had passed him without looking at him. Then Dutton hurried out of the car with his bags.

A moment later, Winkler and the conductor stood in the aisle as they looked at the image of Dutton on Figby's phone.

"Okay, yeah, I know him to see him."

"I made a picture of the other one too but I don't know how to work this thing yet so I guess I ruined it when I took the second picture."

"We appreciate your help, ma'am," Winkler said. Then he and the conductor walked toward the end of the car to talk more without being overheard.

Dutton stopped in the space between cars outside the door to look back through the windows to see if Winkler was pursuing him. "I need to get rid of this fake stuff but since I have a little time anyway I should try to get the most mileage out of it by getting this other guy caught with it. It'd be even easier if I still had the original suitcase but I'll make do. Where is he?"

* * *

Dutton entered the fifth car and immediately spotted Pernell at the far end of the car. Pernell ducked down when he saw Dutton. He looked around as he did so to assess what chances he had to hide.

Dutton stopped by the restroom just inside this car and looked around as if he didn't see Pernell. He made a bit of a show of placing his two bags in an empty seat before he entered the restroom, thus leaving them unguarded and in full view.

The conductor announced over the PA system. "The train's next station stop will be in two minutes. Remember to take all your bags with you if exiting the train."

Pernell considered the situation, made a decision, then hurried down the aisle toward the bags and the door off the train. Dutton held the restroom door ajar enough to see what was happening.

Before Pernell reached the bags, Gladys Adams bustled in the end door of the car and saw the bags. She slid into the seat with them and put a defensive arm over them. She looked up as Pernell hesitated beside the seat. "I don't know where my new friend went but I'm protecting his bags until he gets back. I want to tell him about the excitement in the other car. There's a government agent on board who knows him to see and is looking for him to see what's in his bags."

Dutton fully closed the restroom door and turned the lock so the In Use sign was obvious on the outside.

Looking through the window in the end door, Pernell saw Winkler who had just entered at the far end of car four obviously looking for someone.

The conductor announced over the PA, "This station stop is Deerfield Beach. Watch your step leaving the train."

Pernell looked at Adams and Dutton's bags, at the closed door of the restroom, and again at Winkler. With a sigh that things can be so confusing, Pernell exited the car and the train.

Outside, Pernell walked quickly forward and reboarded the train at a forward door saying to himself, "This doesn't add up. Unless he's just worried about being caught with the goods, why did that guy give me that conspicuous chance to steal back the money? Was he setting me up for something? It doesn't make sense to me."

Inside, when he was pretty sure Pernell was gone Dutton came out of the restroom. He smiled nervously at Adams who, surprise, was eager to talk. Dutton glanced into the next car and saw Winkler approaching. Dutton looked back and forth between the bags and the door leading to the car ahead and at this moment the direct route off the train.

Dutton grabbed up the bags and stepped in by the front seat but facing Adams over its back and said to her, "When you really want to know what's going on, you have to go to the source."

Winkler entered and hesitated, looking over the people at the far end of the car, not noticing Dutton standing unmoving a step behind him. Dutton nodded encouragingly toward Winkler. After a second Adams got his drift.

Adams reached out and half-dragged the startled Winkler into the seat beside her - while Dutton dashed out the door with his two bags. She gushed, "This is all so exciting. Do you men still call yourselves T-men? What do you think is happening on here?"

Taken by surprise, Winkler settled into the seat lest he fall on the woman or the floor while resisting her hard tug even though he had no intention of staying here or explaining himself to this woman. He looked from her to the disappearing Dutton - and suddenly was more interested in this garrulous possible accomplice in crime after all. Important incriminating information was always useful.

In the fourth car, Dutton stopped long enough to pull the store logo bag from one of the gym bags and put the two of them inside it. Then he glanced back toward the fifth car regularly as he hurried at almost a run through this car. He whispered to himself, "The Pernell guy didn't have the plaid bag so he must have stowed it here on the train. If I can find it and take it off the train with me I should be all right. They can't arrest me for having that but this stuff is a different story."

Dutton reached the open door off the train at the end of the third car. He looked back and saw Winkler coming his way through the fourth car at a good pace. He looked the other way and saw a determined looking Pernell coming after him from the other direction at a good pace.

Hauling the gym bags in the store logo bag, Dutton hurried off the train between the third and fourth cars and ran toward a cab at the taxi stand near the platform.

Pernell stepped off the train between the second and third cars, saw Dutton, and tensed to chase after him - but looked around first. He looked left and saw Winkler hurry off the train by the door that Dutton had used holding a cell phone to his face. Pernell looked right to find two local police cars pulling to emergency stops by the station. The officers jumped out to intercept Dutton - who saw them, dropped the bag, and put his hands in the air with a resigned groan.

Pernell looked back left to find Gladys Adams leaning out of the train door to watch all the excitement. He looked back right to find Mrs. Figby leaning out of the train holding out her cell phone to get a picture of the arrest. Pernell got back on the train, hoping none of them noticed him.

Winkler signaled to the conductor. That man waved back to show he got the message and would hold the train here for another minute. Winkler walked Dutton and the bags back to and onto the train. Then the conductor called, "All aboard. Next station stop will be Fort Lauderdale in about eighteen minutes. Miami an hour after that."

* * *

Winkler sat on the aisle seat in the rear set of the fourth car, Dutton beside him in the window seat looking unhappy. The store logo bag was at their feet.

Winkler shrugged, "I'd go looking for that other mug but I have to babysit you. We'll keep the evidence within reach since trains have that effect on me and I may nod off. Don't make the mistake of trying to leave."

Pernell watched those two through the window from out in the space between the cars at the end of the last car out of their sight.

Then he moved to the other door to check out the third car without entering it, assessing his possibilities. "I have forty-five minutes at the most to figure a way to switch the junk in the plaid bag for the money in the bags they have. But how? Once they take the bags off this train I've lost the game."

He moved from side to side, straining to see every spot in the car. "Wait, there was a long coat and a scarf on the seat in the other car. Maybe I could borrow those to disguise myself as an old lady and get a closer look at where the bags are without either of those two recognizing me. No, if the owner starts yelling 'cause I'm in her coat I have a whole bunch of new problems."

In spite of his good intentions, Winkler nodded off in his seat. Moving slowly, Dutton carefully stretched up a bit to see over the tops of the seats to see what was going on without waking the agent.

Pernell watched the two from the space between the cars.

He muttered to himself, "That mug should realize that if he helped me get away with the bags there'd be no evidence against him but it's probably true that if he did try to help I'd be too suspicious of his motives to take advantage of it."

Pernell bent a bit to look up through the window but no, that didn't give him a better view of what was in the overhead rack from here. "It'd be easier to see where the bags are without being seen by them by getting close from behind them. I could get off at the next stop and move to the end of the car outside the train to do that. But from behind I couldn't see when the Fed's asleep."

Gladys Adams entered from the other end of the car. When she saw Winkler and Dutton she took a seat beside another woman of her age and started to whisper and point at those two. The other woman wanted to hear all about it.

Pernell moaned, "Okay, it's over. Damn! With chatty Sue there watching them there's no way I can do anything except go in there with gun drawn and take the bags by force and I don't own a gun which I wouldn't use except in self-defense anyway."

* * *

Later when the train was at the Miami Station, Pernell watched through a window as Winkler walked Dutton along the platform and into the building.

Now Pernell moved quickly into and through the third car. He grabbed the second plaid bag from the overhead rack where he had stowed it. "It'll be safer if I take this with me. If I leave it to be found here there may be a way they can trace it back to me and get me mixed up with the funny money cops. It finally dawns on me that this is clearly marked play money from a game. It was never intended to be passed. That means it's not illegal to have it so I don't have to worry about being seen with the bag if that T-man's still around."

He left the train with the plaid bag but with a less than jaunty step. This hadn't been his favorite train trip of all times.

Chapter 14

Gargoyle sat at his desk feeling good about himself and looking out the window. He was alone here when Shallwee Bee entered quietly carrying some papers for his signature. His back was to her and he didn't know she was there. She stood just inside the door to wait until he was off the phone.

Gargoyle said into the phone, "Yeah, I'm makin' good use of this loser. He picked up trash paper in Savannah to bring back. I wouldn't send one of my guys to get this stuff 'cause I got a tip that the Feds are expecting this shipment to be moved on the train. If they pick up this guy he's on his own and can't lead back to me except on his word which ain't worth much in court. I sent one of my own to pick up the real cash at another place and drive it back while the Feds are distracted. His train should arrive about now, I don't know the exact time. I haven't heard about the Feds or the locals making any arrest on the trains yet so I guess making the shipment two days earlier than we originally planned made a difference. So how are things with you?"

Bee exited quietly without being noticed.

* * *

It was 6:40 P.M. when Pernell greeted Bee with a big hug and a kiss outside the Miami train station. "It's really great to see you, Shallwee. This hasn't been a good day for me but I kept it from being a total downer by thinking about you ever two minutes or so."

"You look tired and worried," she said.

"I'm both, but you take my mind off all the unpleasantness to come. Did Gargoyle send you to meet me?

"No, it was my idea. He doesn't know where I am. After office hours I'm none of his business."

"So you're not...? You know..."

"As I told you the other night, I'm his office assistant and eye-candy but we're only employer and employee."

"I wasn't sure."

"As I also told you, his jealous wife makes sure of that. He knows she has spies everywhere but he doesn't know who they are. Besides, he's not someone I could bring myself to do that kind of thing with. I have more taste than that."

"Still if you work for him..."

"I don't tell inappropriate stories out of school as it were but I'm not personally loyal the way his body guards are at least alleged to be. He knows that so he doesn't trust me with information that might be used against him - which keeps me out of the mire."

"But he keeps you around because he enjoys seeing the way you walk and all. I respect his good taste."

"I'm not just a pretty face and other parts, I'm also efficient at the office jobs that I do."

"I never doubted it for a moment."

"Let me let you in on a secret bit of my history here where we're probably not being overheard. Some time back the police tried to persuade me to spy on Gargoyle for them by threatening to make him suspect me with the expectation that he would then have me have a lethal accident somewhere away from his property. They were fairly blunt that I would rat him out or be set up to be killed by him."

Pernell was incensed and could barely hold his tongue at this claim. She gestured for him to contain himself and let her finish.

"I told them that I had nothing to tell them about my employer and didn't expect that to change in the future. Then I made my boss recognize what was likely a police sting that he hadn't been paying enough attention to. He made some changes and neatly avoided the trap the authorities were setting for him. That screwed up the cops' plans long-term. Because of that Mr. Gargoyle trusts me and the cops stay clear of me lest I tell him the details of that incident and make him even more wary of certain people and situations. Knowing things makes me valuable but also helps protect me as long as no one knows what all I know."

"Wow, you're more fascinating the more time I spend around you. Can I interest you in dinner, Shallwee? There's enough left of my incidentals money left to pay for a decent meal."

"I know a nice place. I need a safe place to tell you what I overheard Mr. Gargoyle bragging about on the phone. You should know this before you meet with him. I also know a nice hotel where we don't need to worry about the room being bugged the way some at the Dorkman are. Are those bags all of your luggage?"

"Yeah. The one with my clothes was checked for the ride. My laptop I kept by my side the whole day in case I wanted to check on anybody with an online search. This other sorry little bag is a big part of my long, sad tale."

"This red plaid softside suitcase is what the unpleasantness to come is about?"

"What's in the bag is anyway. Yeah, the day after tomorrow will be the true test of my skills. For tomorrow - I'm taking a day off. I'll call it train lag. Why should jets get all the credit for stressing us? I didn't agree to a time schedule for getting back with what I picked up. I do need to make a stop and put the red bag in safe storage until I'm ready to deliver it. I know where I can do that with little chance of being seen going in and where it's all coin-operated so nobody needs to know exactly where the goods are out of sight. My own bag I'll keep with me and just leave at the restaurant coat check area until we go to the hotel after dinner."

They walked off arm-in-arm, each pulling a wheeled suitcase.

* * *

After dinner they checked into the hotel of Bee's choice but since there was only an hour of visitors' time left she urged him to go visit Beebop in the South Miami Healing Hospital which was not far away and do her another favor while he was there. Then they both agreed he should hurry back for a mutual well-deserved reward.

* * *

At the hospital Pernell searched out nurse James Fullard.

Pernell had met him on his way out at the end of visiting hours two nights before and had explained then that he had learned enough about Beebop to guess that the fun of pulling something off would motivate her enough - plus she was more than sick enough of being sick to want a cure although she would resist saying that.

He thought about the fact, but didn't explain all this to the nurse, that he did this because he could tell that making Beebop happier and healthier will make his friend Jack Dimple happier by making Jack's lady friend up in Philadelphia happier. Plus he had the time and opportunity to take on the challenge of getting this woman back in the game between doing Gargoyle money moves.

The nurse understood when Pernell explained the on-going game and had promised to find a way to let Beebop snitch some forbidden yogurt from an unmarked container he would leave in a convenient fridge as if part of his own lunch. That was working fine. She made a point of leaving the empty container in there as a mystery and Fullard quietly (i.e. mostly for her to hear) played that up.

Talking about it with Fullard she had laughed at how Pernell had used her quirks against her but was smart enough to embrace what worked so she intended to keep eating yogurt to get healthy. But it tasted a tiny bit better if she was sidestepping a rule while she ate it.

She was now actively ambulatory after several days of not even leaving her room, only getting up and into the chair in there. She fully understood the game they were playing but found it amusing even if it was silly to anyone else. They expected that some staff person not fully involved would eventually and probably inadvertently give away the ploy but maybe not too soon so she could enjoy the very minor thrill of it for a time. The beneficial bacteria were nicely resolving her GI problems. Reconnecting with old friends was quickly pulling her out of her deep depression.

Fullard had explained to Pernell that Beebop's relatives - not her parents or only sister - were founding donors of the hospital. Then they lost most of their money in bad business deals. She had never depended on them for money so she wasn't directly affected by their downturn. She had good hospital and long-term care insurance.

That company would never agree to those terms today but did years ago when they were new and eager to get their first customers. Those terms dissuaded them from trying hard to cancel her policy once it was clear she had a sharp tongue and knew how to attract public attention about what she felt were rip-offs and to praise what she felt were companies who honored the deals they made. It seemed safer and cheaper to let the policy stand as long as she never missed a payment - which with automatic transfer from her bank account was unlikely - and hope she never got sick for long. Until recently she had been keeping them content.

For PR purposes the South Miami Healing Hospital kept her on the premises as thanks to her family - and because the insurance company still paid in full for her care. Another week and attitudes were likely to change.

Since his visit two nights earlier she has been in phone contact with her old friends with whom she had lost contact. She felt better right away when she could do that. In fact she had announced this afternoon that she felt good enough to check herself out the next morning - to the relief of the doctors. Fullard would drive her home since he wouldn't be on duty that early.

Fullard also had agreed to take her shopping for a computer on the way home and to help her set up the machine to make contact her friends via Skype or a similar system when she chose. She wanted a Halloween mask to wear on her first video calls to surprise her friends and show she was back in the game. Since it was coming up on that big costume day they should have no trouble finding those for sale and he predicted that she would be fascinated with the range of choices.

Upstairs, Pernell surprised Beebop with frozen yogurt, a nice variation on what she had been thinking of as medicine but was flexible enough to now enjoy as dessert.

He had timed his arrival tonight to have a good session alone with her to talk over her getting involved in things that were now coming together. At this point he could predict the need to find someone who could keep secrets but would seem loose enough doing so to parry official and non-official attempts to pressure her to tell what she knew.

He told her that she impressed him by being an example of passive resistance. She declined to become loud and aggressive when others wanted to provoke her and thus make her vulnerable in one way or another. He didn't approve of acting that way all the time but he could see that it was useful in some instances.

After considerable discussion since she wasn't about to be anybody's patsy including his, they reached tentative agreement. The final situations weren't jelled yet so what he expected to need might not be called for after all but after this talk they could nail down the details quickly if she was interested in the final challenge.

As a gesture of his confidence in her, he gave her a ticket for the Florida state lottery that would be drawn several days later when he expected all the pieces to be in place for what she might get involved in. Any winnings from this would be entirely hers since he was confident she would have plenty of uses for any money that came under her control no matter how much that was.

The lottery depended on selecting the correct four numbers between 1 and 47 and a lucky ball between 1 and 17 drawn that evening. He had used her birth date, July 28, 1952, that he read off the chart at the foot of her hospital bed to select the numbers, manipulating them a bit as needed. So 07/28/1952 became 07, 28, 19, 05 - with the lucky ball 02. She was amused and promised to make him proud of how she used the money she surely would win since he had gone to the trouble of betting on her.

At Shallwee's urging, while he was in the hospital that night he also delivered a paperback book to another patient that would seem entirely innocent and was except that it was a title with sentimental significance for the recipient who would understand there was a coded message of encouragement in it. He simply put the book beside the dozing recipient and walked out. When she woke and found it as if delivered by an angel it would spark her rally from a serious medical slump.

Then he hurried back to the hotel so Bee would could rejoice at the good deed she was responsible for - and thank him.

Chapter 15

Pernell took today off before going to Gargoyle's office in part to confuse the man whom he was sure had spies at least trying to keep tabs on him at all times but who wouldn't be on high alert since they would expect him to report in as soon as he could. Also to make the point that he hadn't agreed to a specific time table for delivering the goods from his trip to Savannah. And because he had a substantial list of other things to do today including a variety of tasks in preparation for tomorrow before he would finally go see Gargoyle.

Across the day he shopped in a variety of stores - including two different second-hand shops and a hardware store. He also revisited and checked out the big transfer pickup and delivery sites, inside and out, and reconsidered the route between those places. All of it rather casual. All of it with him very alert and noting the details, especially any changes since his last visit to each spot.

At midmorning he called from a payphone and told the agent all was go for the big transfer. It was then agreed that he would get two keys he would need at the pickup location inside a bag of potato chips. He was told the store (where the staff would have no idea there was anything special about the chips since they weren't in on the operation), the brand of chips, and the special mark on the bag to identify it as the one of importance. Those could be available by the time he could walk to that store location if he wished. He did.

That pick up went smoothly. A casual customer entered with a tote bag of what looked like laundry, bought a bag of potato chips - and also placed a bag from the tote bag on the rack - and left. Minutes later Pernell entered, found the marked bag, paid for it and left. He ate the chips as he walked, neatly pocketing the small plastic bag in among the chips with two new keys in it. He was a good citizen and put the empty bag in a street trash basket so he didn't litter. No one would ever know how he got the copies of the keys that someone was paid to make without that being noticed because the plan called for him to use them but then get rid of them where what they opened couldn't even be guessed at so if anyone found them before they were recycled for the metal in them they would reveal nothing.

    Then he was off on his one scheduled paid job of the day. He was contacted about this by one of his local contacts from the past who knew his skills. This caper had an anti-Gargoyle aspect and that person correctly guessed that since Pernell was known on the grapevine to be dealing with the mobster that might be an inducement.

    As it was explained to him to get him interested, Gargoyle had a financial interest in a company that represented various artists. Like their backer, the company tended to play loose with the rules - in this case by contacting companies that might have an interest in the latest hot star on the rise and claiming to be the exclusive reps of that person without bothering to get the artist to sign a contract with them first.

    The specific task he was challenged to pull off was to pick up a demo CD at a post office box that had a combination lock rather than a key and get that CD played live on the air and the Internet during a special "open mike" session radio show being broadcast from a city mall today. The complication was that goons were said to have been hired to intercept that delivery (that had to be made by overnight mail to take advantage of this opportunity that the singer only just learned of) and destroy the disk - and maybe rough up the singer or whoever was the delivery person to send the message that the only way the singer would get to a recording contract was by signing a ten year deal for lousy terms with the rep company.

    Since he had no previous connection to the singer, the idea was that Pernell wouldn't be recognized as significant by the goons as he walked the disk to the site and persuaded the DJs to play it. He was expected to create a diversion that would attract media attention in the process since that's what he was famous for in certain circles.

    That attention would include the name of the singer and in a sense put him more on the map and make the rep companies attempt to force him into involuntary servitude put them on the map in ways that wouldn't help them.

The first part was easy. The post office was laid out so that the P.O. boxes were easily accessible inside but not visible from outside. On his way in, Pernell easily spotted two sullen tough guys annoyed that their aggressive looks scared so many people that they had to stay outside to avoid having the police called about suspicious loiterers. Pernell's clothes were so neutral as to be nondescript. Anyone calling ahead a warning to watch for him would be challenged to mention any feature that would set him apart in even a small group. Even his laptop carrying case handing by its strap from his shoulder blended in.

He knew the combination to open the appropriate box and did so, putting the padded envelope with a CD in its jewel case into his laptop bag after a mere glance to confirm the addressee. He was out and away behind other people leaving the post office building without the watchers paying him any attention.

At the corner he got on a city bus and sat in a back seat where he opened the envelope and slipped the jewel case back into his laptop bag but rolled up the padded mailer and put a rubber band on it. When he got off the bus he would deposit that in a trash container where someone would have to go to the trouble of removing the rubber band to see who it had been addressed to or the return address.

He was amused to note that the title of the disk was "Crazy Moola or Loony Lucre". The liner notes identified the singer and that the backup was the Wisconsin Harmonic Orchestra. It also said very specifically and in large print that, despite some false claims, the singer was not under contract to any representation company. Pernell was now more interested than he had been to hear the music. He made a cell phone call to Bee to say he was on time and the planned surprise should come off at the time they had agreed on. He was close enough to the mall to be certain of being in position in plenty of time.

He had checked the radio show site at 7 A.M. when the mall unlocked its doors for exercise walker. A temporary booth was set up on a small stage so the DJs and their equipment were visible but the noise of the mall space would be minimized when the DJs stepped inside and closed the booth door to speak live into their microphones. The area was in the process of being plastered with signs identifying the radio station, the DJs, and the special live show from 11 to 1 today.

As mercenary cross-fertilization, the mall's music store was of course having special sales. They would have several tables of CDs and two cash registers on rolling stands and employees to operate them outside their doors where they were easily accessible to those standing around to listen to the radio concert without blocking the way.

Two off-site used-goods outlets were setting up a CD/DVD *Swap Fest* not far from the stage. That merchandise would be on eight tables, each three foot by two foot on top, inside a waist-high white picket fence for a subtle degree of crowd control to keep the swappers from blocking the path of those passing by.

The advertising invited everyone to bring in a used music CD or film DVD and take one of their choice, one for one. Sorry, game cartridges wouldn't be included. The swap would be largely on the honor system with no employee involved, nothing to hand to a cashier or other middleman. There would though be people enforcing the *Bring one to get one* requirement. This would make the outlets known while refreshing their stock and moving out items that had been on their shelves for months not making money for them.

When Pernell arrived back at 11:15 the music store sidewalk sale tables were in place and the swap fest tables were covered with jewel-cased disks standing on edge to challenge the truly patient to sort through the myriad of titles for ones of interest. Fifteen people in a range of ages were doing so. The radio show had begun, the DJs doing the chatter they were paid for as they introduced a series of relatively new to never-before-aired numbers submitted in advance by various groups to justify this as an *open mike* event.

The crowd in the mall central area was estimated to be more than 200, mostly teens and early-twenties. They were well-behaved and enjoying themselves. Everyone was happy. There was interesting music although so far nothing that produced a big reaction.

The change was subtle but this audience was sensitive to the movements so it was widely noticed. A scattering of listeners checked new text messages on their devices. Their excited reactions prompted demands from those around them to know what was going down.

The word spread fast, the excitement of it eclipsing much of the interest in the music. There was a brand new rumor on local social media that someone had hidden $20 bills between jewel cases at this event. It was the San Francisco and New York phenomenon come to them but not out in an open air location, here in this space. Few in this audience were desperate for $20 but many of them would be happy to find and claim that amount - as much for bragging rights to being one of the lucky ones as for what it would buy them.

The several mall security guards went on high alert as dozens of young people looked around and called encouragement and then directions to one another as they headed at a run for the tables of stacked jewel cases and the possible free money between them.

In a startlingly short time there was chaos. The music store's employees stared and wondered what to do as thirty eager seekers mobbed their outside tables. The swap fest helpers faced a similar problem but from more people coming their way and without the option of running into a nearby store and closing the doors to keep the strange horde from ransacking the whole place.

The first searchers tried to handle the jewel cases with care but the later comers just grabbed for as many as they could reach and shuffled through them, too bad about the ones that got dropped to the floor. The ones now on the floor made for tricky footing. That meant people trying to get near the tables or to get away from them were stumbling and grabbing onto anyone and anything within reach to steady themselves. More chaos.

The one thing that was quickly becoming obvious was that no one was finding any money among the cases. A few then started to open the cases to check inside, tossing them carelessly aside as fast as they could move without properly closing them.

The DJs signaled the station which went to commercial back in the studio, then they changed the mike switches to be heard in the mall area without it going out on the air. They urged calm and they cautioned people about the underfoot hazard within the picket fence and near the music store where the effort to protect the fallen cases and disks was becoming more vigorous.

The swap fest helpers also became vocally defensive, shouting at the mindless ones to stop opening the cases and letting the disks fall out to be damaged. As the moment passed without anyone finding any money, most of the searchers backed off and tried to act as if they hadn't been part of that wild scene which all knew had been recorded by dozens of visitors plus the mall security cameras.

As the confusion seemed to be ebbing - and the studio kept on signaling that they needed something to air - the two DJs who had been staring in confusion and some amusement reset the controls to broadcast the music from the console but only from their mikes when they were inside the booth. They both crowded in there to exchange on-air comment without the substantial noise of the area. All the security people in the area were busy dealing with the milling crowd.

At that moment Pernell quickly climbed up the steps onto the stage, inserted the demo disk, and pushed the button to start the first track playing over the speakers here and over the radio and Internet. He then leaned against the booth door (that opened out) thus momentarily holding the DJs prisoner - but doing so with a look of innocent rapture at the sound of the orchestral introduction to the number that fooled many about his intent.

The DJs shoved on the door but tried hard not to make noise that the wide radio audience who couldn't see the situation wouldn't understand. They didn't even shout at Pernell. They focused on getting out of their confinement to shut off the unauthorized music.

Then they looked at the audience reaction and relaxed.

There would be plenty of questions to answer later but for now the musical number was a literal show stopper so they were content to let it continue. The audience there loved it and the larger one almost certainly did too.

Pernell handed the DJs the jewel case with the liner notes, then hurried off the stage and away. The DJs largely ignored him once it was clear he was returning control to them. They read the notes and prepared to identify the piece and the performers to the listeners everywhere. They would have a bit of fun revealing that the first track was titled "Crazy Moola or Loony Lucre". If they did their job right they could restore the fun atmosphere of this event and salvage the station's name for sponsoring it by word-playing with the title.

They did that, then read the on-site audience mood and played the second and then the third tracks on the disk. They were happy to have stumbled on a chance to be part of the start of a new sensation. It wouldn't hurt their career a bit to be mentioned over and over again as the first ones to air the music.

As those things happen, within hours the singer would be in high demand with several recording companies vying to sign him to contracts. So Pernell got paid and in the process thwarted Gargoyle, a win-win as far as he was concerned. He was grateful that Bee knew people who would know how to plant a rumor on the social media to have a pretty immediate effect on those in a specific location. He would be even happier to do her another favor later today.

* * *

Shallwee was scheduled to secretly meet Pernell but as she walked toward the rendezvous spot she realized she was being rather clumsily tailed. She recognized the person as Des, as in Desdemona, a female Gargoyle security department employee. Bee slowed but didn't stop while she alerted Pernell by text message to abort the meeting without being too open. She had warned him that she had overheard the boss grumble that he was unhappy that he hadn't ordered tighter surveillance of Pernell - and then of her -when he got word that she had met with him outside the office and their one dinner at the Dorfman hotel. They weren't playing the sit helpless except when told to do things for him game he expected.

Pernell read the text and phoned her.

When she took the call he said, "It's gonna be okay, I have this figured out and I'm ready to make it work. Walk two blocks ahead, speeding up for the short last short bit as if hurrying to a critical meeting. Turn right at that second corner. Look for me."

She didn't argue, she walked. She sped up for the last quarter of the block. She never looked behind her.

She turned the corner and was waved into the back seat of a waiting taxi with Pernell. They then drove in the nearby entrance of a ground floor parking garage for patients in the medical center above that and straight through and out an exit on the opposite side, which meant a block back and thus behind the spy hurrying to the corner to see where Bee went in a hurry. They turned left and drive away in that direction so they didn't go by the corner the two women had passed. That way even if Des looked back that way there was no chance of her seeing them.

Desdemona the spy was confused and distressed that she couldn't explain where Bee had disappeared to. Having to report that wouldn't put her in well with her boss who didn't like to hear that what he had ordered hadn't been done to his satisfaction.

* * *

Later, as a favor, not a paid job, Pernell set out to deliver some sensitive material with political overtones. Bee had asked that he help as a favor for a friend and watched from a distance but wasn't directly involved in this herself.

Political figure Monroe Coleman was scheduled to make a much anticipated public appearance in an indoor downtown public space today to show the public documents that he said would prove his opponent Rupert Rumpster had cheated in a recent election - and had lost anyway. Rumpster was continuing to smear the winner and this was to show why the elections commission refused to delay certifying the winner since the vote count wasn't close. If this forced Rumpster out of politics and made him the poster guy for crude cheating that would be a plus.

Defeated candidate Rumpster had been the one to call for this public presentation and he was determined to keep shouting for it. This because he knew that his supporters had stolen those documents from Coleman's office so there was no longer any evidence of his people's misdeeds. He would now publicly - with cameras rolling - demand that the declared winner show those papers right there and then as he said he would or shut up. A smugly neat strategy.

What Rumpster and his people didn't realize until only an hour earlier was that the evidence they had stolen had been restolen two hours before then by a Coleman supporter (although the operation had been planned the day before). Those documents – along with a surprise - were what was in the manila envelope Pernell would deliver by switching bags only a short distance from the podium.

The recipient, a backroom Coleman supporter but not someone known to Rumpster's people, would get the bag from Pernell and hand it directly to the newly elected man as the cameras rolled. Coleman would open the bag and present the documents on an overhead projection system for all to see - and record.

Because of the close timing, Rumpster supporters were on the alert ready to do almost anything to intercept any known Coleman assistant seen carrying a large manila envelope since they were assured that the newly elected man hadn't yet received the material and probably expected to be given it at the meeting site.

The meeting site was the central area of a shopping mart happy to get the free advertising of having their name mentioned in a ton of news reports about this public exposure event. The open space would accommodate a large audience of news people and the public.

When Pernell casually checked out the site early that morning he noted where all the security cameras were and also a feature that would be useful. He phoned a request of those who were depending on his scenario to make this an event for everyone to remember.

Across the three hours leading up close to show time a series of innocuous people walked by what caught Pernell's attention earlier, a small set of shelves and an adjacent tall bucket-shaped object by a visible but not gaudy sign that asked, Is this your lost item? Each person stood a tall umbrella in the bucket which now seemed rather obviously intended to receive them. Not far away was a standard bench for the weary to take a short break off their feet.

As the audience grew, with the news media people vying for good positions, Coleman's people and the mart tech people made sure the microphone and image projection system were ready to go. A deliberately nondescript middle aged woman walked up and sat on the bench of interest. She sat a well-filled gym bag by her feet. That had the name of a local high school printed on it and what seemed to be an extra cloth skirt that hung down and would have hidden something the size of a remote control toy car stuck on the underside of the bag if such a thing were attached there.

At the same time, a young man casually holding a device that might have been the control box of a remote control toy car - or who knows what else in this day of electronic toys of all descriptions and sizes - stopped by the wall a short distance from the bench to watch what was happening here today. Soon the activity on the temporary stage signaled that the man of the hour had arrived and was entering.

Pernell, in a wide-brimmed hat, dark rimmed glasses, and a big enough wad of chewing gum to somewhat distort his face, walked into the area and stopped not far from the bench and its occupant - who ignored him.

He looked around as if confused about what was happening. He sat down a duplicate of the high school branded gym bag in the same state of well-filledness but with no added skirt a few feet from hers.

He now noticed the nearby lost and found stand and began to examine the dozen tall umbrellas in it. Thoroughly examine them.

That meant opening each and locking it in that position, then setting it on the floor while he examined the next.

Nudging already opened umbrellas aside with newly opened ones, and putting some roughly on top of others so they became a two tier layer, he continued to examine the rain protection. Soon there were enough open umbrellas to block the view of the bench area and those gym bags from any camera except one directly overhead - and he had checked in the morning that there wasn't one there. Now the young man off to the side stopped pretending to play with his device and actually used it as the remote control it was to activate the toy car under the woman's bag with the end of its antenna exposed.

As if reacting with mild annoyance to the wall of umbrellas, the woman shifted down the bench at bit. That got her feet out of the way so the toy car could shuffle her bag to a spot farther from her than from Pernell's bag. Pernell blithely continued to pick up and put down opened umbrellas like a devoted shopper checking for a bargain.

Coleman was now at the podium and being introduced. The woman stood, picked up the bag closest to her, stepped around the umbrellas, and walked casually to the podium without anyone paying her much attention or trying to stop her. She handed the gym bag to Coleman's right hand man who was on the stage and expecting that.

Back at the bench, Pernell quickly closed all the umbrellas and returned them to the display, picked up the skirted gym bag, gave it a sharp bang on the floor (which, as intended, shoved the toy car up inside its space which was otherwise filled only with crumpled paper) and carried the bag away. The youth with the control box went closer to enjoy the show now playing out on the stage.

Coleman opened the gym bag, took out the manila envelope, and handed the bag back to his chief assistant. That man smiled as he held the bag and waited for the moment of surprise.

Coleman emptied the several documents onto the podium and placed a first one on the image projector. He said, "I promised the people of Florida a look at the evidence and I'm keeping my word."

Rumpster and his people were all in a dither about what to do now - with many cameras and voice recorders documenting their agitation and many lip readers studying the images being aired live in anticipation of being asked to reveal what was said if any of it avoided the microphones. They had expected Coleman and his staff to do everything straightforward and therefore open to easy interception and destruction of the evidence even in a blatant way if that's what was needed. They weren't tuned to the idea of a sly move by someone other than a known major Coleman worker, not a mere backroom envelope stuffer, so the delivery was unexpected and thus they made no move to block it until too late.

Coleman said, "I'm going to show you all the documents but of course there'll be claims that they don't say what you'll see is in them but you'll only get a brief look now. To avoid that confusion I've paid out of my pocket, not campaign funds or donations, to have all of these scanned onto a computer and then downloaded onto CDs so each news organization or concerned group can have a copy to study to their heart's delight. Someone makes a claim, you can go to the primary evidence to check on that."

He nodded and the chief assistant held up a handful of jewel cased CDs from the bag. Two other team members stepped over and took some of those and moved to different spots around the stage to hand them to the eager news people and others.

Coleman said, "No need to fight over them. We have a hundred of them which should be enough to go around. That also means that any attempt by the agents of the man who didn't win the election to hog them all in order to keep the rest of you from getting a copy are likely to fail. Come on, news people, watch for that. There's a story in them trying that. Ah, there he is all asputter. Now he's going to further embarrass his backers by saying that I've accused his camp of skullduggery before they could fully implement that strategy and because of that he is declaring the election nullified. Note that I'm realistic enough not to say he could embarrass himself rather than his backers. Not after some of what he did during the campaign."

When the CDs were distributed, Coleman showed each paper on the projection system as he explained its significance.

During that, a Miami top cop in dress uniform was off to the side in animated conversation with Rumpster. Neither looked happy.

When all of the documents had been shown and explained Coleman said to the audience, "I see we have a visitor from the police department. I'm told he bragged on a blog earlier today that he would mess me up by showing up here and confiscating these documents by claiming them to be evidence in a criminal investigation that he would ever so slyly not specify. You have to wonder about people who tell their plans on the Internet before they carry them out and then get upset about their lack of privacy when they get quoted back to themselves. No, he's leaving. I guess he doesn't think he'd get away with trying to confiscate all the CDs as he was being urged to do. I'm betting that you'll be able to see the cell phone video of their little chat on the Internet within the hour. Probably with good sound since the equipment's so efficient these days. There will be the lip readers if there's any doubt about what they said."

Pernell waited outside for things to wind down inside and Bee to join him. He had proposed the switch and then the umbrellas, the CDs were the idea of Coleman's people. He thought they had worked well together. Shallwee would be happy and Florida better off.

Chapter 16

The next morning, Pernell and Shallwee sat in the back of a taxi stopped at the curb outside Gargoyle's building as she prepared to get out. Pernell said, "I probably still only know half of what's going on so I'm better off playing it as straight as I can make myself do after all these years of lying at most turns." He pointed to the red plaid suitcase beside him.

"I wish I knew more that would reassure you but I don't," she said with a sad shrug. "At least you won't be surprised by some things even if you decide to pretend to be."

"Last night was terrific. At least I can die a happy man if it's my time."

"Don't say that! I'm only getting started so I want more."

"If I can, I'll call you later and we can see what the possibilities are. Don't put yourself in any danger asking too many questions."

They kissed passionately while the driver politely concentrated on the Sudoku puzzle in his newspaper.

Shallwee got out and walked to a side door of the building.

Pernell said, "Driver, cruise around a bit then stop back here in ten minutes. I need a few final minutes to collect my thoughts so I might as well confuse any spies who are watching me right now."

* * *

Twelve minutes later Pernell stood in the lobby facing Harri and Paulie at the reception counter. He carried the red plaid suitcase. He said briskly, "I have an appointment with Mr. Gargoyle."

"Why should I care what you have?" Harri sneered.

"Because you're in charge of this entrance way and I'm not challenging you on that. Am I authorized to go up?"

"You can try it if you want." She made a small gesture that brought Paulie to his feet, eager to break some body parts.

Pernell shook his head that he was disappointed in her.

Behind his back where those two couldn't see the move though, he pushed the button on an electronic pager.

Harri's phone rang. She grinned at Pernell while she refused to hear it. She was annoyed when Paulie stepped over and pointed to the ringing phone, assuming she must not hear it.

Pernell waited calmly, smiling pleasantly.

Harri gestured her annoyance when Bee's voice blared over the PA system. "Please send Mr. Gargoyle's guest upstairs to his office immediately. Thank you. We're waiting - and watching."

Paulie gestured rudely at first one, then a second, and finally a third wall-mounted TV camera.

Bee said over the PA system, "Shame on you for that, Paulie. That merits a time out. Fifteen minutes."

At a gesture from Harri, Pernell moved toward the elevator.

He stopped and stood aside while the sulking Paulie tramped past him and sat down hard in a chair facing into a corner.

* * *

As he waited for Pernell to reach his office to give his version of what had happened about the package from Savannah. Gargoyle mulled over the fact that his spies on the hotel staff had reported Pernell out of the hotel and therefore of their sight for hours the night before he went to Savannah. That time was unaccounted for since he had been expected to stay in the hotel and maybe mess around with Bee since he was clearly taken with her so no one had been assigned to follow him if he went out. Where had he been in that time period? And the night he got back to Miami from Savannah, all day yesterday, and again lost night since he hadn't followed the expectations and checked into the comped room at the Dorkman?

As the boss, should he demand to know or at least ask casually - thus admitting he was keeping tabs on Pernell? He hadn't dictated where his bagman had to stay and when he had to deliver what he had picked up. Those had been mistakes although this guy who had wrapped himself in the protective shield of the Code might have refused and that would have created a kind of crisis that it seemed better to avoid for now.

* * *

Pernell entered Gargoyle's private office and stopped facing the desk. No one else was in sight although Gargoyle's high-backed chair faced away from the desk so he might be in it. Pernell didn't look around, only waited patiently.

The voice came from the area of the chair that remained facing the windows. "Did you bring me the bag of money?"

"No, I didn't. I brought you a bag of top quality play money bills but they're probably not what you were expecting. I'm not sure what's the best way to explain that," Pernell responded.

Gargoyle turned in his chair as Oscar and Webber stepped into view from behind a draped-off space at the side.

"Savannah handed over play money?" Gargoyle asked.

"That'd make it too simple," Pernell said. "In my experience things like this are usually complicated. They often make good stories even if those don't exactly fit with the facts."

"You gonna tell me a story?"

"I've thought about it. For instance I could claim that a crew of weird alien creatures attacked me in a dark alley. There I was running full tilt down this trash-strewn space with three werewolves chasing me but I was determined not to let them stop me from delivering the small suitcase I was holding onto with such grim determination."

"Interesting setup," Webber said, then remembered that he wasn't supposed to speak.

Pernell continued, "I could tell you that those werewolves were clever and resourceful and in spite of my brilliant defensive moves they managed to corner me. Not being a total fool, as two pairs of slobbering jaws with teeth the size of grizzly bear fangs snapped close to me I shoved out that bag to fend them off - and one bit it and shook it so hard it's head would have snapped off if the bag were a man but since it was only a cloth bag it simply tore open."

The two guards smiled and nodded that they liked this story.

"I could say that to my amazement those werewolves promptly lost interest in me and concentrated on ravenously stuffing the bills into their mouths. Instead of making man-sushi of me, they ate your money instead."

Gargoyle looked at Oscar and Webber. All three shook their heads that no, they don't find that last part an interesting claim.

"Or I could play a different angle, the sex card," Pernell said.

"Sex usually gets our attention," Gargoyle agreed.

"I could say I gave your money to a beautiful woman who came onto me in the hotel lobby and promised me the best night of my life. The fantasies that produces are worth a lot."

"You ain't much of a shopper if you paid that much for to get your rocks off," Gargoyle said with a dismissive sneer. "I'd expect a guy like you to know that fancy claims don't make for good deals."

"I guess you had to be there to appreciate her allure," Pernell said with a shrug.

Oscar had his eyes closed, all smiles, lost in his fantasies that had him running his hands over an imaginary figure in his arms. Embarrassed, Webber stepped over to discreetly nudge his buddy to bring him back to reality. Gargoyle pretended not to notice all that but did give a loud cough that brought Webber back to full attention.

"Those are stories you're not gonna try to distract me with, right?" Gargoyle said to clarify the situation.

"Right. I'm also not gonna blow smoke at you by claiming that the money magically sprouted wings and flew away like a cloud of butterflies although I like that image."

"I don't like butterflies or any kind of bugs," Gargoyle said with a grimace of distaste."

"Too bad for you. They're beautiful creatures that give grubs and worms reason to hope," Pernell said.

Gargoyle gestured dismissively. Pernell gave a resigned sigh and shook his head at the sad situation he found himself in.

"My last story, and surely my best, could be that I was chased by a posse of treasury agents who suspected the money I picked up for you was counterfeit and wanted to use it against you in court. I could tell you that six men in dark suits and dark glasses waving badges chased me down a long, long deserted street. I could say that as I ran like the wind to stay ahead of them I pulled stacks of funny money from the bag that hung by a shoulder strap around me and ignited those bills by flicking my Bic lighter and then ran on with the flaming paper singeing my fingers until there was too little left to make a case with when I tossed that stack aside and got out another stack and repeated the whole process. You can see why it had to be such a long street. The bottom line would be that when I finally stopped to ask what they wanted, what had been potential evidence against you was all ashes of no use to them."

"That one's a sort of beautiful image and a beautiful sentiment," Gargoyle conceded. He got up and walked to the large window as he gestured for Pernell to join him. "Let me show you something."

Gargoyle pointed out a building in the distance. "See that place over there? That's the local office of the treasury department. You're right that they'd love to get their hands on me with some reason to mess with my operation."

"It's nothing personal I'm sure," Pernell said since it seemed like the thing to say.

"You're right that they'd love to have caught you with the counterfeit bills you picked up."

Pernell did his Academy Award performance shocked reaction, "I was actually carrying counterfeit stuff?"

"It seems so. Of course I wasn't supposed to know that's what I was being set up with but I do have my sources of info."

Pernell played the angry wronged man routine. "I went through all that for worthless stuff? You knew it would be some kind of funny money but sent me anyway?"

"Don't raise your voice, it irritates me."

Pernell continued his sputtering innocent routine.

Gargoyle said, "You had a job to do and you did it well enough for my purposes since you didn't give the T-men a reason to arrest you. You did good so I'm gonna give you a chance to make good on what you owe me."

"No, you're wrong about that. I don't owe you anything, it's the other way 'round," Pernell said firmly and without hesitation.

Gargoyle gestured that he was being reasonable about this. "You were entrusted with my money and you didn't deliver it to me. Ersatz, or whatever it is like the Romans said, you owe me the amount you lost because you weren't careful enough. Plus of course you don't get any reward for that bag job since you didn't finish it with what you signed for in Savannah to turn over to me. And since you didn't deliver what you were sent to get, the payment of what you asked for to take to Lumbago will be delayed a few weeks at least until I have the money on hand."

"But what was lost was funny money."

"So I'll cut you some slack and take payment in either that same stuff if its good quality so it'll pass on the street, even if the bank people will eventually spot it - or in regular cash."

Pernell grumbled, "Situations like this are why there's a Code of Honor but for the moment I'll play along and ask what you're proposing I should do to make good."

"You set up the people who tried to set me up when I sent you to Savannah," Gargoyle said and let himself think about the pleasure he'd get from accomplishing this.

"What are you talkin'? That's absurd. I can't set up the U.S. Treasury Department."

Gargoyle backhanded that aside. "Not them, the people who arranged the switcheroo that put bills in the bag at Savannah that would have been big trouble for me if you were caught with them."

"By the way, the Fed took those bills. He nabbed the guy who switched bags with me on the train."

"Yeah, my guy at the train station reported they took some guy away in cuffs."

"Of course you had a guy at the station."

"He took some pictures, then found out the guy's name. I'm waiting for my chance to pay him a visit but he's small change, not high priority."

"Who tried to set us all up? Do you have names and faces?" Pernell asked.

Gargoyle smiled, always happiest when he knew more than those he was jerking around. "People you know in fact. They got you involved in this whole thing."

"Louie Lizardo Lumbago?"

"At least those who use that name as a cover for certain of their operations."

Pernell's mind was in full swirl mode as he processed all this new information looking for pitfalls and possibilities. "Interesting. What am I supposed to do to set them up?"

"I don't care as long as it doesn't lead back to me. Which means you can't use or implicate me or any of my people. Connect those people with some funny money and sic the Feds on 'em by any scam you want. I don't care how you plan it or if you pull it off yourself or have somebody else do the leg work, I only care about the results."

Pernell nodded then said, "But let's be clear about this, the original demand for payment to Louie Lizardo Lumbago still stands. The Code's clear about that. This doesn't get you out from under that debt under any circumstances."

"I was hoping you'd forget about that since I'm lettin' you off the hook for what you owe me."

"We'll clarify that in a minute but first let me refresh your memory. You owe Lumbago two million real legal tender dollars. I've thought more about it and I've set up an account so that I'll accept a thousand good $100 bills and you can transfer the rest between bank accounts. That way you don't have to have as much cash on hand. I'm making it easy for you to pay up but yes, harder to delay. No apologies for that."

"Also then you never have to carry that much cash with you."

"Certainly a consideration. Even a hundred thou is more than I'd keep with me for long but I'd feel better being sure I wasn't going to have as much trouble getting my cut from the other end as I'm having getting any of what I've properly earned from you."

"According to you. I have a different rating of your success."

"Thank you for getting us back to that point. No, I don't owe you a penny since you wanted and expected the Savannah package to be grabbed by the treasure people. You've said too much and made too many people aware of your plans so the whispers and comments about it are on the grapevine whether you want that or not. That means I'm owed for the percentage of the real value of what I risked jail time and muggers to pick up. Owed by you. Now you want to hire me to setup this other thing. To stick this pair with funny money that they'll get caught with and that'll seem to tie them to the other guy and somehow in your fantasies that'll confuse the Feds so they'll believe you had nothing to do with the bad bills. And to top it all off, you think I'll do both the planning and the execution for free. You wouldn't, so why should I?"

Gargoyle smiled a lazy, superior smirk and started to reply that the man should do it because he, the boss, could make it nasty if he refused. But Pernell cut him off as he continued. "Why should anyone depending on the Code to keep things on the up and up while we mess with everybody else do so? You're the one who asked for this and the main one benefitting from it if I agree to figure out what to do and it works so it's your operation and therefore you should pay for it."

"What if I disagree?" Gargoyle asked as he leaned over closer to be as intimidating as possible - which was a lot.

"Then I decline to have more to do with you and since a whole big bunch of people know I was here, the Code either protects me or destroys you."

Gargoyle looked at him for a long moment as he did the math in his head. In the last two days he had been sampling the anonymous grapevine postings. He was forced to conclude that if bad things happened to this little creep or if he simply disappeared there was no chance Alfonso Gargoyle wouldn't be believed to be responsible by those he wanted and often needed to work with. This wasn't something that could be argued in a court, he'd be blackballed by the worst of the worst which would leave him isolated. Until this guy showed up in his office and somebody started posting about it on the grapevine nobody gave more than lip service to the idea of the Code. It was a joke but you didn't dare say that out loud. Now it was on the mind of everybody who was important to somebody like him and that was more than a nuisance, it was a near disaster. No, he had to deal with this Pernell carefully and be aware of what his own people saw him do and heard him say. The best plan was to use this guy and hope to find a way to screw him over during that with minimal bad blowback for himself.

"Since you suggested that you'd enjoy doing this thing to mess with those two…"

Pernell rolled his eyes but didn't rush to contradict the man.

"…I can see where it might fit with what I'd like to see happen to them for the trouble they've caused me in the past. Okay, I'll let you do that if you want to. Not a lot I could do to stop you…"

"Please stop spewing bullshit before you ruin the rug. Let me get this right, you propose I somehow let those two find out that I'm delivering a bag of cash to a contact for you with the train as the mode of transport. Correct?" Pernell said.

"Right. You have to do it by the train for them to have a chance to steal it and get caught with it. It's not vulnerable enough any other way."

"How much real bait money will you supply? It wasted effort without that. Surely by now those two know what the other guy was caught with that the Fed took him in to book him. Because of that they'll check what's in the bag before they take it far enough that they can't make a convincing case for a simple bag mix up. So there has to be enough good money clearly visible to pass a fast inspection. I'd suggest a single good bill as the top and bottom of each banded stack."

"How will only those be convincing?" Gargoyle asked.

"What denomination bad bills are they to get caught with?"

"Hundreds. Pretty good but not good enough to fool anybody who's paying attention. Better than the twenties of the other batch."

"Okay, let me run some numbers. They'll be in banded stacks of a hundred bills. The bag I have in mind will let you pack them three stacks long and four stacks high and three layers like that will fill the bag. That's twelve bills showing on the top and bottom of each layer."

Pernell held off an objection with a gesture.

He said, "Thirty-six stacks of bills, twelve per layer. Each stack would be ninety-eight bad bills and two goods with overall face value of $360,000. But the actual value will only be $7200 - that's twenty-four $100 bills per layer and three layers."

Another gesture to hold off an objection.

"What will make it work is that the bundles of each layer will be shrink-wrapped together for fast, easy handling. Of course on a quick inspection you can only see the top and bottom bills without opening the shrink-wrap and we all know how hard that is. Definitely they won't be able to do it in a hurry. They see the real bills and have to decide whether to believe the others are the same because things are happening fast."

"Not bad, Pernell. Kind of iffy off the top of your head but I won't reject the idea out of hand. A few alterations are needed. The shrink-wrap's a cute idea but there's no reason to put real bills except on the top of the top layer. That's means only $1200."

"No deal. Almost guaranteed to fail. No, I won't run the risk of being caught with the counterfeit bills when all they have to do is look at the middle layer. As they'll be sure to do since it'll be easy.

Play it cheap and you play it yourself. Send one of your regular guys to try it since I can't claim I own the patent on the procedure. I'm out before I'm in."

"I'm an agreeable guy. We'll do it this way. We include the whole $7200 that you want but it's your money, your payment in full for doing the Savannah bag job. Agreed?"

"I congratulate you on trying that although of course I resent you for doing so. You try to cheat me two ways and make it seem like you're doing me a favor. No wonder everybody counts his fingers if he ever has to shake your hand on a deal."

"I could resent you saying that I'm dishonest, Sylvester."

"Which would make the point in capital letters since on the websites you pay to have flaunt your claims about you supposedly being such a hotshot that's the kind of thing you brag about and claim makes you a big guy."

"I don't claim to have any websites."

"Probably true. Certainly not as far as I know anyway. But you pay people who know how to hint broadly enough to make it clear to anyone paying attention who the hooded guy in the spotlight is. If we're only gonna waste time talking about your vanity shows here I have other stuff to do. It's decision time for you. Do you want to mess with those two badly enough if it's gonna cost you the bait money plus my fee payable in advance since I don't trust you to pay me later?"

"There you go with the negatives again."

Pernell ignored that and said, "It should only cost you another failure to have some other guy try what I proposed."

"Here's how we'll do this," Gargoyle said. "I don't like or trust you either so if all seventy-two hundreds real bills aren't found with the funny money by the Feds, then that amount comes out of what I decide I owe you."

"No way. Cute double talk though. Your reputation for doing that is justified. First, how much you owe me doesn't depend on what you decide it is at some point. We negotiated a price for each job I've done for you. As for any of the money that might end up as part of the evidence, in the short run which is as long as I'm planning on dealing with you, there'll only be your word about that. It's already widely talked about on the grapevine that your word can't be trusted so why would I agree to that?"

"I resent your words and your tone but I'm willing to try to work out a deal..."

Pernell cut him off. "No, I won't agree to have you deduct the bait amount from what I'm to be paid to meet Lumbago's payment request. I don't care if you want to make some claim that the pair you want to mess up are connected to Lumbago. That's irrelevant to the IOU I presented to you. You don't have to mess with them but if you want that done you should be a man and pay for it. If you were the one being hired to do some job you'd insist on that."

Gargoyle reluctantly nodded agreement.

He would treat the bait money as a necessary business expense for dealing dirt to Hill and Taylor. If this ploy also made the Treasury people doubt his involvement with this batch of counterfeit bills that he was tricked into investing in and now couldn't bring himself to simply walk away from that would be a plus.

* * *

Shallwee Bee hurried from a side entrance of Gargoyle's office building to join Pernell when he came out the main entrance.

"How did it go?" she asked anxiously.

"I dodged a really unpleasant situation. He let me off easy." Pernell nodded at a pad of paper in his hand. There has an ear drawn on the page.

Bee wasn't sure to make of this. "Uh, well that's good to hear."

Pernell flipped to a page showing a crude drawing of a parrot. Bee looked up at him as he made a small head gesture in the direction of the street – then flipped back to the first drawing.

Bee got the idea now. "Got it. How easy did you get off?"

"I have to do one more job for him, then I'm free of the mess."

"What kind of a job this time?" she asked.

"Another bag job. I have to deliver a suitcase full of cash using the train since again that can't go through airport security. The person I'm to give it to may decide to claim it with the right password on the train rather than wait until we're at West Palm Beach station itself. I'm not supposed to tell anyone about this of course but I don't see a problem with telling anyone who asks since they won't know the important details."

"I hear what you're not saying." Bee smiled but resisted the urge to look around to see who was listening to them from nearby. She also found being part of a fake-out amusing.

"I knew I could depend on you to get it," Pernell said. "From in the building I spotted the vultures circling, looking for a lead."

"It's a good day for bird watching."

Pernell waved his hand in the air. "I have to go buy a twenty-inch black Studly-Built suitcase for my trip. Talk to you later by landline phone."

A taxi pulled up, Pernell got in and they pulled away. Bee waved and walked off down the street as if nothing were going on.

Before Bee had walked far, Hill and Taylor, dressed as tourists with dark glasses, bright printed shirts, and wide-brimmed hats, pulled their car to the curb and got out. Bee stopped with a pleasant smile to talk to them.

"Hi, we were just passing by and saw you talking to that man who got in the taxi. Do you know his name?" Taylor asked.

"We're asking because we thought we recognized him as someone we used to know and wanted to say hello to but we didn't want to embarrass him if he's not the person we thought," Hill explained.

"I know what you mean. You want to do the friendly thing but if it's the wrong person it's so awkward," Bee agreed.

"He looked like someone we know as Sylvester," Taylor said.

In the distance, Dutton, out on bail, sat in his parked car and aimed a concave plastic dish sound collector in their direction.

"Oh yes, yes, yes. It must be the right person. He'll be so happy to hear that somebody else that he knows is in the area. Good, sweet Sylvester," Bee gushed.

"But I can't remember the last name," Hill said hoping to get the most from this fishing trip without scaring off the fish.

Dutton kept the sound collector, a round object the diameter of his head, aimed at the trio, the earplug in his ear, straining to hear every word being said.

"Parsons. Isn't it Sylvester Parsons?" Taylor asked.

"No, Pernell. Sylvester Pernell," Bee corrected her.

"Of course. I have no head for names," Hill said.

"What's he up to these days?" Taylor asked since this woman seemed almost eager to share all she knew.

"I suppose it's okay to tell you, he's getting ready to do what he called a bag job, whatever that means," Bee said with a giggle.

Dutton flailed about trying to hold the collector in place to be sure to hear every word while also getting a note pad ready to write down the important details.

Hill slipped a small voice recorder from his pocket and held that nonchalantly in his hand as it were nothing of importance. "A bag job?" he said, all feigned innocence. "Strange term. I think you have to do those for someone else but who's he working for?"

Bee pointed to Gargoyle's building with a pleasant smile. "I think this company right here. He did one job of some sort for them so they offered him another one. I don't know the details."

"When will he be doing this new job?" Taylor risked disaster to ask. "*Uh*, I mean we don't want to interfere with his plans by trying to contact him to invite him to dinner."

"He said he's taking the next train to West Palm Beach. I guess that's tomorrow but I'm not sure about how the trains run," Bee said, the epitome of a helpful stranger.

"Train rides can be nice. We're always saying we should take one," Hill said with a hint in his tone for Taylor.

Bee gestured that she'd just remembered another detail. "He said he's to meet somebody on the train or on the street at West Palm Beach who'll give a secret password so that he'll turn over the twenty-inch black Studly-Built suitcase he'll have with him to them. I don't understand the details."

"Probably he'll be delivering money for the company here. It's safe to do it that way if no one knows he's carrying a lot of cash," Taylor said.

Bee shrugged. "Maybe that's correct but he didn't tell me what would be in the bag. He wouldn't want me to say too much. He says I do that at times."

"You're sure he said he was getting the train tomorrow?" Hill asked.

Again Bee shrugged. "He said the first train he could get. Is there one in the afternoon? I just assumed he meant tomorrow or the next day."

Taylor glanced at her watch. "Wow, look at the time. We'll be late meeting our tour group if we don't hurry. Nice to meet you. Bye."

She half-dragged Hill back to their car. Bee walked on wearing an airhead's innocent smile.

"What's the matter?" Hill demanded of Taylor.

"There's an 11:50 A.M. train north. He could be on it. We need to be ready," she answered.

"We know he didn't get caught with the counterfeit money on the train yesterday but some other guy did. That means he survived his initial meeting with Gargoyle and he also didn't lead the Feds to Gargoyle. So what's Pernell doing now? Maybe escaping with it if he got our money out of Gargoyle."

"He sure as heck wouldn't bring the money back to Lumbago. We knew that from the get-go."

"Besides, he's only going as far as West Palm Beach."

"Assuming his girlfriend knows what she's talking about and isn't deliberately throwing us off," Taylor cautioned.

"Could a giggly airhead like that pull the wool on experienced cons like us?" Hill said. "I don't think so."

In his car Dutton made notes with one hand while trying to keep the other pair lined up with the listening device.

"I guess not," Taylor said, not completely convinced.

Dutton whispered to himself, "Don't be too sure."

"We need to move fast and get ready to pull a bag switch on him," Hill said. "If he's got Gargoyle's money in his bag we're at least partially repaid and maybe we'll double the take as fair payment for all the trouble the big guy gave us in collecting our due."

"We should try to make the switch before he gets on the train," Taylor suggested. "It's easier to get lost in the confusion in the station if he realizes what happened than when you're cramped and trapped on the train between stops. Not that we'll let him realize what we're doing."

"Whoa, I just remembered the Feds. Ten days ago we tipped them in that anonymous call to expect somebody to be carrying a bunch of funny money on a train today," Hill said.

"Then this guy that we hoped to recruit as our suitable chump came south two days earlier than we expected him to. Suppose they interfere. It was pure dumb luck that they caught that other guy on the train from Savannah," Taylor said.

Dutton stared angrily at the pair in the distance.

"That jerk deserved what he got and a lot more for messing up our setup of Gargoyle," Taylor growled.

Dutton shouted out loud in his empty car, "The treasury guy who nabbed me was on that train because of you? You two rats deserve any punishment you get and I'll be happy to try to see that you get some."

"We need to hurry and buy a bag and prepare our plan," Hill said. "It was real helpful for the airhead to spell out what kind of bag he'll have or we'd have been forced to try more dangerous schemes to separate him from that money."

As Hill and Taylor drove off, Dutton fumbled the listening equipment into the back seat and acted nonchalant as a local police car cruised by. "Nothing in here you need to be interested in, officer. Just listening for bird songs. I'm out on bail that I don't plan on reclaiming now but it was worth following up on these people. I lost everything but now I may be able to get whatever's in this latest bag for my trouble and screw these two up deliberately this time. I've got nothing against Pernell, he's just trying to do a job for people who can't be trusted."

He drove away once the cops were out of sight. "It should be useful to have another of those black Studly-Built brand suitcases to confuse them with. Surprise will lead to confusion which will lead to me coming out of the whole thing ahead - unless I lose track of which bag is which too."

Chapter 17

What would be a big and potentially profitable but risky day began early for Pernell. He had spent the night in the Dorkman hotel after checking that his room there was still being comped. It meant he was under constant but limited observation since he knew where the cameras were and could work out where in the room he would be beyond their visual range - or could be made so by a small shift of the lamp on the dresser with the camera in its base or by moving the comfortable chair three feet to the side.

It was to his advantage to allow Gargoyle to check on him to this degree so the man didn't feel a need to have people whom Pernell wouldn't recognize out looking for him. When he left the room at 4:15 A.M. he left the Do Not Disturb sign on the outside doorknob. He had put that out there when he first entered the room days earlier and made sure it was still there when he came in for the night last night so it would establish the pattern.

He left the covers heaped up on the bed now so the overhead camera could see what looked vaguely like him with the sheet pulled up to his head at the edge of its view. Then he positioned the waist-high footed circulating fan that he had requested when he first checked in so that at the right hand end of its slow 160 degree sweep the air would slightly ruffle the bed clothes enough to suggest that the person under them had moved.

He wore clothes bought two days ago at a used goods store - and three layers of those, which had the effect of looking like a fat suit. Dressed like that he was unlikely to be recognized by any hotel staff or assigned watchers as himself. He expected the fire stairs to be wired to alert the front desk if those doors were opened so he walked down the main stairs wearing a full-head Halloween mask of Richard Nixon but stayed against the wall rather than holding the outer railing to avoid providing a good view to the security cameras along the way.

At the lobby level, without moving into easy view of the front desk, he went around and, after taking off the Nixon mask, walked through the kitchen to leave the building. All the other ground floor doors should be either locked at that hour or alarmed - and not being noticed was the goal. There wasn't much going on in the kitchen yet but the first deliveries had been made and the first preps for the day begun so the doors to the outside were unlocked and the few workers busy, which let him slip out unnoticed.

His next stop depended on his observation days before. He went to a coffee shop and bought a tall decaf coffee - to which he added an OTC sleep-inducing medication. He calculated the quantity and the specific material to make the drinker drowsy but not enough for the man to think it was other than routine. There was little chance it would do any significant harm to the man and wouldn't produce a large enough effect to lead to an investigation. Pernell checked the time and waited.

Soon a man in a security guard uniform entered and waved to the woman behind the counter. She waved back and poured a tall cup of regular coffee to go, his daily order. She put the lidded cup on the counter and went to move a tray of sweet rolls to where the guard could see them better and choose the one he would buy.

Pernell walked by the counter and smoothly switched the doped cup for the beverage the guard - on his way to work at the site where Pernell would be moving the special item - would enjoy on the job. A little extra insurance to reduce the man's alertness without doping him to a suspicious degree.

At 5:05 A.M. someone who looked like an overweight street person pushing a beat up cart holding his few possessions arrived near the building where the art object had been standing for days or weeks, no one except those who put it there knew exactly how long. It was time for the real action to begin. Not suspiciously early for a street person to be active, but still before the full morning activity began.

After a look around Pernell stepped to a closed, locked door.

His action seemed like that of any wary person wanting to avoid muggers or hassles. He used one of the keys from the chips bag to open the door with no trouble.

He stepped inside with his cart and closed the door, careful not to let it bang. Every move was now a cautious one to avoid giveaway noise. He stood and let his eyes adapt. It wasn't pitch blackness in there but it was dim with only a few security lights on.

Once he could see to avoid what might have changed since his last inspection visit, he went directly to the small door to the four-story-high utility and storage space at this level. His attention to detail when preparing paid off with silent well-lubricated cart wheels. A squeak at the wrong time could lead to disaster.

He opened this door to the utility panels as well as the rest of the space with the second key from the chips bag. He would be certain he disposed of those keys right after he left this place for the last time so they couldn't trigger questions it was best for his side in the game not to have asked. If he did this right, few would even be able to guess where Funny Money had been recently.

He temporarily removed two outer layers of clothes to make it easier to move, pulled on latex gloves so he wouldn't accidentally leave any fingerprints behind, and set to work. He moved the ten-foot-tall wrapped item from against other stored tall materials by the outer wall to by the sets of metal stairs that went up to the utility panel landings for each of the four floors. As he had tested to verify on his earlier visit, it was lighter than its bulk suggested it would be. He moved slowly and carefully to avoid noise and to be sure that none of the paper or cloth coverings of the other stored items caught on the one of interest so he might move or pull over more than he intended. When ready to leave he would deal with the wrappings removed from the art work of interest. The ideal was to leave nothing behind that would arouse suspicions.

The art piece consisted mostly of thin metal tubes that had been individually wrapped in decorated paper strips to suggest there would only be base metal, not real gold, underneath. The tubes were two secrets of the piece. First because, despite what the original owner (not the creator) had hinted, they were not solid gold, only gold covered. And two, they were a very strong alloy that made them much stronger than they looked for their diameter. The whole stored unit was a bundle of upright tubes with other smaller parts in individual plastic bags taped to those tubes. Wide Kraft paper was then taped around the whole unit just tightly enough to form a thin closed-umbrella shape to keep it bundled for easier handling. There was nothing underneath the unit which sat directly on the floor and the Kraft paper sheath ended two inches above the floor which allowed a first hint view of what form to expect the contents to be.

Pernell had thought long and hard about that sheath of Kraft paper. It would inevitably be somewhat noisy to remove. And then what could he do to stop it from raising questions? His answer to the first was to come prepared with a telescoping aluminum tube to which he taped a box cutter at the upper end. With that he started at the first floor level and sliced open the wrapper, then climbed to the second floor platform to complete the slice to the top of the tall, thin cone in several moves. He then reached out from the stairs and carefully removed the heavy paper wrapper intact. For the moment he taped the top of that to the stairs support to keep it from collapsing to the floor where it would be in his way and would likely make avoidable rustling noise doing that.

This left the bundle of tubes exposed. To his relief the paper wrapping on each tube was only attached at its ends, not its whole length so it would come off fast and cleanly. Online research on material for that kind of use had primed him to expect this but if the product used here wasn't like that he would have an additional major headache. No need for that aspirin tablet.

Based on what the principal had told the agent and that man passed along to him, he anticipated that the tubes would be designed to interlock and therefore to be taken apart if that was needed. He eyeballed the longest tubes guesstimating how many lengths each would likely come apart as if he assumed the artist aimed to make that an inconspicuous aspect of the overall design. His best guess was three sections, not necessarily of equal length.

With the whole bundle close to the stairs so he could easily reach any part of it by going up or down a few steps and bending or stretching up as needed, he removed the decorated paper coverings on one tube, thus exposing two places where exterior decorative bumps and markings hinted something more could happen. Working with care so he didn't wreck his back in the process, he pulled hard on the topmost section of the tube and that came out of the lower part. He put the freed piece aside and pulled on what was now the new top - with the same result. The ten-foot tube became three tubes, one four feet long and a pair of three-foot lengths.

He then considered other tubes in the bundle and guessed where any separation points would be on each. Knowing what to feel for, he could then verify his guesses without removing the decorated coverings. He noted with gratitude that in most cases the points he needed to get at were near the ends of paper coverings so he could disassemble the lengths without removing most of the paper covering. As he had hoped when he planned this, he could leave those in place to prevent damage from the parts rubbing against one another while he moved them - and disposing of that paper would be easier at the destination site than here.

He had work to do now. One at a time, starting with the tallest tubes, he disassembled the bundle and the individual tubes. As he had hoped, and to a degree depended on, no piece was more than four feet long. They would all fit in his cart without sticking up enough to attract attention. The small bagged items would be no transportation space problem either. He would be able to move it all in one trip since both the bulk and the weight were within workable limits.

In no more time than he had planned on, the whole art work was in pieces in his sorry looking but carefully reinforced for strength cart. He had alternate plans worked out in his head in case it would take two or even three trips but no one but he would ever know what those were since he didn't need them.

Time to deal with the Kraft paper cover. He smiled as he took a kid's water soaker type play gun and filled it from a faucet in a ground level corner cleaners' tool storage space. He had bought and brought this oversized water pistol in with him as his solution of choice to the paper tent matter if things fit in the cart as he hoped.

Starting at the top, he slowly wet down the Kraft paper as it hung from the outside of the stairs. Initially the paper resisted the water but with continued exposure it began to absorb it - and then did so readily. By the time he got to the ground level section, what water had drained down its length from above had made the whole thing slightly soggy. He worked with restraint to keep it from getting too wet when it might either fall apart or create a water trail on the way out of here.

He untaped it at the top and let it fall almost silently into a damp mass on the floor. After he put a plastic drop cloth he came prepared with over the cart, he laid the mildly sodden paper mass on top. He silently cheered that there was no drip and even if someone got close and touched it, the paper layer didn't seem suspiciously wet.

He made sure the water soaker was empty and wiped the outside of it with a tissue that he made sure went back in his pocket. He left the soaker out of sight among the remaining stored items where it wasn't likely to generate much interest whenever it was found.

He took the sleepy guard's empty coffee container from the trash with him on the way out. That way the dregs couldn't be tested if for some reason questions were asked even if that didn't seem likely.

He redonned the extra clothing layers to become the heavy set guy with a cart and cautiously left that space and then the building without being seen. He was a third of the way to success.

By walking about three times the distance of the most direct route to the destination site he avoided every government and private security camera that would include a view of the streets and sidewalks that he had spotted during his preparation tours of the area. If anyone followed him with no idea why he was going the route he did they might have questioned whether that plump fellow was all there. That was part of the purpose of the extra clothes layers and the cart that said he was on the street without any clock to punch and maybe a loosened hold on reality.

By the time he reached the destination it was 6:15 A.M. so the building was officially open although not yet open for business. It was a tourist attraction and this arrangement let those eager to take a few photos to show they had been inside to do that and get on to the rest of their whirlwind seeing of the sights with only a few security staff present.

This final part of the transfer would be the trickiest precisely because the place was open so unexpected persons could walk in at any moment.

Along the way he left the Kraft paper at a small neighborhood recycling center that wouldn't question where it came from or its damp condition. He also left his two outer layers of clothes in a recycling bin for rags there. By those simple moves he changed the appearance of himself and his cart if they were being recorded and he didn't know it. There were two cameras here at the recycling center but he saw them and played them so it wasn't too obvious what had happened. It was too early for anyone else to be around there.

He has chosen today as the day for this transfer since, to focus attention on a large event in another area of the city, activities at this site would be curtailed until one P.M. The city fathers had officially designated the morning hours today as a "sacred memorial time of inactivity" here. They were careful to make clear that morning visits were discouraged but not forbidden though. No one would be hassled or turned away at the doors. That wouldn't be tourist friendly.

A second lucky chance was that this would be one of the last days for a display of colorful banners suspended overhead in the large central area. A display that someone had noted on a blog commentary about it that then got wider notice blocked the view of several security cameras of much of the central floor space.

The city people in charge admitted they knew this but chose not to let it prohibit the ten day display since there were plenty of other security measures in use. One official refused to apologize for calling the blogger names for making the world aware of this minor problem since otherwise almost no one would have known there was even a small reduction in security coverage to try to exploit. Pernell thanked the blogger and those always eager to point an accusing finger at officialdom for making enough of a fuss to cause him to learn of the exploitable glitch.

There was no way that he could have arranged either of those situations but he was quick to take advantage of them.

Pernell entered by a rear door left unlocked for employees, then opened a locked but not alarmed door from inside and pulled in the cart he had left outside there. He was alert for anyone but didn't see anyone. He used that door because he knew from his earlier poking-in-the-back-corners-like-an-innocent-but-nosey-tourist inspection there was no security camera aimed at that site.

Inside, he transformed his look by removing his current top layer of clothes and donning a Santa's elf type costume from the cart. He had estimated it would be too hot to work in this outfit until now.

He kept the removed clothes that were his visible garb on the streets from the recycling center to here folded with the cart since he would need them to wear when he left here. The pants were sweats he had been wearing turned inside out and the top was made to be reversed for a different look so he was set.

The elfin ears and hat which he now put on could go out under his tucked-in top. Thus costumed, if someone saw or photographed him he would be taken as a playful artistic type caught in the act.

His window of opportunity was six to eight A.M. so he went to work in the open where today he was out of view of security cameras.

He knew where the tall ladder he needed was stored and as a first step padded its legs for quiet movement. Noises would still bring a guard to check even if they saw nothing on the security center video monitors.

He knew what to do, so he did it.

He unwrapped the tubes, joined sections that would be parts of a single length, then followed hints he recognized on the tubes themselves to attach those with pieces there for that purpose (some of which were in the small plastic bags) to make a three dimensional piece that hadn't been seen for more than a decade and only for a short time when it was first presented to the world. In fact a time so brief that in its peculiar history it was much talked about and in some places raved about in the art world but as a PR stunt had only been allowed to be photographed by one man - so the press weren't allowed in to the initial private showing.

Then a fire in that man's photo studio reportedly destroyed the film before or after it was developed. In any case, no one ever publicly claimed to have seen them. Many assumed that was more PR untruth but when the piece disappeared overnight it stopped being a subject of public interest no matter how a few tried to fan the flame of mystery into a conflagration. The end result was that there were a few verbal descriptions of the details and several drawings but those included enough discrepancies to which each source swore their version as true beyond doubt and the others the result of blind troublemakers that the closest thing to a depiction of its overall shape was an eight-inch high simplified version shown in a gallery with a sign claiming it was made by the artist who said it was a good but very simplified version of the big piece.

Interpreting certain bumps, raised lines, and a few thin linear depressions as guides for what should be attached where, Pernell assembled the pieces. Several sections had been attached, not just taped to one another in the storage bundle, and he didn't try to take those apart but now he recognized that when properly freed up some parts could be rotated out as arms, making the overall occupied space much larger than the bundled unit suggested. With those "arms" opened it seemed too flimsy to hold together but the alloy was strong.

He had disassembled a fairly solid looking ten-foot-high, three-foot-thick bundle of tubes, moved it in pieces none of which was more than four feet long, and rearranged it into a twelve-foot-high, ten-foot-wide spindly armed mobile on a tripod base. He used some clothes line and a pulley he brought for the purpose since he had foreseen he would need them to raise if into the upright configuration, then used the tall ladder to add the other parts.

Some small flat parts that were hardly visible in the bundle now hung down like Christmas tree ornaments but only once it is upright and stable so those don't fall off and break. He used long-handled "grabbers" which he had seen in the janitorial supply closet where the ladder was kept to adjust those parts along the spindly horizontal tubes. Also to hang the additional items from plastic bags. The six-inch-long melting money sign emblems went on at spots marked by pairs of bumps. He didn't know or much care whether he got those in the original spots since it was unlikely anyone could prove they weren't as he placed them.

He looked up at his work and thought it was good.

He now returned the ladder and the grabbers to the store room, only taking the pads off the ladder legs once in there. He gathered all the thin coiled paper that had wrapped the tubes and stuffed that into his cart. He took off the elf costume which he would take with him and he put on the clothes he had worn here from the pickup site inside out but now right side out so he looked like a different person.

As a last special gesture not called for by his agreement with the principal, Pernell taped four photos downloaded from the Web site touting Gargoyle's art collection without naming him at eye level on the returned art work. One showed one of several small simplified souvenir copies of *Funny Money* that were known to have been sold to collectors at the first showing. The others were blurred images of small groups of items in the collection that Shallwee had recognized from her visit to the Nana residence. He didn't even leave it to those who would rush in to authenticate the newly returned work to wonder about where those photos came from and where the items in them were or had been. He printed the web address on the back of each of the photos. He felt certain that art experts would recognize them and the photos should be enough for the authorities to get a search warrant for stolen art objects in Gargoyle's building.

That was intended to point Interpol to Polly Nana and her late husband and his acquisitions. From her they should learn how her items were commandeered by Gargoyle, thus connecting the mobster to the original art thefts. He likely had nothing to do with those but the evidence would make it hard to believe he didn't and all but impossible to disprove he didn't since most, if not all, the people who could say otherwise were dead.

He left one additional item hanging from the reconstructed art piece. Another mystery photo. It dangled at eye level for himself and others on the shorter end of the height scale. It showed a flat metal artwork depicting two connected standard dollar signs with visible lines marking where those could apparently be separated. This was the only photo encased in a plastic sleeve and the only one in sharp focus so words engraved on one half were blurred on the second half but in a way that suggested they were readable on the item itself, only messed with on the photo. Those two details set it off from the other photos - and thereby guaranteed word of it would be leaked to the news media no matter what the investigators to whom it made no sense would have preferred.

He took the paper wrappings away packed down in his cart. He fitted a very different looking cover he had with it the whole time for that purpose over the cart changing its appearance.

He threw the paper and the cart in a trash dumpster several blocks away, hurrying to do that as the trash truck was approaching on the schedule he expected based on his observations days earlier.

Rid of all that evidence he went to a diner to have breakfast where he could see the activity out a window as police rushed up to report on and secure what an anonymous tip from a payphone told them to look for. The transfer was complete; the public awareness that it had been done under the radar had begun.

While Pernell was making the big transfer, Hill and Taylor and also Dutton were looking for him. Those trackers distracted Gargoyle's people as well as the Interpol agent and FBI agents and local cops from their searches for Pernell. All of those searchers were looking for him because he might be carrying money or engaging in illegal activities that could be tied to and used against Gargoyle. None of the groups had any reason to suspect anything about the big transfer so they weren't looking for him with that material. Pernell didn't know about all that and couldn't have arranged it but he would be delighted when he inevitably heard about it later.

Chapter 18

At 9:20 A.M. that morning Pernell walked to the lobby desk in Gargoyle's office building. Harri glared at him with a hint of a smirk.

"I'm here to pick up a package from Mr. Gargoyle. I'm to pick that up here in the lobby, not in his office."

"What's your name?"

"Mister Sylvester Pernell."

"Your home address?"

"Irrelevant. Mr. Gargoyle, are you really going to let this minor worker mess up our deal? I expected better of you. Have you no control at all of what goes down in the building with your name on it? Under these silly circumstances I can't even bring myself to call it your building."

Pernell said this in a slightly louder than normal conversational tone since he was sure the boss was monitoring this with audio and video feeds and he didn't need to shout to be picked up by hidden microphones.

To her obvious annoyance, the computer by Harri emitted a distinctive *pay attention* sound that she obviously wanted to ignore but knew she couldn't. She tapped a key to acknowledge that signal, then reached down beside her, grabbed up a black twenty-inch Studly-Built suitcase and literally threw it in Pernell's direction. It hit the floor but didn't open or dent, thereby making the Studly-Built people proud.

Pernell tensed while it was in the air but once sure it wouldn't hit him directly or on the bounce he stayed calm and in place.

The computer made that sound again so Harri had to shift her glare from Pernell to the monitor for a moment. Then she made a face as she had to look around her to find the clipboard that held the receipt form he was required to sign. That was a detail she should have taken care of before she gave up possession of the suitcase and would be in trouble about if he grabbed the bag and ran and she couldn't get over the counter fast enough to grab him.

But he made no move to even touch the bag, much less run with it.

She held up the clipboard, then banged it down on the edge of the counter with an emphatic gesture that he was to sign it. He made no move to approach to do that. She picked it up and banged it down again and pointed at it. She was a firm believer that noise was a sign of strength and an easy way to get a demand across. He didn't move or change his expression.

Finally she felt compelled to shout, "Sign the receipt to show you took the bag."

"I require that a company employee open the bag and visually verify what's inside while I watch," he said calmly. "I have reason not to trust what's in any closed container based solely on the word of Mr. Gargoyle. Since there should be a significant amount of cash in the bag I need to see that but to have him or his rep present to attest to what's in there so there won't be any false claims later that what's not in there supposedly was."

Harri was taken aback by this blatant refusal but tried to hide that in a sneering taunt. "You want somebody to *attest* to it? What's that mean?"

Pernell firmly grabbed his crotch as he said, "Swear on the family jewels that it's true. Sorry if that means you're not literally qualified. I can see how that might frustrate you." Was that just a hint of a grin?

"You will sign the receipt," she demanded.

Slowly so it couldn't be taken as a threatening movement, he pulled a document from the laptop case hanging from his shoulder that seemed thick enough that the computer could be in there. "Of course. But only when the man himself signs my receipt listing the face value of the money in the bag. Yeah, that'll happen. So I'll be okay with his designated company rep signing. He probably should know that but being prudent and a doubter I'll only proceed when I've watched him show and count the bills. Any questions?"

Harri stared. She was having difficulty processing his flat out refusal. Seldom in her adult life had anyone dared to tell her no.

"To be clear, Mr. Gargoyle, I emphasized the literal meaning of *attest* to your doorkeeper but I don't object to her doing the verifying if she has your approval. Her assistant is clearly not competent for the task though." Again he spoke to be picked up by microphones without the need to shout.

Harri glanced at Paulie and sort of shrugged. Paulie looked around no more confused than he had been for several minutes.

The computer made its *pay attention* sound. Harri looked at the monitor and broke into a big smile. She said, "The boss says screw you, no. *Uh,* in not exactly those words but ones like them."

She knew enough to be wary of misquoting the boss. After an incident in the past she knew she was free to interpret him but not to indicate she was quoting him.

At that an inconspicuous door at the back of the lobby opened and Oscar, Webber, and two other hefty bodyguards stepped into view but stayed back there. Paulie stared at them, then at Harri who hadn't turned to look so it was impossible to tell if she knew those men were there although her slight smirk suggested she did and therefore felt she had backup.

Pernell felt in his pants pocket and after a moment pulled out a cell phone. He pushed a few buttons and waited, looking at the device.

Gargoyle said over the PA, "Oh my, there's no cell reception in the lobby right now. How unfortunate for you, Sylvester. It seems like you have little choice but to take my word about what's in the bag and everything else. Too bad about what you want to claim we had agreed to at some previous time."

Pernell slowly and calmly took another device from his pocket. "Not a problem. I anticipated you so I sent a signal with this beeper that's on a different frequency range. An associate is at this moment releasing my prerecorded message onto the grapevine about your attempt at cheating and your defiance of the Code."

"More of the damned Code baloney," Gargoyle grumbled.

At the back of the lobby, Webber and Oscar now held up their personal devices to confirm that Pernell's message was already hot on the grapevine where it was fast generating lots of negative reactions against Gargoyle - and them.

"Shoot, shoot, shoot!" Gargoyle grumbled from the ether.

By now Harri was so enraged that Pernell was getting away with telling them he wouldn't do what he was told to that she lost it. With a shout she jumped onto the counter and off onto the floor in front of it in full attack mode. The five men watched this but didn't move for the moment.

As she got within range, hesitating a bit to think of viler things to shout at him and more terrible things to promise she was about to do to him, he smoothly pulled out a Taser from his over-shoulder laptop case and dropped her writhing onto the floor. The men still didn't move as he quickly shoved a plastic gag in her mouth and then bound her hands and feet with plastic strip flex cuffs. Paulie tensed and waited for her to tell him what to do but she was gagged and he wasn't conditioned to do anything much on his own.

The four bodyguards finally came forward and released her while Pernell stood back and calmly watched. Then, instead of turning her loose to savage Pernell, the two extra bodyguards hustled Harri out the way they had come despite her profanity-laced protests and vigorous physical resistance. It took Webber stepping in close to face her and quietly but very firmly threatened her with dire consequences to force her to take control of herself. Finally she let the men lead her away but everyone understood without her needing to state it - even though she did that loudly and in colorful language and imagery - that she would hold a grudge about this forever and Pernell would never be safe near her again. Paulie was taken away with her since he would be worse that useless left here on his own.

Webber now took on the task of examining and counting the contents of the suitcase (without opening the shrink-wrapped layers since Pernell agreed that it was unlikely there are any additional good bills that didn't show). Webber had brought one stack of the play money with him to count out and compare the thickness of the stack to what was in the wrappers and Pernell agreed that he didn't need to have the bad bills exactly counted. Webber then signed Pernell's receipt and Pernell signed Gargoyle's.

Oscar and Webber exchanged nods of admiration for Pernell as a brave operator and of satisfaction that they had covered themselves with the way they conducted this matter so they didn't need to worry about being falsely accused by Pernell. It was peculiarly comforting to know that Pernell wouldn't lie to cause anyone trouble. It would be reassuring to know that no others would lie about them but this was the world they were stuck with. They watched him get into a taxi outside and privately wondered how this would work out.

* * *

The clock inside the Miami train station showed 11:20 A.M. The next train listed for departure was going to Lakeland, Florida and points north to Boston. It was scheduled to leave at 11:50. One of the listed Florida stops was West Palm Beach. There was not a departure gate listed yet.

Pernell stepped away from the sales window with his ticket, glanced around to get oriented, then headed at a leisurely pace for the center of the room. He pulled his wheeled black twenty-inch bag with a two-inch-diameter Smiley Face sticker on the top where only those close by could see it.

Hill and Taylor stood where they could see but not easily be seen by most people. A black bag like Pernell's - except with a red ribbon stuck in the ID card pocket on the back and no Smiley Face sticker - was between them. Each held a large store logo bag of items.

Dutton stood where he could see Hill and Taylor and Pernell. He had a bag like theirs by him, his with two paper ID tags on strings attached to the handle. He muttered, "This is amazing but really a mess. How did whoever did this do it?"

He was reacting to the forty other people standing or walking slowly around the room with identical black Studly-Built suitcases. More people with the same bags entered the station regularly.

Taylor explained to Hill, "I asked somebody. This is a special promotional thing for a local radio station and Studly-Built brand bags. Show up here between eleven and noon today with one of their bags of this size and color and you get a chance on $5000 cash. Each bag and person gets stamped with ink visible only under UV light to limit them to one chance per person and bag. It'll be a total madhouse here in a few minutes."

"Damn, it could get really confusing," Hill grumbled. "But let's think positive, this is an opportunity, not a problem."

"Let's not waste time. I'm going for a switch. Be ready to help if he starts making a noisy fuss."

Taylor put on her dark-veiled hat from her big store logo bag and adjusted it, then hurried by Pernell pulling her Studly-Built bag. She stumbled dramatically, using that move as an excuse to swing and release her bag so it knocked over Pernell's bag, resulting in them landing together.

Taylor quickly recovered her footing and grabbed Pernell's bag intending to hurry on with it - but found a retractable dog leash attached to his bag. "Sorry, that one's my bag. I like to stay attached to it in a crowded place like this," Pernell said pleasantly.

So Taylor grabbed her own bag and hurried on without saying a word or looking directly at Pernell - who smiled a tiny bit.

Moments later, Pernell stood in the open center of the room, bag by his feet, in full view of the security people and everyone else.

Hill whispered to Taylor, now in a different jacket, hat, and sun glasses to alter her appearance, "I recognized right away that the kid's a born thief so we'll use him. He'll do the dirty work for twenty bucks. Be ready to get out of here fast."

A large woman, pulling a Studly-Built bag and looking angry at being inconvenienced, stopped not far from Pernell.

Sixteen year old Gary zipped down the room on his skateboard, right at Pernell's back. Other people saw him coming and got out of the way. A uniformed police officer started after the teen who was moving away from him.

As he got close to Pernell, the thrilled and excited Gary crouched and prepared to grab the man's bag as he went by.

Just before Gary reaches him, Pernell, without any indication that he realized what was about to happen, stepped to one side with his bag – which put a waist-high trash container between himself and the teen.

Gary shifted for all he was worth and now found himself zooming right at the large woman as she turned to glare at him, swinging her obviously heavy bag from beside her to in front of her to let her get at him better.

Gary had to make a quick decision - run into her or into her bag since it seemed unlikely he could avoid both.

Gary wiped-out disastrously as he bent too far to the side trying to avoid the unpleasantness waiting for him. He skidded across the floor in one direction, his skateboard in another, while people jumped out of the way and cringed at the thought of what that must feel like. Injured but with no broken bones, he was quickly up and running, his skateboard abandoned for now, since the woman and the cop were both moving at him.

Dutton watched all this happen from a corner. "Ouch, that had to hurt, kid. I hope they made it worth your while to try it. I'd have interfered if you pulled that off to be sure those two don't manage to switch bags with him here though. I myself won't pull a switch until we're on the train. There are too many people watching here that might be paying special attention - like cops or the mobster's people."

Pernell looked around, nonchalant and innocent. "Somebody here must be Gargoyle's guy but I have no idea which one he is."

He shook his head in wonder and said, "The other pair are pretty determined - which bodes well for me."

Eight nuns in large old-fashioned habits, and each pulling a black Studly-Built wheeled bag, walked solemnly in pairs down the center of the room. Pernell was ahead of them, his back to them, his bag at his side.

Hill urged Taylor, "C'mon, this is our chance. When the nuns pass by him they'll block the view of most of the people in the place. If we run between them, the confusion'll let us get away. I've got my penknife ready to cut that darned leash on his bag."

"Nuns scare me," Taylor said. "I heard stories about them when I was in grammar school."

"So using them to pull this bag switch'll be perfect payback for you having been afraid of them all these years."

Hill and Taylor moved in behind Pernell on his right side since the eight nuns were lined up to pass on his left side.

When the nuns were almost upon him, Pernell stepped to his left, seemingly unaware of them. The pairs of nuns separated and walked around him, effectively protecting him from both sides. This left Hill and Taylor out in the open and feeling as conspicuous as they were. Pernell, smiling, turned slowly, giving them time to hurry off to the side to hide.

Pernell watched as Agent Winkler stumbled into the station in the distance looking like he was half-asleep and hardly functioning. The agent went immediately to the door to track three where the sign now indicated the train to Lakeland was boarding.

Chapter 19

Pernell entered at the rear of the first car of the Lakeland train, put his Studly-Built suitcase on a seat and hurried forward, stopping two seats from the front end of the car. Without being too obvious he leaned forward to see Winkler slumped sound asleep and snoring softly in the front seat.

Pernell retrieved his bag and took it into the second car where he put the bag in the overhead space and settled to enjoy the ride.

Dutton, wearing purple colored-lens glasses, a wig, and blond fake beard which had the same effect as so many of his attempts at a disguise of making him more conspicuous when he wanted to not be noticed, entered from the third car and sat several seats behind Pernell in the second car.

Half an hour later the conductor announced, "Our next station stop in about three minutes will be Hollywood, Florida."

Dutton slumped in his seat to be less visible when Pernell stood and got his bag from overhead rack. Dutton whispered, "Okay, he's obviously planning to get off the train at this stop. This can be my opportunity. He may be pulling an off and get back on again trick in case anyone is following him but I can use that against him."

Dutton pulled an open newspaper up over his head as he leaned against the window as if napping while Pernell came down the aisle with his bag.

Dutton slowly lowered the newspaper to peek and be sure that Pernell was gone. There was no sign of Pernell in the aisle ahead of this seat or beside it - but when Dutton turned enough to see the aisle behind his seat there was the man standing, looking back the way he had come - with a tiny smile. Dutton jerked the paper back up. Pernell smiled more broadly as he walked to the end of the car and waited as they pulled into the station.

The conductor announced, "This stop is Hollywood, Florida."

Dutton started to jump up but slumped back into his seat when he saw Pernell still at the back end of the aisle and looking his way. Dutton told himself, "I'll pull a bag switch on the platform and then use the train to my advantage. If he's staying here I get on the train and I'm gone before he realizes what happened."

The train stopped. Pernell exited by the door between the first and second cars. Dutton jumped up, grabbed his own bag, and ran to follow, saying to himself, "If he's just getting off to stretch his legs I pull the switch, he gets on the train but I stay here and again he doesn't realize what happened until he's miles up the track."

Out on the platform, Pernell walked about half the length of the second car before he stopped to stretch and look around, not in a hurry to go anywhere, his bag at his feet.

Behind his back, Hill and Taylor leaned out the open door without stepping off the train to watch him. "What's he up to? Can we do this as a team? I'll distract him while you switch bags," Taylor said.

"I'm hoping we can do it that way but I'm not sure yet. He's staying out in the open where other people can see what's happening. Let's see what he does before we let him see us," Hill recommended.

Dutton reached the end of the car with his bag, ready to rush off and after Pernell. He came to a screeching halt when he found Hill and Taylor hanging out that door where he could see them but they hadn't seen him. "What are they doing here? They must have been in the second car. I can't risk having them recognize me and raise an alarm to keep me from getting the money since I'd be beating them to it. They might figure it's better to ruin my chances in order to give themselves better ones."

He slid into the empty seat on the platform side as close to the door as he could find and flattened his face against the window trying to see along the platform to check on Pernell. "What's he doing? I can't see him from here."

Dutton jumped up and rushed to the door at the front end of this first car and cautiously peeked out. Hill and Taylor hung out the door at the other end of this car, looking in the other direction so he could see them but they didn't see him. "Darn, they're staying there. I can't get off the train or even see where he is without them seeing and maybe recognizing me."

He took a stun gun from his pocket and hefted it without firing it. "I have a new option this time. I figured I might need to use this on the money bag man but it could also be useful if I need to get these two out of the way. I won't use it on any of them out in the open though since I know there are people watching him but I don't know if these two are the only ones. There were lawmen before and could be this time too."

Outside, Pernell ambled toward the conductor who stood outside the doors between the second and third cars. Hill and Taylor leaned farther out to watch him.

"What's he going to do?" Taylor asked.

"I think he's playing games with us," Hill said.

Pernell stopped as if he had heard something and looked back but he telegraphed his move enough that Dutton, Hill, and Taylor all had time to get back out of sight. Pernell smiled and walked on.

Dutton hurried through the first car and into the second. He stopped to look out at the platform when he found an empty seat on that side. Outside, Pernell nodded to the conductor and reboarded as the train crew exchanged waves to indicate they were ready to depart.

* * *

Pernell sat at a table in the lounge car with a cup of coffee, his back to the door, his bag on the aisle by his feet.

Hill and Taylor stepped into this car and stood by the door. Hill whispered to Taylor, "Okay, he's set himself up for us. He'll recognize me but you were never with me when I talked to him so he shouldn't have any idea who you are. It's not crowded in here so we should be able to pull it off. I'll walk by him carrying our bag."

"I'll be behind you but I'll trip and half fall on top of him."

"Don't get hurt though," Hill said.

Taylor said, "Of course not but if I wiggle around on there playfully that should distract him long enough for you to switch bags while I'm apologizing profusely. You continue out the other end of the car, put his bag out of sight back there until we get off with it at the next stop. If he notices the switch before then, and there's no reason to think he will, we can create another diversion until we're off and away from the train."

Hill pushed up his collar and ducked his head to signal he was ready to go. Taylor silently pulled him around and fixed his collar better while tapping the dark glasses in his jacket pocket to remind him that he had those to wear.

Hill put on a pair of those large-framed dark glasses. "Good, I almost forgot we bought these for exactly this kind of use."

Pernell telegraphed his move, then turned to look back toward the food counter. Taylor grabbed Hill, turned him so his back was to Pernell and smoothed his jacket while she peeked to see what Pernell was doing. Pernell had turned back to his coffee.

Hill and Taylor exchanged go-ahead nods and Hill started down the car past Pernell.

As soon as Hill was beside him, Pernell stood to leave. He smiled and hummed innocently as he gathered his coffee cup, his computer bag, and wheeled his Studly-Built bag as he headed for Taylor. She turned aside to check the passing scenery. He hesitated beside her long enough to prompt her to turn farther away to avoid making eye-contact, then finally he exited. He was having fun.

* * *

Pernell walked the length of the third car. At the far end he stood resting his Studly-Built bag on the seat for the moment as if considering whether to put it in the overhead rack. He took a sheet of paper from his jacket pocket and glanced over it, further delaying his move to stow the bag.

During this, Taylor and Hill stood between the cars watching him through the door window, their store logo bags at their feet,

"We can do it right now," Taylor suggested. "I'll hurry down the aisle and bump into him. 'Sorry about that, the train movement gives me problems'. If I'm lucky I'll knock him all the way into the seat. I grab his bag and hand it back to you while I take ours from you and shove it into his hands. You come back this way with his bag while I continue on through the car and out the other end in case he notices the switch and comes after me. I don't have his or any bag so there's nothing he can do. All an unfortunate and confusing accident on a train."

"That's good," Hill agreed. "Nobody else in the car can say they saw you bring in a bag so we're covered. I take one in and bring one back out. Let's do it!"

Pernell nodded to himself and pocketed the sheet of paper as Taylor entered the car at the far end with Hill close behind her. Both of the pair wore their large sun glasses and light-weight jackets with different sports team logos on them. Hill had their Studly-Built bag.

The pair moved quickly down the aisle toward Pernell who gave no sign that he noticed them. But just before Taylor reached him, Pernell tossed his bag into the empty seat and slid in beside it.

It is too late to make the planned switch so Taylor went to some trouble not to attract his attention by bumping into Pernell, almost falling in on him as she tried to avoid doing exactly that.

Hill dropped their bag so he could grab Taylor from behind and help steady her, then he grabbed up their bag and hurried back the way he had come. Taylor looked both ways, debating her move before she followed Hill back out. Pernell seemed not to notice.

* * *

Pernell checked the time and the train schedule. They were only a few minutes from West Palm Beach, the end of his train ride this time. He went into the restroom and used his penknife to remove the shrink wrap which he balled up and shoved down into the waste paper container. He put the real $100 bills in the flat box in his laptop carrying case that hadn't had the computer in it the entire ride.

Back in the seats, after a quick look around to be sure no one else was within hearing distance, he placed a cell phone call. "Hello. Is this the U.S. Treasury Department tip line?"

In the first car, Winkler was shaken awake by his vibrating cell phone. He answered as soon as he cleared his head enough to know where he was. "Yeah, Winkler here. What do you have for me?"

He listened, nodded with determination, and disconnected. He stood and put his badge in full view on his coat pocket and moved slowly down the car looking closely at each person and at every bag in the overhead racks or by the people.

In the third car, Pernell carefully wiped the exterior surfaces of his bag with a disposable cloth, then put on flesh-colored cotton gloves before he got up and took his bag with him as he walked to the back end of this car and on into the fourth car. Of course he acted as if nothing of consequence was going on.

When Pernell entered at the front end of the fourth car, Hill and Taylor settled back into their seats and ducked their heads, then peeked over the tops of the seats to see what he was doing.

Pernell placed his bag flat on an empty seat and spread a newspaper over it to claim the seats. That done he entered the nearby restroom, locking the door behind him.

Hill urged Taylor out of their seat and down the aisle, dragging their bag with him. "Good, coffee makes you need to pee. This is our chance. Move. If he comes out too soon I'll shove him back inside and hold him there while you get out of sight in another car with the bag."

Over the PA the conductor announced, "Our next station stop will be West Palm Beach in about three minutes. West Palm Beach, Florida is next." That meant it was close to 1:30 P.M.

When Hill and Taylor reached Pernell's seat they noticed Jim Harvey Ringalet in the seat across the aisle, cell phone in his hand, watching them with suspicion.

Hill whispered to Taylor, "A little blocking action, thank you."

Taylor let Hill get around her while she looked back the way they had come as if expecting a signal from back there. She moved side to side a bit, effectively blocking Ringalet's view while Hill switched their bag for the one under the newspaper.

Hill hesitated when he now saw a ten-inch-diameter sticker with a distinctive pattern stuck on the side of Pernell's bag. He tried to pull that off to transfer it to their bag but it was firmly attached to Pernell's bag. He muttered to himself, "I didn't see this on here earlier but I don't have time to worry about it right now."

Hill led the way out the door toward car three saying to Taylor, "Okay, we're on our way."

"Right off the train," she agreed. "That's called perfect timing."

Taylor continued to block Ringalet's view while Hill exited at the end of the car, then she followed him out.

Hill and Taylor entered the third car, all smiles. "We're slowing already. We've pulled it off," Taylor said with glee and relief.

Then Winkler, who had his back to them while he checked a bag in a seat, turned to face them. He looked at them, then at the bag in Hill's hand with its conspicuous sticker. He pointed to his badge, then at Hill and Taylor and said, "Federal treasury agent. You two are under suspicion of involvement in illegal activity. Sit down here."

The train was coming to a full stop. Taylor glanced toward the door behind her.

"Don't make this even harder on yourselves," Winkler said. "There are police waiting outside at this station."

Hill tried to sound calm. "There's a misunderstanding here. Who's accusing us of doing anything illegal?"

Winkler pointed emphatically to an empty seat. "Sit. And open that bag. If I'm wrong you'll receive a full apology."

"I think there's been a mistake. That doesn't look like our bag. We must have picked up the wrong one," Taylor said.

Winkler pointed to the seat again. "Your failure to sit when told to can be taken as resisting arrest. There are penalties for that."

Reluctantly Taylor settled into the window seat, Hill on the aisle with the bag on his lap.

Winkler opened the bag so they could all see the contents - stacks of the same kind of bad counterfeit bills that Dutton had ended up with. Not shrink wrapped which meant the bundles were readily available for him to examine. Also no good $100 bills.

With a mix of confusion and relief Hill insisted, "See, it's only a kind of play money. Someone's playing a joke on us."

"There's a lot of this stuff floating around these days and we in the treasury department are very interested in knowing everybody who's involved with it," Winkler told him.

A happy-looking Pernell got off the train at the fourth car with Hill and Taylor's bag that he had picked up when he came out of the restroom. He headed into the station without looking behind him.

A determined-looking Dutton got off the train at the rear of the fifth car carrying his own matching bag and stalked after Pernell.

Taylor insisted, "We never saw this money before."

Hill jumped in too. "Yeah, we picked up the wrong suitcase. Ours is just like this one - except for that sticker thing."

Winkler gave them a *who's kidding whom* look. "Yeah, this sticker that's like half the size of the darned bag but somehow you didn't notice it until just now. Interestingly, this sticker's what a tip alerted us to watch for. You'll have plenty of time to tell us all about how you confused this with some other bag."

Taylor shouted, "The other bag! That'll prove this one isn't ours. But that's…"

Hill moaned, "I have the sick feeling that we were set up."

"We picked him 'cause he's good but we didn't figure on him being too good for our own good," Taylor said.

"Who's that?" Winkler asked.

"It's not necessary that you know. We want our lawyer."

"Happy to oblige you, sir," Winkler said. "We're getting off the train now so it can continue on its way. You'll get a free ride in a police car to West Palm Beach police headquarters. Surely you have cell phones. You can call your lawyer and tell him to meet you there."

* * *

Pernell entered the West Palm Beach train station pulling Hill and Taylor's bag like he didn't have a care in the world. He looked around and got oriented, then stood outside the men's room to make a cell phone call, the bag a few feet from him.

Dutton entered cautiously and then stopped to watch Pernell disappear through that door. "Okay, mister, it's time to end this. You've been more trouble than I should have to put up with. You've got the bag of money and I'm gonna take it." He took the stun gun from his pocket and tested it, looking around nervously since the *zap* sound seemed loud in here but no one else seemed to have heard it.

Dutton pulled his own bag as he hurried over, grabbed the bag near Pernell, and took both into the men's room - where he stopped and stared at Gargoyle's bodyguard Oscar and two other large and notably muscular men. Those two men gleefully stepped forward and took Dutton by the arms. He turned his head and saw Pernell quietly exiting the room without the bag he had brought in.

Oscar said, "My boss sent us to make you an offer that you don't really get the option of refusing, Mr. Terence Dutton."

Dutton stuttered, "I don't... I didn't..."

Oscar shook his head sadly. "Yeah, you inconvenienced him and got yourself into trouble with the law too. You're out on bail and not planning on showing up for trial and my boss is happy to have us make sure you won't have to worry about the consequences of that."

Dutton tried to scream and shout loudly but all that came out was a whimpering, "Help me. Mommy!"

"For whatever consolation it might be, you're gonna contribute to the advancement of science," Oscar told him.

"Sci...science?"

"The boss is paying the professor to find stuff to make pain worse so he'd enjoy inflicting it even more. But the professor stumbled on stuff that seems to stop pain instead. Since the drug companies will pay way big bucks for what he's found, the boss has him continuing the research. He needs people to test for sure if it works though."

Dutton stared at Oscar, then the other strong men who had him firmly held as he thought about that.

Oscar took Dutton's bag and opened it on top of a sink to show it was filled with stacks of newspaper cut to the size of dollar bills. "What could it mean that you're dragging around a bag full of stacks of worthless cut newspaper?"

Dutton made like a goldfish, gulping but with no meaningful sounds coming from him. His eyes bulged when Oscar placed the bag Pernell had with him on another sink and opened it - to reveal more stacks of cut newspaper.

Oscar chuckled, "Newspaper seems to be the theme of the day. Can you explain that to me, Terence?"

Dutton leaned as far forward as the men holding him let him, staring in disbelief at the contents of the bag Pernell had with him.

"You can think about it a lot but you'll get to do that in a lab cell, not a jail cell."

"But I didn't do anything illegal," Dutton protested feebly.

Oscar removed the stun gun from the man's pocket. "But you sure tried. This little tool suggests you were ready to get tougher about your money chase too."

Oscar held the stun gun up in front of Dutton's face and tested it. Dutton now leaned as far back as the men holding him would allow as he stared at that device. Oscar asked almost casually, "Do we have to use this on you and carry you out as a drunken buddy who passed out or will you walk out without raising a fuss? We don't much care which way we do it. We won't get more jollies one way or the other."

Dutton slumped resignedly in the men's grasp as Oscar closed up the two bags and lead the way out, him pulling both suitcases.

Pernell was already in a newly rented car making the two hour drive back to Miami to deliver an additional surprise or two.

Chapter 20

A bit after 4 P.M. Gargoyle sat in his chair in his office facing the window and enjoying the view.

Pernell quietly entered by the side door, carefully closed that behind him, and moved to the center of the room undetected. He carried a gray softside suitcase. He checked his watch, took a deep breath and said, "Mr. Gargoyle, I have business to finish with you."

Gargoyle spun around in the swivel chair, startled. "How the heck..? Who let you up here without letting me know?"

"That's irrelevant. But please, by all means, get some witnesses in here. The only matter of consequence to me is the payment I was sent to pick up and have already formally requested."

Webber and two other hefty bodyguards rushed in the main door in response to the signal Gargoyle sent by pushing a button under the desk. They had guns in hand. Pernell didn't turn to look or react at all.

"How'd this guy get up here?" Gargoyle demanded to know.

Pernell took one step forward to get everyone's attention. "You're wasting time which makes it seem that you're delaying to avoid meeting your obligation. I'm determined to get this finished and over with in timely fashion right now. Therefore I politely repeat my request for the immediate payment of the money owed to Louie Lizardo Lumbago, invoking the Code of Honor by article and verse if you want me to repeat those."

Gargoyle shrugged. "It's on the grapevine. Lumbago has been permanently neutralized."

"But the debt hasn't and can't be - except by being paid in full to the person who presented the I.O.U. *Uh*, that would be me. So I'm repeating my respectful request for immediate payment under the terms of the Code. I'm also repeating so these men can hear it that to expedite the matter I'm willing to take a thousand $100 bills in cash and have the rest of the two million you owe transferred to an offshore bank account whose number I will provide."

"Come back in a couple of weeks, I don't have that much on hand," Gargoyle grumbled with a dismissive wave of his ham fist. Then he made a show of taking a handgun from a drawer and laying it within easy reach on the desk top.

Pernell turned slowly to face the other men. "I'm sorry that you gentlemen had to hear your boss lie like that. You know from his bragging that there's more than enough money in his private safe to meet this obligation under the terms I mentioned yet he lies and therefore defies the rules of the Code."

The men's expressions showed they knew Pernell was right and were disturbed by this turn of events.

Pernell turned back to calmly face Gargoyle. "Shame on you, sir. I invoke the protection of the Code, Section five, paragraph six. This is clearly an outrageous attempt to avoid repaying a debt that you agreed to before witnesses."

The bodyguards muttered among themselves and shifted around uneasily, obviously distressed by Gargoyle's actions. They also conspicuously kept their own guns ready for use.

"I wanna know how you got to my office without being stopped," Gargoyle shouted. "I didn't have to tell Harri not to let you up here, I could hardly have kept her from tearing you limb for limb on sight because of how you defeated and humiliated her earlier."

"That's irrelevant to my request for payment which has been on the table for several days now. You leave me no choice," Pernell said with a sadly resigned shrug.

Gargoyle glared at him, daring him to go there. The bodyguards gasped at the possibility of what Pernell might do.

"I invoke Clause nine. This may be the first time in the history of the Code that that needed to be invoked."

Gargoyle jumped up, his fast move bringing the guns of all three bodyguards up to aim right at him. Gargoyle, now appropriately afraid of his own men, pushed his gun farther from him with his fingertips to reassure them. "Okay, you've got me, Pernell. I'll get the money for you right away. There's no need for what happened here to ever go beyond this room."

Pernell stepped forward and placed his bag by the desk. "Please be sure none of the funny money gets mixed in. That would be a violation of the rules."

"I know, I know. But how did you find out I'd have that much good money here tonight? I don't understand that," Gargoyle said.

"Like yourself, my success depends on knowing stuff others don't think I have any way of finding out. Your required compliance with my request doesn't require me to explain my methods."

Gargoyle called to the others, "You guys get outta here."

Pernell objected. "Thank you but I need their protection until I'm out of the building. I'm concerned that some faction of your employees might not get the word and might try to take back what I have the right to take with me."

"My word that you'll be okay should be enough for you."

"In a more perfect world that might be the case," Pernell agreed. He gestured that he had no choice about this. "Gentlemen, I am invoking the protections of the Code for Bagmen so if you're ready to swear to the Brotherhood that you have never known Mr. Gargoyle to give his word as assurance and then do what he said he wouldn't I'll be happy to have you leave me here alone with him. Your honor under the Code is at stake here."

The bodyguards shuffled their feet and stared at the carpet. They muttered among themselves since they weren't ready to put their honor on the line like this.

"Okay, okay. They can stay," Gargoyle said.

A short time later, an angry Gargoyle watched Pernell leave with his bag and the two bodyguards. Gargoyle whispered to Webber who shrugged but showed no enthusiasm for what he was being told.

* * *

It was almost standard closing time. Harri was looking forward to getting out from behind the lobby desk of the Gargoyle building and into the gym where she could work up a good sweat trying to beat the stuffing out of the large punching bag to release some of her pent up frustration and rage. She was alone here since Paulie had been so upset by the earlier fuss he had been sent home.

Then in strolled two fit looking young men with big grins that spoke a challenge to her whole persona. From the minute they stepped into the vast lobby they were staring at her, laughing, and exchanging comments. They were dressed alike in dark blue windbreaker jackets with something printed on the fronts but all Harri saw was red. This was the kind of trigger she needed to snap and snap she did.

With a growl that would have terrified most people not sort of expecting something like it, she vaulted over the counter and ran at the pair when they were still yards away. She expected - craved - looks of terror and the smell of fear since those were appropriate reactions to her onslaught. Their response was to brace for action and calmly step apart so she had to decide which to grab first.

She chose. She shifted. She saw. She cursed. She fell to the floor when the Tasers fired by the two of them reached her and jolted her while they were both still beyond her reach.

As Pernell had done earlier, the men quickly bound her hands behind her back and feet together with flex cuffs to keep her down but didn't bother with a gag. Only now as she squirmed and flopped about did she read the *FBI* on their jackets.

Everyone gave her a wide berth as she thrashed as much as she could with the result that she squirmed on her side in a circle on the floor as much to see what was happening as to release some fury.

Now two dozen strangers were moving across the lobby and on the elevators - people in jackets marked Interpol, FBI, and Miami Police.

She had been drilled in the procedure.

If anyone dressed like that or claiming to be with any of those organizations came to the counter there was a button for her to push to sound alarms all over the building. She hadn't pushed the button. Her bad.

Had those two guys come in the way they did hoping to evoke the response they did for exactly this purpose? She could only wonder about that and continue to polish that circular spot on the terrazzo floor since she was too hyped to stop moving. Or shouting. But that was a different matter since her verbal challenges seemed to amuse and encourage the intruders.

There was another complication. Harri had been watching a live feed from a third floor lab of the torture of Dutton and hadn't blanked the monitor before she jumped the desk to attack the smug visitors. The first of the raiders to reach the desk saw that and gave a few orders that resulted in a six man rescue team forcing their way into that area - the exact location indicated on the video feed - to find Alfonso Gargoyle there as a full participant in the torture.

That changed the raid's calculations. The charges for actively torturing someone would likely delay Gargoyle's request to be released on bail – which was a highly desirable situation in the eyes of the law enforcement people. They wouldn't take him away immediately though, they would give him a chance to show them his private art collection and tell them all about how he came to possess those items. At the least it was likely going to be a long and unhappy night for the boss.

* * *

Half an hour after he left the Gargoyle building, Pernell got out of the front seat of a taxi with the gray softside suitcase at the Miami train station. There was a second passenger in the back of the cab but no one outside the vehicle could see who. The taxi pulled away.

Pernell, looking a bit chunky, hesitated long enough for everyone standing around to get a look at him if they choose - as several tough-looking men did. Then he entered the station.

Pedro, a street-tough lounging there, glanced from a picture cell phone to Pernell and back again. The phone message showed a head shot picture of Pernell and the text message: *Carrying much cash. G says okay to intercept.* Pedro flipped his phone closed, and headed inside after Pernell.

Almost simultaneously five other street-toughs flipped picture phones closed and moved toward the station after Pernell.

All of those men smoothly turned aside and casually walked out of the immediate area as three Miami police cars, lights flashing, pulled up and six officers hurried inside the station after checking that their guns were available for prompt use.

* * *

A few minutes later, two Miami cops stood by their cars talking into the car radios. A small crowd of the curious stood back watching the activity which seemed to be going nowhere.

Pernell had entered the train station wearing the last of what he at that point thought of as his "been seen in" clothes over new to him but used clothes he had bought while buying the ones for his disguise while he made the big transfer.

He changed his appearance in the men's room by taking off that outer layer of pants and shirt and leaving those in the trash there. Soon, without his bag, and wearing the different clothes of a different style that didn't suggest the man who had gone in, a too big sports cap that slipped down over his ears, and a fake short beard, Pernell ambled out among several recently arrived people who were carrying or pulling bags. The cab he had arrived in pulled up (although few realized it was the same one) and Pernell got in the back seat and they pulled away without incident.

The other cops now came out of the station bringing a man in a hoodie with them as their prisoner along with a gray softside suitcase. They got in their cars, and drove away. No one in the area got a look at the hooded man to ID him.

* * *

A few minutes later Pedro held his phone with the picture showing as he scanned those still in the area for any sign of Pernell. The other toughs were in here doing the same. None of them could find a match for that face now.

* * *

The taxi drove smoothly through the growing night with fares Pernell and Shallwee Bee in the back and the divider up between the front and back seats.

Pernell congratulated himself carefully and quietly. "Yes, I've still got it! Leave 'em guessin' for the price of a cheap suitcase. I let the first mug who wanted it steal the bag that had one of those tracking gizmos attached. I had called the cops and said it was being stolen and had that on it before I went inside. They drive up with their trackers and there's no place the guy can hide but I'm just the guy who hurried away and can't be found after he was robbed. Whatever happens to him I'm thinking that he and a lot of those toughs will suspect that Gargoyle set them up."

Bee signaled the driver and said by way of the intercom, "We're going to the airport, driver. No special rush."

"Where we'll fly off to a new life," Pernell stage whispered.

"A new life together. I have a lot of places I've never been," she stage whispered back.

In a real whisper he said, "With the cash in the bag at your feet we can afford to go anywhere we want to. Technically it belongs to Louie Lumbago who hired me through his agents to pick it up for him but now I'm assured by a man who would know about such things that Mr. Lumbago is permanently neutralized. Considering the source I'm confident that means he's dead. I know that those who were using those names have become unavailable so I can't deliver it to them. Therefore it's mine. And it's only five percent of the take. The rest has been transferred to an offshore account from which money-hiding pros I'm paying are already moving bundles of it around like a big shell game to confuse whoever wants to track the money and me. I didn't leave until I got the confirmation that the funds transfer was made and couldn't be reversed without my approval. I was sweating things playing it so close time-wise to the probable arrival of his unexpected visitors but I knew I couldn't trust him half an inch."

"Mr. Gargoyle will be furious when and if he finally figures out that I was the one who got you inside without him knowing you were coming."

"But he won't try to do anything against us himself. That would violate the Code and he can't survive if word gets out that he's even trying to do that. He might try to sic other lowlifes on us as he's already tried this evening but even that'll be a strain on him since they can be a trail that leads back to the Code."

"Where did you buy tickets for us to go tonight?"

"I thought New England might be a stimulating change for a while." He nodded slightly toward the driver, who was watching them closely in the rearview mirror, then pointed to his small pad of paper in his hand where he had written Dallas in large letters while he winked and silently mouthed that city name for the benefit of the observant driver.

"That's a good idea. I've always thought that if you're going to go to a new place it might as well be as far away as possible."

"We need quiet time together to plan for the longer term."

"We've earned some quiet time together.

"I have things I've never let myself think I might ever get to do but things have changed."

"That sounds like the story of my life," Bee agreed. "Change is good, especially the kind we've experienced. New England will be nice."

"We'll be snow bunnies and call ourselves the Joneses."

"But every so often we'll change and call ourselves Mr. and Mrs. Smith. Nobody will ever find us unless we want them to."

* * *

Soon after the taxi left them at the airport they had a rental car.

Pernell drove, Bee beside him. He said, "We'll never know for certain but it was worth the trouble to go to the airport like we intended to fly out and played a game to give the cabbie hints of two places we might be headed for if anybody comes around later to ask him about that."

"Plus a good tip," she noted.

"Right. He did follow directions about dropping me off and then coming back to pick me up a few minutes later. But after all that we rent a car and drive off into the night instead – but to a place where we'll switch to an inconspicuous used car I bought for cash from a private citizen earlier so there's a minimum paper trail. This way we don't have to worry that our movements are being reported to our former employer, a man noted for being a sore loser, so that he can send people to intercept us and relieve us of our cash."

"Will you miss pulling things over on people?"

"I always enjoy a challenge but I've only risked legal penalties when I needed money and that's no longer a problem. Between the Lumbago money, what Gargoyle was unhappy to advance me on the payment for bagging for him to use as the bait on the last train trip but that I was careful to remove before I gave up that suitcase, and the reward for helping a mystery person pull off an art shuffle and return to claim a reward I'm set. We're set if you're interested. Besides, you'll keep me on the straight and narrow won't you?"

"Unless there's something worthwhile to be gained if I want to persuade you to do something you hadn't planned on. Then it might be fun to watch you in action."

"I like you more every moment."

"That's what I want to hear," she said.

Chapter 21

Two mornings later, Pernell and Bee sat in a diner at the edge of Valdosta, Georgia where they were over the state border and therefore beyond the reach of Florida authorities while things worked out. They were lying low in what they thought of as their *wrap up the loose ends time* by letting the combination of the various media keep them up to date on all that was happening that they were now safely away from - they hoped. Keeping up on the details of developments, not just the headlines, was the safest way for them to know when they needed to move on and maybe where to go and whether another change of identities was called for.

They had found this place at the intersection of routes 78 and 81 with enough long-distance traffic to not be noticed while they watched CNN and other TV news shows to learn what was happening while they ate. Nearby they had found major newspapers from around the country available because there was enough interstate traveler demand. That print news awaited them when they got back to their motel several miles away where they were registered as Mr. and Mrs. Justin Newlies.

The first night they had driven for several hours in their newly bought used car, stopping finally at a motel by the highway between Ocala and Gainesville. The next day they drove on north, making minor celebratory noises when they crossed the state line and settled in for a few days stay at Valdosta.

Yesterday's top news story for them had been that Alfonso Gargoyle had been captured literally red-handed by the Miami police torturing an unnamed person whom they deduced was Terrence Dutton in a laboratory equipped area of the building owned by the alleged torturer. Then a search of Gargoyle's office suite in the same building found a number of what were tentatively identified as stolen art objects for which Interpol filed additional charges against him.

Pernell admitted that from the minute it had been suggested that he invoke the Code to pressure Gargoyle to pay up - and did so and wasn't immediately shot dead - he felt he was safe as long as he didn't push things too far. And that he made sure some Gargoyle employee saw them the whole time they were together. Gargoyle's men, all believers in the Code, were Pernell's protectors. He also from that point figured that if he survived, he would get all or most of the Lumbago money so he wouldn't have to work or scam every again. Not a guarantee at the start, but something to reassure him in the scariest moments.

Regarding the raid, Pernell took credit for Bee's ears only for phoning in an anonymous tip to Interpol about items in Gargoyle's offices and residence that would be of interest to them. He even made the call from a payphone on the street near Gargoyle's office building. He left it to the authorities to conclude that the art was stolen by Gargoyle from someone who probably bought it knowing it was stolen. Gargoyle denied knowing that part of the story - but everyone expected him to say that.

Gargoyle had a website, using a fake name, where he boasted about and exhibited items he believed were legit and properly his from his personal art collection - but that included several stolen pieces from this source. Alerted by the tip, the Feds identified the stolen art items on the website and got a court order allowing the raid on Gargoyle's whole building plus his residence.

The gangster had refused to say anything about the torture allegation but he believed the Feds were at his office that evening about something else (that he had been tipped about and had had removed) and was confident. Then he was told that what they had the search warrant for was the art. While they are there looking for that, they took the opportunity to seize all his records as part of a valid search for stolen or purchased stolen art.

In a fascinating twist that the authorities were still only starting to recognize, Polly Nana, from whom Gargoyle stole that art, died of a heart attack the night he was arrested so she couldn't testify about any of it to clear him. The topper was that all of her and her husband's personal papers were lost in the fire that started when she keeled over and knocked things over that started the fire.

What caused her sudden death wasn't known but the shock of surprise news of some sort was suspected to have been a factor. Mrs. Nana would surely have at least been glad that few art objects were lost in the conflagration - since they had already been hauled away by Gargoyle's people over her objections.

The pair agreed that this could hardly have been better for them. Gargoyle would always believe that Nana got her revenge by tipping the authorities so he wouldn't suspect them. There was a reward for information on the stolen art that could be claimed anonymously but they agreed that with the moneys coming from several sources now they didn't need that amount. They also had little doubt that claiming it would put you under law enforcement microscopes despite the promise of official anonymity.

For the same reason they wouldn't suggest that someone like Beebop submit a claim. She had a more important role to play and it would be best to not complicate her situation.

They did suspect, as proved true over the next few days, that several people with no actual connection to the matter would file claims so Interpol would have enough to keep them busy sorting out those false claims while they identified and authenticated the many art objects.

All that while Gargoyle insisted he was innocent of any wrongdoing, that he had merely borrowed the items at the request of the widow Nana to give them a safe home until she refurbished her house to show them properly to the world. There may have been a few innocent souls who believed him about that.

Bee claimed her own coup in the matter. Her anonymous phone tip pointed out that a photo in a two year old interior fashion magazine spread on Gargoyle's lawyer's fancy house showed several items Interpol art experts should recognize as listed on the secret inventory of works in the man's collection that were now identified as stolen but that hadn't been found in his office or residence.

When a team showed up at the attorney's door while he was busy trying to think up a persuasive argument to get his client out on bail, the lawyer claimed not to remember whether those had been gifts to him or were only lent to him. Suddenly his much vaunted incredible memory failed him. He declined to say for certain but said he seemed to remember those being lent to him by his client to add to the decor for the magazine photo shoot. In all the confusion of his busy life he had apparently forgotten to return them since he hadn't been hounded to do so.

He was outraged, *outraged*, at any hint that he might have involved in their theft and would certainly have reported them immediately if he suspected they were stolen. But he was a top notch defense lawyer, not an art expert no matter what he had said during the interview for the magazine article. After all, adults understand that lies are common currency in puffery. Alas, there were no papers documenting him getting them from Gargoyle - and therefore Polly Nana. Those should be in his files, not hers, so the loss of her documents was irrelevant unless you let a fast-talking lawyer with a vested interest in the subject convince you otherwise.

As to why Interpol only recognized them as important after her anonymous tip, Shallwe Bee suspected that since this lawyer was a consultant to Gargoyle but never personally went to court for him, he wasn't widely known as one of the gangster's lawyers and thus wasn't on Interpol's radar for every little thing like an interior design magazine puff piece.

The pair had to combine bits from several sources to feel sure that the photos left on the returned *Funny Money* piece helped lead Interpol to Polly Nana and Gargoyle's art collection and questions Gargoyle couldn't answer without incriminating himself. The web address source clearly printed on the backs of those images made it almost impossible for those people not to get the message but there was no official mention of that last part.

If the authorities had had their way there would surely not have been any mention of the photos, much less of what was printed on their backs. But anonymous phone tips to several news outlets had photographers at the site recording such details ten minutes before any police arrived with orders to clear the area and prevent any photos being taken.

Once Pernell was away from the transfer site, and before the return of *Funny Money* was international news, Agnes Beebop had shipped the second half of the photographed dollar sign artwork to Armand Clanger by overnight express. She expected, as happened, that as soon as mention of the mystery photo of the engraved attached dollar signs found taped to the art piece made the news despite official efforts to keep it a secret the billionaire would recognize it as the ID of the person who had arranged the transfer and won his bet. Her return address on the package was her ID.

Clanger was amused and thrilled but he didn't explain that to anyone or report it to any authority. He had a discreet agent contact her. Yes, she had the other half of the item, the half on which the inscription was known. Clanger accepted her claim and arranged with her how to pay off his half million dollar bet. He was content that the item was back but the world didn't know how and Interpol didn't seem to be moving to arrest the person taking responsibility. It was fun to be rich enough to make bets like that and create a new mystery to keep those who would obsess about the details occupied.

Armand Clanger hadn't and wasn't expected to tell anyone there was a valid claimant for his challenge bet and his behavior in the past suggested he would fight not to reveal any information about the person if there was a leak.

Beebop was quietly waiting to see what authorities would eventually find their way to her door and what they would have to say for themselves since there were some unavoidable paper trails from that money. Clanger turned it over to her special bank account. She arranged for all but her handling fee to become available to the agent. The agent pocketed his fees, arranged for the payment to Pernell of the rest of his fees, and deposited the remainder to a bank account where the anonymous to everyone but him principal who had lined up the whole thing could get it as her reward.

There was real headline news about Agnes Beebop though. She had recovered and left the hospital days earlier, then on the night that Gargoyle's big troubles began she won $1.4 million State lottery money on the ticket Pernell gave her.

Pernell claimed that was uncanny proof that he was right in depending on Beebop to do the right thing in getting the proper proportions of the Clanger money to the agent and himself. He didn't know or want to know who the principal who hired him was, he was content that he had fun with the challenge and was well paid for it.

On the blog Beebop had set up when she had a new computer - in part as a way for Pernell to anonymously keep tabs on the latest news about her and her doings - she noted she was in the process of adopting nurse Jim Fullard's family, including his special needs son. Fullard was being helpful in a variety of ways but was barely making it financially so this was appropriate. She subtly emphasized that it wasn't a romance, she had procured a whole family for herself in order to make better use of her talents and money and to make fuller use of their talents.

With lottery money and Clanger money being directed to her by inconspicuous routes she was well heeled but would be generous to charities. She had already pledged a generous donation to the hospital since her stay there helped her back to good health. Yes, that was more because of who she met there than because of what the doctors wanted to do. But she wouldn't talk about that detail and didn't expect the hospital administrators would either.

In her most recent posting she announced that she was suing Selma's great-niece Irene for libel. Her new lawyer agreed she could seek every penny of Selma's estate as Irene's penalty so her dumb actions would end up not profiting her.

Beebop would specify from the start that the money was to go to Selma's favorite charity - which is what Selma's last will and testament specified but somehow that document supposedly now couldn't be found. Beebop had hired someone to follow the paper trail and see if a copy of that will wasn't in the files of Selma's now deceased lawyer who drew it up.

At a seemingly innocuous web site, specific wording signaled that his payment from the principal for pulling off the big transfer was in the process of being delivered by the route Pernell had chosen.

Prepaid $2000 credit cards would minimize any paper trails. Those were purchased a few at a time in different locations and on different days to make the trail as hard to follow as possible. They were conveniently anonymous, not requiring a bank account or the name of the person using them. They could be mailed anywhere with minimum risk. He only needed to supply an address each time he wanted the next batch to reach him at a new location. He started on the road with the first five cards in his pocket. Sixty-five to go. How many to have in his possession at a time was his call.

The pair agreed that the fee for pulling off the big transfer might stay a secret but once the authorities checked Gargoyle's recent financial records the bank transfers of Lumbago's money to Sylvester Pernell's offshore account, plus Gargoyle's reluctant direct payment for Pernell's services as a bagman, would all come to light. Pernell was having the offshore money moved around as fast as he could arrange it to have it lost in the paper trail jungle before the regulators tried to interfere or at least track him by those paper trails but he knew there were no guarantees that he could succeed at that.

He was realistic enough to expect a few reporters, government agents, and/or general snoops to devote much energy to identifying him and tracking him so it was best for Sylvester Pernell to disappear and live out his days in simple but comfortable anonymity.

That is, under some other name and content with a wife.

Pernell and Bee expected that as soon as he learned she had gone missing, Gargoyle would spin out yarns to blame Bee for all his problems and would try to get others to get revenge on her so it would save a lot of problems if the person using that name disappeared too.

They agreed that if it could be arranged for suspicions to float that someone, likely Gargoyle who would overtly deny it but secretly bask in the notoriety of it in his prison cell, erased Pernell for harm done with the Code - with his body never to be found since the gators had feasted - that worked for Pernell. If it could be hinted that Shallwee Bee met a similar end then they were both a bit more in the clear. It is too late to worry about the police or others having their prints or DNA, they would just try to be careful in the future.

She revealed in that context that Shallwee Bee was a faked name she had used for years but she had maintained her legal name in active form so since all her connections to Gargoyle were by the Bee name she couldn't be easily traced and could have unknown bank accounts. Pernell could be traced by social security number and bank accounts but he could arrange to have part or all of the Lumbago money offshore transferred to a new account that Bee controlled and thwart at least some attempts at tracing him.

With the idea of disappearing never to be found, Bee had left all her clothes and other belongings behind to support the idea that she intended to return but had disappeared involuntarily. She took no clothes that anyone might recognize her in. She had bought a few new things and would buy anything else she needed new since she had her own money and was assured that money would be no problem. She had never been into extravagances except as part of a role she was playing to stay safe and get ahead.

Pernell retrieved the items he had put in paid storage when he arrived in Miami and then left all the clothes and the suitcase he had brought south in the comped room at the Dorkman hotel along with his laptop in the room's safe. Not the computer's carrying case though since he still had uses for it and it was inconspicuous.

On the day he was making the big transfer, someone he trusted was thoroughly wiping his laptop's hard drive and then putting a bunch of individually password-protected files back on it to keep either Gargoyle's people or the cops busy finding a way in only to find nothing of his files left on there. He bought a new machine and set up a new online access account under a new name during their lunch stop yesterday. The Internet was too useful to be avoidably without access to its information resources for long.

In a month or two he would try to find out how much he was now on various law enforcement radars, but he would continue to use fake names and pay cash until he felt it was safe to do otherwise. He didn't expect to ever need to run scams for money again. He would miss the excitement but was confident he could find new outlets for his creativity that wouldn't put him in danger from the law or the lawless.

Each agreed that their whirlwind romance had been a high point of his or her adult life. Each had finally met someone who clicked but after years of deceptions and play-acting it took time to test and then to fully trust someone. Each admitted there were incidents and secrets from the past that could be stumbling blocks so it would work best if each warned the other when a touchy subject came up and neither swore to be totally open and honest about everything in the past. Not even in the present when that would risk opening sealed closets that wouldn't clearly benefit them in the present and the future.

From one Miami area criminal prosecution focused website they learned that Dutton had been rescued from Gargoyle and was expected to make a full physical recovery. The current plans were for him still to be prosecuted for possession of the counterfeit bills he was caught with unless a clever lawyer could blame it all on Gargoyle, currently the ogre of the week.

The defense attorney for Hill and Taylor was rumored to be collaborating with Dutton's defender. This man told a gaggle of reporters outside the court house that he would show it was all Mr. Gargoyle's doing, that all three people caught with the counterfeit bills were innocent dupes. Obviously that lawyer liked a challenge.

What wasn't said but seemed clear to the pair was that it was to the advantage of all of the defendants not to mention Pernell since that would almost inevitably expose how they worked to get those bags of money from him. Very possibly he was safe from being dragged into that matter in court but there were no guarantees.

Also those three defendants didn't want to be linked in any way to the suspicious death of Louie Lizardo Lumbago which was being closely investigated.

And the final bit, Hill and Taylor would hate so much to have to admit publicly to being setup by Pernell whom they hired to setup Gargoyle for money for them.

All three were currently out on bail and there were serious doubts about whether any would show up for trial.

A newspaper mentioned an FBI raid on Savannah Movers and Fakers, Inc. but their reporter could get no official word on what that was about beyond the comment that it was part of an investigation about the distribution of counterfeit money. Pernell and Bee thought it likely that those people held Gargoyle directly responsible for focusing attention on them by dealing with them.

More distant plans for the pair definitely involved the use of new names but beyond that were still fluid. They needed to give it time to see how much they needed to hide (and from whom) and how the money access would work out. But they had one another, no desire to be ostentatious or notorious, and lots of memories to chuckle about.

Printed in Great Britain
by Amazon